CUT YOU DEAD

SAMANTHA WILLERBY MYSTERY SERIES - BOOK 4

A.J. WAINES

ALSO BY A.J. WAINES

SAMANTHA WILLERBY MYSTERY SERIES

Inside the Whispers

Lost in the Lake

Perfect Bones

STANDALONE PSYCHOLOGICAL THRILLERS

The Evil Beneath

Girl on a Train

Dark Place to Hide

No Longer Safe

Don't You Dare

Enemy at the Window

WRITING AS ALISON WAINES

The Self-Esteem Journal

Making Relationships Work

In memory of sweet little Lucy,
our feline bundle of loveliness,
who was by my side when I wrote this novel.

HAZEL

Eight days ago

Is it you again? Are you following me, you dipstick? I've had this prickle under my scalp ever since I came out of Harrods. Is that your reflection in the shop window, your shadow blocking the light, your manky breath on my shoulder, just like yesterday?

I skirt around a woman selling *The Big Issue*, nearly tripping over the wheels of a child's buggy. I stare into the open doorway of a mobile phone shop and wonder about rushing in and making a fuss about you. But, you'll keep out of sight and everyone will stare at me as though I'm a nutter. I'll feel even more of a dufus. Then you'll be there waiting for me when I come out.

I hate you for making me feel like this, you creep. Whoever you are.

I hurry along the pavement, keeping my head down, glancing up only to cross the road. I'd rather not know which lamp post you're leaning against, which display of designer sportswear you're pretending to be interested in. Nevertheless, a single figure wearing an army-style jacket stands out from all the rest, in spite of me training my eyes on the traffic. Is it you? Have you come past me, somehow? I can't keep track.

You must be up to something because unlike everyone else you're not on the move, you keep stopping, watching. Are you waiting to see which way I'll go?

I think about waiting for a bus or a lorry to come by, so it will block the view and I can double back, but I'm already late for the photographer. I *must* get the shots done today; the competition closes tomorrow and I *know* I'm in with a good chance. It's not every day you get through to the final round in a top modelling contest.

I break into a run and I'm almost at the tube entrance. I can no longer tell if you're there; too many other things are going on – cars jumping the lights, a man handing out free newspapers, the screech of a bus.

The pedestrian light is green outside Harvey Nics, so instead of going straight down to the tube, I cross over the road to the more recent entrance on the far side. It might throw you.

It's crowded in the foyer. Even so, I wish it were busier so I could blend in. I hurry towards the barriers and glance up before I take out my travel pass. Sweat coats the back of my neck. I can't see you, but that means nothing. You could creep up on me any second; there are so many corners and corridors.

I join the shortest queue at the barrier, but I feel someone right behind me, way too close. I daren't turn round. Once through the other side, you step beside me. Your hood's up so I can't see your face. But, I'm really freaking out now, because it looks like you've got something tucked inside your jacket.

Everyone's pushing past and no one's seeing what I can see. The glint of metal. Jeez – is that what I think it is?

I join the escalator up ahead, squashing behind an overweight woman. You slip out of my line of sight. Should I call out? Am I being paranoid?

In a sudden movement, I dart to the side and join the flurry of commuters passing those who are standing. I make it to the steps down to the platform, my boots clattering on the stone like cascading skittles. I can hear the train rocketing through the tunnel and feel the suck of air as it approaches.

I need to be on this friggin' train. I need to get inside and hide before you catch up with me. The wheels grind to a halt and I don't care that I'm rude, shoving people aside using my elbows and the edge of my bag to break through the cracks. Instead of using the nearest door, I race further up the platform. I want you to think I've doubled back, to faff about and miss your chance.

A woman carrying a small child gives me a dirty look. But I've made it. I hurtle through the last set of doors and they swoosh behind me, sealing me inside. I can breathe again. There are no spare seats, it's a hot and stuffy crush, but I don't care. I'm on the train – and right now that's all that matters.

As we pull away, I catch sight of your khaki jacket out there on the platform. You're speaking to a woman with a toddler and I start to wonder if I've got it all wrong.

1

SAM

The Present – Thursday, 10 January

It should have come as no surprise to find the lift was out of order on the one day I was running late. It wasn't a great start to my final day of training. Not after my brolly had blown inside out on the way over and I'd got my heel caught in a drain cover, sending me straight into a puddle.

Not only did I have one sopping wet foot, but my thighs were burning when I reached the seventh floor. I was gasping for breath. Mid-thirties and I felt ancient. Too much sitting down since I'd started this course at Guy's Hospital; thank goodness it was nearly over.

From the following day, everything was going to change. No more Kit Kats with morning coffee. No more sitting at the back of the lecture theatre with a bag of crisps stashed away for those yawn-inducing moments. Once I'd got my certificate, my daily commute back to work would have to be on my bike again.

Professor Landy must have spent the initial five minutes trying to set up the PowerPoint because the lecture theatre was still buzzing with chit-chat when I peeled open the door. By the time the first slide came up, I'd found a seat.

I was glad I hadn't missed anything, because the final day of lectures turned out to be the best yet. As soon as the professor mentioned the forensic applications of 'delusions of grandeur', I felt my spine snap up straight.

'Such delusions are a common trait in serial killers,' she said. 'They drive individuals to believe they have special powers or are being given secret instructions to kill.' I shuddered at those last two words. I'd worked with several delusional patients in my own practice, but none where their behaviour had ended in murder. At least, not as far as I was aware.

During the break, I wandered over to join the queue for coffee. I had half an eye on a plate of chocolate digestives on the table, but as I pulled out my mobile, my appetite absconded. A missed call. A hot wave of nausea rolled over me when I saw who it was from. Someone I hadn't expected to hear from ever again: Detective Chief Superintendent Elsa Claussen from the Metropolitan Police.

What did *she* want? Keen to get it over with, I stepped out of the queue and called her straight back.

After a few pleasantries, DCS Claussen weaved her way to the point. 'So tell me, Dr Willerby – how did you feel after the Aiden Blake case?'

Claussen's familiar brisk tone brought her into my mind in full colour. The speckled grey short-back-and-sides haircut, the ample bosom kept at bay under a formal shift dress – invariably buttoned-up to the chin. Not forgetting the black 'hospital ward' lace-ups, as if she'd come straight from breaking in new army recruits on an assault course.

How did I feel?

'Well, it was very – how can I put it – *challenging*,' I said, my body recoiling as I relived a flashback to the ordeal last summer.

'As it turned out, I was also within an inch of losing my life... but...' My words fizzled out. Why was she asking me this now – six months down the line?

'Your expertise as a therapist saved the day, did it not?'

'That's... I–'

My mind whirred.

The last time I had a call out of the blue from the Met I lost my annual leave. I was forced to trade in a long-awaited trip to Greece for drifting up and down the Regent's Canal on a narrowboat. On reflection, it was a poignant, life-affirming case to work on, but it still ruined my holiday.

She continued. 'I'm not sure how we'd have proceeded without you, if I'm honest.'

Okay, now I really was worried. Why was she talking to me like we were in a Nancy Drew novel?

'After some initial hiccups,' she added, 'you blended into the team admirably.'

Initial hiccups, eh? Is that what they were? More like unacceptable and abominable arrogance from a number of police officers who should have known better. And insensitivity that was bordering on bullying towards a vulnerable witness. And a lack of respect for my professional input. My list could have gone on.

She cleared her throat. 'We were impressed by your handling of the situation – most particularly your dogged tenacity. Some might say you were a true asset.'

Was someone holding a gun to her head?

I didn't want her praise. 'Listen, I've got to go. It's nice of you to let me know, but is there anything else?'

A short silence plummeted between us.

'A little bird told me you have some new training under your belt,' she said, her voice almost childlike.

'Not quite. My last lecture is today. In around two minutes to be precise.'

The little bird was no doubt Terry Austin from my PhD days in Manchester. Surely he hadn't dropped me in it again. Then came the words I was dreading. The ones that had meant trouble, last time.

'I also understand you don't have any patients bocked in at St Luke's for a couple of weeks?'

My lungs felt like they'd collapsed.

That was the problem with detectives – they tended to find things out about you behind your back. I gave her a non-committal 'Hmm...' in response. Let her lay her cards on the table first.

'Come to my Camden office in the morning and we'll chat more then.'

'About what, exactly?' I snapped.

'I have a proposition I think you'll be interested in.' Without further explanation, she was gone.

2

Elsa Claussen greeted me in the reception area of Stanhope Street police station with something resembling a smile. It was tight and short-lived, but nevertheless, it was the closest she'd ever got to one during our prickly acquaintance. It startled me, robbing me of the polite entrée I'd rehearsed on the way over. Instead, I stood before her with my mouth open, looking like the new girl at school.

It didn't take Claussen long to resume her customary severity. She looked me up and down, then turned away. At a brisk pace, she led me to an office I'd not seen during my visits the previous year. Her own personal domain, by the look of it.

'Thank you for coming in,' she declared, striding behind her desk and offering me a plastic seat at the other side.

She remained standing. Just as I'd pictured her the day before, she wore a high-necked outfit that looked more like a uniform than a dress. Whilst I'd layered up, in keeping with the chilly weather, she seemed impervious to the cold, clad only in short sleeves. A woman who, by being perpetually poised for battle, evidently generated sufficient heat inside her own body.

I sat tentatively, perched on the edge of the seat, waiting.

Everything about the space was austere; no pictures on the wall, only a clinical map of Camden. No photos of loved ones on the desk, only a laptop, papers, a scattering of pens. With relief, I spotted a single plant, a hydrangea, standing on the filing cabinet, but the more I peered at it, the more I was convinced it was artificial. All the while, I felt a latent twisting in my gut as I wondered what my summons here was all about.

She cleared her throat and leant forward, spreading her hands flat and deliberately on the desk, like a sprinter in the blocks. 'I won't beat about the bush. We'd like you to look into some cold cases "off the record".'

I stared at her. 'Cold cases?'

'We'll give you access to our database and you can see if you can offer any insights with reference to delusional behaviour.' She examined my face. 'Now that you're an expert.'

Was this Claussen's attempt at a joke? I didn't know whether to smile or not, but she rescued me from my indecision by speaking again.

'As you have no clinical work for a couple of weeks, we thought it might be a good use of your time.'

It was true, I hadn't got anything lined up at St Luke's for a while.

'Might even pep things up. Stretch you a little.' She made it sound like a test.

'For two weeks?'

She shrugged. 'Starting Monday. Should be long enough to find something, I reckon.'

I stopped to think. I'd barely had the chance to let my newfound knowledge of delusional behaviour sink in. Did I want the responsibility of having to prove myself in this area so soon after my training? 'How would it work exactly? What would I have to do?'

She straightened up, exuding a breezy air of victory,

assuming she'd won me over, even though I hadn't yet agreed to anything.

'Simple – you flick through our files and use your psychological expertise to find links we've missed.'

Something inside me burst into a full-scale firework display. 'Like a profiler, you mean?'

'Kind of – we prefer to use the term Behavioural Investigative Adviser.'

I'd always dreamt of having a go at profiling, but never believed I'd get the chance. Normally, you'd need a master's in forensic psychology and two years' experience to be taken seriously. But I knew that would have meant a complete change of direction in my career some time ago. I'd always thought it was too late. Claussen was dangling a very juicy carrot indeed!

I kept my face straight. I didn't want to fall into a very large hole, then find myself immediately desperate to climb out of it. 'What sort of links do you mean?'

'We know that serial killers often display delusions of grandeur. It makes sense to bring in an expert who can skim the files and spot the signs. You'd be joining our Serious Crime Analysis Unit.'

3

———

'Why now? Why for only two weeks?' I asked.

Claussen scratched her ear in the way people do when they're slightly embarrassed. 'We get injections of funding from time to time. Small amounts usually, that have to be used within a certain timeframe.' Her lips were thin and resumed the bitter expression around her mouth. 'That's all I can say.'

A thought occurred to me. 'What about Dr Herts, the police psychiatrist I worked with last time? Isn't he able to do this kind of work for you?'

She sniffed dismissively. 'He's busy,' she said, offering no elaboration. I nodded knowingly. He'd always been 'busy', I recalled, even when assigned as the go-to psychologist in a case.

I let out an inconclusive sigh and sat back. This was a chance of a lifetime. To work, hands on, in an area I'd become more and more fascinated by. Instead of examining details of a crime scene for fingerprints, fibres or bloodstains, profilers searched for the 'mind trace' left behind by the perpetrator. A different way of looking for a killer. I'd be accessing a hidden trapdoor into the criminal mind.

Inside my head, I was dancing the cancan, but I kept my face like granite.

A shadow clouded her demeanour. 'It's not for the faint-hearted. You'll be trawling through the minds of those who abduct, torture, rape and kill other human beings.'

I stiffened at her words.

She leant closer. 'Are you sure you're up to it?'

If it wasn't a test to start with, it was now.

'Yes, count me in,' I said, before I had the chance to change my mind. 'I'll do it.'

She clapped her hands and another smile almost graced her lips. 'You remember DCI Wilde from the Aiden Blake case?'

I dropped my eyes. Oh, no – the nervy, snappy officer who used to hang around the back of my chair in meetings, driving me mad.

'I'm afraid he won't be with us this time,' she said.

I turned the puff of air escaping my lips into a cough. Thank goodness. I'd be working with someone new.

'DI Jeremy Fenway will be working closely with you, instead.'

I almost flinched. This wasn't what I wanted to hear. DI Fenway had also been involved with the Aiden Blake case and we'd ended up having what could only be described as a humdinger of a falling out. At first, he'd seemed like the one person on the team I could make a decent connection with: he had a soft-handed approach, was welcoming, warm even. But before long, he let himself down. Badly. Mainly due to poor judgement and downright impudence. Unfortunately, he'd never quite redeemed himself. If I was going to be working with him again, things were going to be awkward, to say the least.

I opened my mouth to protest, but the words stayed trapped inside my head. I nipped the skin on my neck; it was too late to back out.

'That's sorted then,' she said, clasping her hands against her bosom. She looked like a tycoon who'd just landed a mind-blowing deal. 'I'll get all the paperwork over to St Luke's right now.' She turned to the printer beside the filing cabinet and scooped up three or four sheets of paper lying in the tray. She laid them on the desk in front of me and held up a pen.

I glanced down to discover the sheets already had my name printed on them. I felt a flush of heat in my cheeks. I see. She'd decided I was a shoe-in for this job before I'd even set foot in here. I managed to refrain from letting out an irritated tut and quickly scanned the forms.

'Fee satisfactory?' she added, hovering over me.

The fee was more than adequate, but I wasn't going to admit it.

'Fine,' I said, before adding my signature with a flourish.

We shook hands and without further ado, our discussion was over.

On the way out, a female officer stopped me at the front desk.

'Dr Willerby, if you wait a moment, I'll get your access to the system authorised.' Either word got around like lightning in here or individuals had been primed in advance about my involvement.

I gave her a brittle smile and leant against the counter. She rifled through some documents on her desk and pulled out a plastic wallet.

'Here you are,' she said, handing it over. Inside was a special pass with a barcode. 'The admin office is at the end of this corridor on the right.' She turned and pointed in that direction. 'You can only get into the system from there. You won't be able to from home. And your level won't allow you to edit any of the files. But you can access all the crime data, such as the methods used, locations, characteristics of the victims, timing, details of the crime scenes and so on.'

I nodded. 'And these are all cases where a murder has been committed in the past, but no one was ever convicted?'

'DCS Claussen suggests we stick to cases in London during the last twenty years.' The officer rolled her eyes. 'That should be enough to keep you busy.'

'So, when do I start?'

'The DCS said Monday, but you can pop in whenever you like,' she said, as if I was going to be dropping by selling sandwiches. 'The office is open eight until eight every day – later, if there's a major case on. Just grab an empty desk and off you go.'

As I left the building, my heart was running wild; thrilled but also a little queasy. My task sounded straightforward, but I wasn't fooled. It was going to take enormous courage simply to look at the files in the first place, never mind try to figure out why certain victims had been selected or what information the killer might have given away through their particular actions.

Was this really what I wanted?

On the way to the tube, I was trying to figure out if Terry knew I'd been headhunted to work with the Met again. Was he the little bird who had mentioned it?

There was only one way to find out. We needed to have a chat, and sooner rather than later. I was looking forward to it.

4

———

Terry was at work when I called, so I left a message to say I'd drop round that evening. On my way, I picked up a free newspaper on the underground. As I flicked through, one headline caught my eye:

Woman Falls to Death Taking Selfie

There was a photo of a stunning woman with long flowing blonde hair down to her waist. I read the full story:

A woman died early yesterday afternoon after falling from a balcony on the 19th floor of a London tower block. The deceased, still to be formally identified, was taking a selfie on her mobile phone when she fell. She was pronounced dead at the scene. A police spokesperson said: "There is nothing to suggest at this stage that this was anything other than a tragic accident." The deceased's remains were taken to King's College Hospital for a post-mortem examination.

"Having taken statements from a number of people, initial indications are that the woman was taking a selfie and lost her balance," the spokesperson added.

Witnesses said taking selfies in dangerous circumstances was the victim's 'new hobby'. They also described gusty winds on the balcony that day.

It wasn't the first time I'd heard about this new trend for taking extreme selfies. I'd seen Instagram shots of people posing from the top of skyscrapers, high bridges and clifftops. Risking life and limb to get that perfect shot. A surge of anger bubbled up inside me. For the sake of a few 'likes' on social media. I looked long and hard at the photograph again. The caption stated it had been taken just two weeks earlier. Such a waste.

5

'It wasn't me,' Terry said, as he chuckled witheringly. He held open the door to his ground-floor apartment, a tea towel slung over one shoulder and a teaspoon in his hand. 'I haven't said a word to Claussen.'

Aromas of some kind of delicious curry wafted in my direction, making me realise how hungry I was. I sighed. I'd spent the afternoon reading up on grandiose delusions and had forgotten to buy anything for supper. Baked beans on toast again for me.

'Come in,' he said, glancing behind him at the kitchen-diner.

'I'm not stopping,' I said defiantly, holding my bag in front of my knees like a barrier. 'Did you know I was on a course at Guy's?'

'I bumped into one of your colleagues at St Luke's; the pushy one with the strong sickly perfume...'

'Ava,' I snarled.

'Yeah, her. She told me.'

'I'll kill her.' I pinned my eyes on his. 'And you didn't tell *anyone* in the Met about it?'

Terry stalled and scratched his nose. 'I might have mentioned it in passing,' he said lightly. He tried to clear his throat, but his voice didn't improve. 'To a couple of people, maybe.'

He saw me open my mouth to rail at him but got in first. 'But I didn't mention cold cases, or you not having any patients or discuss *anything* about how you've always loved the idea of having a go at police profiling...'

By the end of his defensive tirade, he was grinning at me.

I stayed put on the mat, forcing him to keep the door open. Either that, or he'd have to let it spring shut in my face – and I knew he wasn't the kind of man who would ever do that.

'How did you know that about me?' I snapped. 'About police profiling? And I'm *not* coming in.'

'You told me.'

'When?'

'During a sushi meal we had in Soho... in June, I think it was... last year.'

'Flippin' heck.' I dropped the bag at my feet and stood tall, my hands on my hips. 'That's the problem with you,' I said, trying not to laugh. 'You've got a bloody good memory and you're too good a listener.'

He pulled a silly face and blew a raspberry at me.

'So, you told Claussen you're not doing it then?'

'Not exactly,' I muttered, not looking at him, reaching down for my belongings.

Another blast of curry enticed me to linger, together with the strains of smooth jazz and a crackle from the wood burner.

'So, all in all, everything's turned out in your favour then,' he said. 'Is that it?'

I stared at him, trying to keep a straight face.

'Are you coming in or not?' he said, pretending to sound exasperated.

'No,' I said, stepping inside after all.

As soon as he took my coat, my petulant toddler act fell

apart. He accidentally brushed his sleeve against my cheek and I took in the visceral rubbed-sage aroma of his jumper. What was it about this man, who seemed to have the capacity to win me over, like no other?

'It's good to see you,' I said, softening my tone. 'Did I say that earlier?'

'No, I don't think you did.'

He hung my coat in the hall and led me through to the living space. I'd been to his apartment only once before and remembered how different it was from my flat. Situated in a refurbished mansion block in Earl's Court, it was basically a one-room open-plan living space, with an en-suite bedroom. But what a space. Sleek high-gloss units lined the kitchen-diner, with an L-shaped sofa just the right toe-toasting distance from the wood burner. At the far side, floor to ceiling windows were draped with made-to-measure silky curtains. They flowed over the carpet like the gown of a monarch. The words stylish, plush and exclusive came to mind.

By comparison, I rented a first-floor flat within a tatty Victorian house. It had narrow rooms, creaking floorboards, and something different broke down virtually every week. So much so that I had the maintenance guy on speed dial.

The previous week, it was a leaking shower. The week before, the door of the washing machine wouldn't shut. Everything about my home was battered and shabby – but it was my blissful sanctuary. Originally only meant to be a stopgap, I'd put down roots there deeper than I could ever have imagined. It would take a lot to get me to move on.

'It's good to see you,' I said, trailing my fingers over the cool marble of the kitchen island, 'it's been a while.'

'Too long,' he said, avoiding my eyes.

He offered me a seat on the plump sofa and brought over a glass of wine.

When we were flung together the previous year on the case of the Regent's Canal murders, there was definitely a spark between us. I'd known him for an age, since we were students, but I'd always thought of him as a loyal 'brother' figure. Until last summer. He seemed keen on me and we even went on a few 'dates' during the investigation. But nothing happened and our contact fizzled out. I'm not sure why.

Terry had gone to Italy on holiday once the case was resolved, then I started my new training at Guy's and things just didn't seem to get off the ground between us. We exchanged a few texts and phone calls, but they were polite and stilted. Various phrases were batted back and forth: 'hectic at work', 'no time off', 'when I get a moment'. Neither of us was prepared to make the next move. Were we both scared? Not ready for a full-on relationship?

'I've made too much chicken korma, so you'd better be staying,' he said, throwing his comment over his shoulder as he stirred the contents of a pan.

I made a point of looking at my watch as if weighing up his offer. Then I realised he wasn't even looking my way.

'Mmm, I think that would be okay,' I said, taking a sip of wine, tasting citrus and a flinty flavour, but not too chalky – exactly how I wanted it. I had the feeling his choice wasn't an accident.

Since our near miss over summer, there'd been no one else for me, but I wasn't sure if Terry was still single. As he poured boiling water on the rice, I glanced around the flat, looking for signs. Had he met someone by now? Was it all too late?

6

———

Terry beckoned me over to the shiny pebble-dash dining table and presented me with a plate so pungent with cumin, ginger and coriander, I was virtually drooling.

'I've not had anything like this for weeks.'

'You haven't tasted it yet,' he said, offering me a bowl of dukkah for sprinkling. 'These are Moroccan, I'm afraid, not Indian,' he admitted, as if it were a crime.

The flavours burst open on my tongue the instant I tucked in. I sat back in admiration. 'When did you learn to cook like this?'

'Been on a course myself,' he said, holding his knife and fork on end, either side of his plate, like a child.

'The only courses I ever do are for work,' I told him. 'Memory loss, trauma, delusional behaviour – you name it, I've got the T-shirt.'

'But nothing just for fun? Just for you?'

'I used to do meditation and spinning at the gym, but...' I wrinkled my nose. 'I don't know. Things fall by the wayside.'

His hair looked freshly washed. Soft dark hair that hung in sculpted curves. Too long to be on trend, too short to make him look vain. He'd always had something old-school and erudite about him. Perhaps it was the battered brogues he was wearing even indoors, the colour of treacle. Or the turned-up collar on his ribbed M&S sweater.

He offered me a naan bread drizzled in rosemary oil. I tugged off a huge chunk, then put half of it back. 'Sorry, I need to lose weight and get some regular exercise again,' I admitted, pulling a guilty face.

'You look fine to me.' Again, deliberately not looking at me as he spoke.

I shook my head. 'Seriously, I'm so unfit.'

'You don't have to become a copper on the beat for this new project at the Met, you know. You won't be expected to chase suspects down the street.'

I laughed, but having just filled my mouth with garlic pickle, I spluttered like a choking parrot. I could feel my face turning crimson. Terry leapt from his seat and gave me three sharp whacks between my shoulder blades. I took a gulp of water, feeling stupid and self-conscious. If I was hoping to show him my elegant sophisticated side, I was failing abysmally.

'When will you get started?' he asked, sitting down again.

'Tomorrow, maybe.'

'Saturday?'

'I might as well. I've only got two weeks. It's hardly time to do anything.'

'Hey, don't forget, you don't have to *solve* the case in that time, just give the SIO some new lines of inquiry, some fresh pointers, if you can.'

I studied the tuft of coriander on my fork. 'It's a tough ask to search through hundreds of murder files and tease out any that are connected in some way.'

I might have known we'd end up talking about work. It was

the glue that held us together. But it wasn't the only thing. We needed to remind ourselves of that.

Once we'd finished the meal, he insisted on shunting me away from the dirty dishes.

'Put your feet up,' he instructed, sending me back to the sofa with a refill of wine. 'Chopin, Whitney Houston or Glenn Miller?'

I wanted to restore the soft mood. 'Got any Ennio Morricone?'

'Only on vinyl,' he said, finding the cover straight away from a wide row of records on his built-in shelves. Not only did he have exactly what I asked for, he didn't baulk at my choice. I liked that. I received enough derision in my life from my sister, even though I loved her to bits. As he slid the disc from the sleeve, the mobile on the coffee table rang.

Glancing at the caller's details, he picked up. 'Sorry, I need to take this,' he said, his expression sombre.

A rock fell inside my stomach. Someone special?

He disappeared into the adjoining room, presumably the bedroom.

I still had a tickle in my throat, so I slipped over to the sink to top up my glass of water. Terry's laptop was open on the kitchen island and I knew it was wrong to pry, but still I took a quick look.

I was surprised to recognise the photograph. It was the woman who'd fallen from the balcony the day before. The same picture the press had posted. I glanced up, but there was no sign of Terry coming back.

Originally a detective, and a good one, Terry was now involved with crime data management, training officers in the HOLMES 2 system. His change of direction came about due to a shotgun that had shattered his knee in an armed robbery a few years ago. Luckily, he loved his new job and with a passion for trying extreme sports, as well as learning new skills in the kitchen, he'd never let the injury hold him back. He didn't even need his walking stick anymore.

When I looked closer at the screen, I noticed the Met logo in the corner. Of course. Terry must have been working on data connected to the incident when I turned up unannounced.

I quickly scanned the text. The deceased was believed to be twenty-three-year-old Hazel Hart – an estate agent from Kings Cross. A formal identification was being carried out by her next of kin before the post-mortem.

Claussen's team had made it clear to me that I wouldn't be allowed access to current cases, so I knew this was something I shouldn't be looking at. Nevertheless, I was intrigued to know what information had been kept out of the media, if any. I tentatively put my finger on the touchpad and scrolled down. Then wished I hadn't. I had to swallow hard to keep the curry I'd just eaten where it was.

There were a series of photos taken at the scene. Shots of Hazel, a stunningly beautiful woman, after she'd hit the concrete. I looked away. I didn't want to see this. Nevertheless, something drew my eyes back. It was her hair. It wasn't long, like it had been in the press picture, it was cut short into a bob.

I speed-read the police report underneath. The stunt occurred during a party in Hazel's flat where around fifty people were believed to have attended. The police already had a long list of witnesses. The report stated that nothing was found on Hazel's body at the base of the tower block apart from one item. A pair of hairdressing scissors.

I was so engrossed, I didn't hear Terry march back into the room.

7

HAZEL

One week earlier

Is it you again, you slimeball? Loitering at the end of my road, hands in your pockets, trying to look cool? How do you know where I live? You followed me home?

I take two steps out of my gate in my new Jimmy Choo ankle boots and glance round. Sure enough, you're on the move. I still can't see your face, but know it's you from your big strides. What kind of pervy game are you playing?

Whatever it is, I'm getting pissed off. How do I get rid of you? I finger the phone in my pocket and think about calling the cops, but what would they do?

I should tell *someone* though. Until now I haven't been sure – I keep thinking it might all be in my head – but it's been three days. No one's going to help me if they don't know what's going on. On the other hand, I'm going to feel like a total wimp if I have to get one of the lads in my block to walk me to the bus stop and meet me from work, like an effin' bodyguard. Humiliation, or what? In any case, that's no use to me right now, because

I've just checked and you're right behind me, your hood up like a thug.

I toy with the idea of breaking into a run, but I'm wearing the wrong bloody footwear. Besides, it's chucking it down and I'm bound to go flying and muck up the new Max Mara coat I snapped up in the sale. I can't afford to be a mess when I get to work. Not today. Not when I'm showing a couple from New York around a property at nine o'clock. I need to look my best.

The buyers are only in London for a few days and they're interested in the five-bed property with the swimming pool. It's really posh and absolutely top-end for Dentworths. I can't stuff it up.

I'm tempted to walk straight past the bus stop, but I'll be late if I don't catch the first number forty-six. Sure enough, it comes round the corner and I have no choice. I have to get on in full view of you.

The umbrellas go down in the queue around me and I bunch up behind people, but you're not fooled. I hurry to the back behind a tall bloke and slide down in the seat. I'm hoping you won't see me, but you walk straight down the aisle – your face turned away as if I'm of no interest whatsoever. You slip into the seat directly behind me. I make a move to get up, but there are so many passengers that the aisle is full and there's nowhere for me to go.

It's two stops to the tube, the next bit of my journey, and I pray the crowd will thin out, so I can move to another seat. I cringe and sink lower as I feel your stinky hot breath on the back of my neck. I pull the scarf up to my ears to block you out. I want nothing more than to turn round and punch your friggin' lights out, but I don't want to get arrested. Certainly not today, when a hefty commission with my name on it is hanging in the balance.

I watch the raindrops dribble down the glass in crooked

lines. The windows are steaming up with commuter breath and I'm feeling trapped. Pukey too. I want everything to stop. Do you have a knife in your pocket? Or scissors like I thought I saw last time? Surely, with so many people around, you wouldn't dare touch me. Why can't you naff off and leave me alone?

Finally, it's my stop and I get up. I keep my head down and shunt my way through the crush to the door. Once on the pavement, I jerk my head round to look back. I scan the figures who got off and you don't seem to be one of them. I can't quite believe it. I punch the air. The bus chunters off down the road and you're nowhere to be seen.

I walk to the escalator with a spring in my step and can breathe again. Anyone watching me would think I'd won the lottery.

By the time I get to Dentworths, the rain has dropped off to a needling drizzle and everything seems as it should be. I'm more alert than normal, my ears pricked up for the slightest sound behind me, my eyes primed for any sudden movements in my peripheral vision, but I'm fine. And alone.

I shake my wet coat off at the door and peel the scarf away from my neck. Carol brings a coffee to my desk and she's telling me about her new pet rabbit. I listen to her soothing voice, every word sounding like it's coated in buttercream now I'm safe. Then, between her cute anecdotes, I wonder where you went when I got off the bus and whether you'll be waiting when I leave work tonight. Maybe it isn't over.

Carol drops a plastic lid into the wastepaper basket behind me. She says something and giggles nervously as she straightens up.

I snap round at her. 'What did you say?'

'Hazel, your hair! What have you done?'

I reach up with both hands and run my fingers through the back. 'What the f–!'

I stand up straight, then buckle, right there in the middle of the office, bile burning my throat. I have to reach out and grab the chair to hold myself upright.

Carol is already searching in her bag for a mirror and a group of colleagues have formed a small circle around me. They're gawping at me as though I'm one of those baboons with a red arse in the zoo.

Carol grabs my wrist and marches me off to the bathroom. She stands me in front of the mirror on the wall, then offers me the small one from her handbag. I try to line them up to see the back of my head. My hand is trembling the whole time, so the image is blurred at first.

Then I see what you've done.

It hits me like a cannon ball in the stomach. There's a chunk missing at the back. My hair's all one length and now there's a bit where it only reaches my collar. About six centimetres wide. *You bastard!* I let out a piercing scream, the sound bouncing back from the tiles at me.

'My hair – my beautiful hair!' All strength drains from my limbs and I drop the mirror. It smashes and I sink to the floor on top of the cascade of glass splinters.

'It must have happened on the bus... I didn't feel a thing... I had my scarf around my neck, so that must...' My babbling dries up.

Carol's mouth is moving. 'Just stupid kids... a silly game...'

She prattles on, but her words float above me.

My hair. My luscious golden hair that reaches down to my waist. It's my pride and joy. I've put up hundreds of selfies on Instagram and get tons of likes and comments. Everyone says how gorgeous it is. It's taken me over a decade to get it to look like this. Now it's soddin' ruined.

Carol grabs my arm and is more or less propping me up. 'You'll need a really good hairdresser to sort that out...'

Her words fill me with dread. I cradle my remaining hair in my hands as though afraid it will all fall out. 'No... no...' It's the only word I can utter. Over and over again. I'm in a total nightmare. This is the worst thing, like, ever. I've been violated.

I can't. I simply can't get it all cut off.

8

———————

SAM

The Present

As soon as I caught Terry approaching, I swivelled towards the sink and started filling my glass with water. He came up behind me.

'Sorry about that,' he said. 'Work stuff.'

I turned round to face him, holding my glass to my chest. He was standing very close. There was an intensity about him that was hard to describe. As I stared into his lagoon-blue eyes, his pupils seemed to sizzle. It was like stepping into a shallow pool and finding the shimmering water up to my waist by the second step. Then I wondered if he was scrutinising me that intently because he knew I'd been snooping.

I cleared my throat. 'Everything okay?'

He nodded absently, but didn't elucidate. 'Tell me about this project you're starting. What exactly has Claussen asked you to do?'

Since we'd last spent time together, I'd missed his soft velvety tones. He had the kind of lie-back-and-relax voice you'd expect to hear in a Baileys advert.

We returned to the sofa. On the way, I noticed he'd taken his shoes off and was padding around in his socks.

I explained the details.

'And she wants you to look for evidence of grandiose delusions?' He twisted in my direction, his elbow on the back of the sofa.

'Yes. Did you know one of the earliest documented cases of homicidal delusions involved King Charles VI of France in the fourteenth century?'

He smiled, folding his knees up, looking settled and comfortable, as though he could listen to me for hours. I took another slug of wine. It was slipping down a treat. 'The king thought he was made of glass and went on killing sprees to stop people harming him.'

'Seriously?'

Terry seemed genuinely animated, so I carried on. There weren't many people in my circle I could rattle on with about this kind of subject. To be honest, there weren't many people in my circle – full stop.

'A serial killer was recently convicted in America,' I said, 'a guy who believed he was Kojak, the TV detective from the 1970s. The only thread the police could find linking his murders was the fact that he left behind a cherry lollipop beside the corpses. When he was finally caught, he told them he shaved his head before every attack.'

'You're kidding me.'

'It's a fascinating area to explore.' I tossed my hair back, sensing Terry's eyes on me.

'Are these psychopaths we're talking about?'

'No. Psychopaths don't tend to have hallucinations or delusions. These individuals are suffering from psychosis – they're out of touch with reality, but they're not psychopaths. And most people with delusions don't actually kill.'

He seemed to blink in slow motion; it was very sexy and it distracted me. I reached down to scratch my ankle to break the seductive spell he was weaving, whether he knew it or not.

'How the hell can you track down suspects suffering from delusions merely from police records?' he asked.

'Er... hmm... how indeed? That's what's worrying me.' I rapped my nails against the side of my glass. 'Sorry to keep going on about this.'

'Don't apologise. We're chatting about things we both find engrossing, aren't we?' He got up suddenly. 'I've got a book about Jack the Ripper; the psychology behind his rampages. You probably could have written it yourself, but let me go and get it.' Terry flashed an unexpected grin and put his hand on my knee as he got to his feet. The heat of his palm lingered long after he pulled away, sending shivers skittering headlong down my spine.

There was something different between us that evening. Maybe it was the wine. Maybe it was simply the right time.

Despite the risk, I scuttled back to his laptop, taking my glass with me. Back to the woman with the long hair who'd fallen from the balcony. Something was bothering me. As I reread the details, Hazel's radical haircut wasn't mentioned once. That was a lot of hair she'd had removed. And the scissors. Not just any scissors, but they were hairdressing scissors that had been found in the deep pocket of her mini skirt. What about the selfie? Had she taken the picture? I skimmed the particulars. She had lost her balance before the shot was taken. The mobile was found shattered about three metres from her body.

Once again, I was so engrossed in the report that I failed to see Terry come back in. I wasn't so lucky this time.

'Hey, what are you up to?' He was serious.

Caught in the act, I grimaced, swaying a little, still holding my wine glass.

He glanced down at what I was studying.

'You do understand you're not allowed access to current cases,' he said, reproach transforming his eyes.

I nodded, not taking my eyes from his face. 'I was curious – her hair... I mean, who carries hairdressing scissors at a party? It says here she was an estate agent, not a hairdresser. Had she just cut off all her own hair? Look at it here.' I pointed to the shot given to the press where her sleek mane reached down to her waist. 'This photo was taken only two weeks earlier. That's about two feet of hair she's had lopped off.'

He reached across me and shut the lid of the laptop, then leant back against the sink folding his arms. 'You shouldn't be looking at this.' He took a laboured breath as if to imply it wasn't the first time I'd overstepped the mark. 'You're meant to be looking into unsolved murders. Cold cases. This is strictly off limits.'

'But maybe someone pushed this woman? Maybe she didn't just "fall off" the balcony taking a selfie.'

'It's not a suspicious death, Sam.'

'But what about the scissors in her pocket? Were they her scissors or the killer's?' I was on a roll. 'Were they meant to be the weapon? Was the killer a hairdresser?'

Terry shook his head in despair. 'I think maybe you've had a bit too much to drink.'

'No,' I retorted, blinking hard. I stared at the floor working out how much I'd actually had. Three large glasses? Four? I didn't usually drink this much.

I felt my face fall and reached out to take hold of the edge of the sink. The room shifted a fraction to one side. 'What if I have? I'm still talking sense.'

'You shouldn't be talking about this, at all.' Disapproval showed in his mouth and I cringed inwardly at my transgression.

'Shall we get you home?' he suggested, stepping into the hallway and reaching for my coat.

Damn. I didn't want to go. I was enjoying myself and there were too many unanswered questions left up in the air.

Although, one thing was certain. I'd well and truly blown it between the two of us.

9

———

My instant companion, even before I'd opened my eyes, was a hangover. The full works: nausea, dizziness, a mouth like the bottom of a parrot's cage, topped off with a splitting headache. I turned away from the hairline crack in the curtains, as a laser shard of light stabbed my eyelids. It was as if I'd spent the entire night being churned on the tornado ride at an amusement park. Not a great way to start my weekend, but it was my own fault.

I dragged myself in slow motion to the bathroom, trying not to move my head. As soon as I staggered into the shower, I remembered there was something worse. I'd made an out-and-out fool of myself. And I'd violated Terry's privacy. He would never trust me again. All in all, I'd made a complete hash of things.

For a fleeting moment I considered contacting Terry to apologise, but my head was so woolly I had no idea what I'd say. I'd probably only make things worse. I could either go back to bed and feel even more of a loser or bury my shame by getting straight on with the cold case job. With time, caffeine and painkillers, the physical symptoms might shift at least. I might even find myself absorbed in it.

There was no way I was climbing onto a bicycle in my wobbly state – my new intentions to get fit already out of the window – so I caught the next train.

Camden was already bustling with shoppers and tourists by the time I arrived. As I weaved along the side streets, a text buzzed in my pocket. My heart rate shot up a notch. My first thought was that DCS Claussen was ordering me off the cold case investigation after hearing I'd accessed data without consent. Then I realised Terry would need to admit he'd left his laptop open in my presence. I glanced down at the screen and let the breath I was holding go – it was my sister.

Thought we'd pencilled in Friday night at my place. Did you get a better offer?

Shit! She was right. We'd agreed I'd go over to chat about her new venture. It wasn't like me to forget. Another reason to feel guilty.

I called Miranda straight away.

'I'm so sorry. I got landed with some extra work yesterday and I was... following it up.' I cringed at my half-truth.

'Doesn't matter,' she snapped. 'At least everyone else turned up.' Her best friends came from the Camden Community Art Project, where she spent most of her time. It was her safe haven, run and used by those with similar mental health issues.

'I can come over later, if you like?'

I'd been meaning to have a chat with her for a while. She'd been avoiding me and that was usually a sign that there was something I needed to be worried about. She hated asking me for help and her response when there was a difficulty in her life was to retreat from me instead. I needed to get to the bottom of it, whatever it was.

'Where are you?' she asked, undoubtedly hearing background traffic and the judder in my voice from my footsteps.

'Camden, actually. Only a stone's throw from your flat. I'm on my way to the police station. I'm doing some work for them for a couple of weeks.'

'Dragging information from another reluctant murder witness?' I could picture her wagging her finger at me. A familiar gesture.

'No, it's nothing specific.' She was referring to the canal case where the sole witness had been rendered mute. 'I'm just in their office. And Aiden wasn't reluctant – he was traumatised.' I took a breath. 'You okay?'

Since childhood, I'd always had an antenna tuned in her direction, trying to look like I hadn't. I've always had to be more than just her sister, even though she's two years older than me. My parents didn't handle her schizophrenia well at all: my mother gave up on her years ago and my father handled Miranda like a broken doll, making everything worse. So it had been down to me for as long as I could remember.

She didn't answer my question. 'Text me when you're finished,' she said stiffly. 'Can't say I'll be around for definite, mind you. Anyway, can't talk now, got things to do.' With that, the call was over.

Miranda's abrupt approach wasn't new; she regularly blew hot and cold with me. Largely because our relationship was so complex. I'd spent my entire upbringing watching her every move, waiting for the next thing to get broken. It had taken years to establish her condition and she'd reached twenty before she was finally diagnosed.

In the meantime, she'd left a trail of destruction with every manic outburst. Climbing naked onto our roof, smashing tiles, for instance. Riding her bike into a group of morris dancers on May Day. Tipping a sherry trifle over Mum's birthday cake at a lavish family gathering. Inevitably, onlookers were outraged and the rest of us – mainly me, it had to be said – were left to clear up the mess.

These days, Miranda was on the right medication, after numerous trials and false starts. She was just like any other person, only her emotions and behaviours soared and dipped several notches beyond the rest of us. She was more volatile, excitable and conversely, gloomy and disconsolate than anyone else I knew. But she was also funny, imaginative, generous, the life and soul of the party, and far more outgoing than me. In fact, she was more *everything*. The one constant in her life was that I adored her.

10

———

Once inside the police station, my pass was heavily scrutinised by an officer at the desk. After several checks on the computer and a phone call, I was allowed through. I headed along the corridor and encountered a walk-through security scanner before I had to press the card against a small black box on the wall beside double doors. Finally, I was admitted inside a large office.

It was like any other open-plan place of work with long rows of desks and computer terminals. Filing cabinets, a couple of shredders and a handful of parlour palms competed for the remaining space. I'm not sure what I was expecting, but there were no stark crime-scene photos or mugshots on whiteboards, just an overwhelming impression of beige.

I hovered beside one of the central pillars wondering where to go. My head was still throbbing with the hangover and the flickering strip lights didn't help.

Several desks looked unoccupied, but on closer inspection had either a jacket over a chair-arm, a pen on the mouse mat, or a half-full mug on the coaster. In the end, I trawled the room and finally came to a vacant terminal beside a coat stand. I dropped my briefcase against the chair, sat down and slid my pass through a reader attached to the monitor to log on.

It didn't work.

At that moment the woman next to me swore vehemently, making me jump.

'Sorry,' she said, nibbling her bottom lip. 'Just input a pile of suspects in the wrong age band. Don't tell anyone. I'm Prue, by the way. And you'd better get a neck strap for your pass or you'll never see it again.'

I laughed. 'Right. Thank you. I'm Sam. I'm just temporary. Browsing cold cases for DCS Claussen. Or supposed to be.'

'Ah, you're the clinical whatsit.'

'Clinical psychologist – yes, from St Luke's by London Bridge.'

'Oh, my dad went there for a hip replacement. Not your department, obviously.'

I tried the pass again. Still no luck.

'I appear to be locked out of Fort Knox,' I said, scowling at the card.

'Let me give Donald a ring.' Prue reached for her phone. 'There's probably been a hitch getting you onto the system – it won't be the first time – want a coffee while we wait?' she said, all in one breath.

'I'd love one. Strong and black, please.'

She said a few words into the receiver then replaced it. 'It could be half an hour,' she told me, wrinkling her nose. 'Rough night?'

I nodded with a groan. She'd no doubt spotted the slugs that replaced my eyelids and the charcoal smudges under my eyes. She puckered her chin, emanating sympathy rather than judgement, then got up.

Prue gave me a tour of the scant kitchen facilities.

'We're meant to be getting a machine that makes macchiatos

and cappuccinos with frothy milk and all that, but it hasn't arrived yet,' she said, flicking a switch on the wall beside the kettle. 'So, it's basic hot water and instant, I'm afraid.'

'Hot and black is all I need right now.'

'I've got a spare mug you can use while you're here, if you like?' She held it up. 'Don't be put off by what it says on the side.'

She turned it round so I could read it. *My handcuffs are for off-duty use only.* I laughed. 'That'll do nicely,' I said, blowing my fringe out of my eyes. She poured hot water onto a sprinkling of coffee granules and handed it to me.

After a brief chat about the location of the canteen, loos and lockers, we returned to our workstations.

With time to kill before I could get into the system, I looked up Jack the Ripper on my tablet. Terry hadn't actually given me his book last night – my fault, not his.

Since I'd joined the course, I'd been meaning to check if any psychologist had found signs of grandiose delusions behind the Ripper's killing spree, back in 1888. As the first murderer to be named a 'serial killer', it seemed like a good place to start.

I'd got myself embedded in a labyrinth of tangential links involving his victims when Prue turned to me. 'Just got an email. They were expecting you on Monday. You're authorised now.'

I patted her arm with a smile and ran the pass through again.

'Geronimo,' I said and got my head down.

Although I'd been given access to the cold case database, I hadn't had any instruction about how to use it. Perhaps that was also lined up for me on Monday. I didn't want to disturb Prue again, so I simply put the word 'delusion' into the search bar. Over five hundred individual results came up, so I started with the first one to see what kind of information I'd selected. A police report filled the page. It described a victim of a hit and run in Liverpool who'd suffered delusions before her death. It was about the victim, so wasn't of any use to me. It also wasn't in London during the last two decades. I applied London as a filter and restricted the dates, reducing the results by half.

The first of this new list referred to a statement where a witness had complained of persecutory delusions the night before someone stabbed her brother to death. Still, the wrong angle.

I sat back. The delusions I wanted to examine needed to be those of the *killer*, not those of victims or witnesses. Terry and I had touched on this the day before, but I hadn't actually narrowed down the main problem. Now the whopping spanner in the works was plain to see. It was *unsolved* murders I was looking into. Investigators *didn't know* about any delusions that may have been involved, because the killers had never been found. The search term 'delusion' was useless.

So how on earth was I going to find delusional behaviours? I was stuck in a catch twenty-two.

I rapped my fingernails on the desk and found my thoughts winding back to the report on Terry's laptop. Professional hairdressing scissors had been found in Hazel Hart's pocket. As an experiment, I typed the word 'scissors' in the search box. Numerous files came up, but as I trawled through I found they were all cases where scissors had been used as the murder weapon.

It was going to be a long day. I needed to rethink this whole process.

I decided to try something completely different and put in the word 'hair'. Over 800 results came up. After looking at the first two selected files, I realised my mistake. Of course, the word 'hair' would get countless mentions in the reports; it would be linked to DNA found at a crime scene.

I put in 'disturbance to hair' and got no results at all. The wording was too obscure. Then I tried 'haircut'.

Two records came up. At last. I punched the air and almost whooped with joy. I was getting the hang of it. Then it occurred to me. Of course. I was going to have to look for clues in the *methodology*; find traits in the *ways* in which murders were carried out. Either that, or find common themes in the backgrounds of the victims involved, or common themes in the way victims were selected. My euphoria dissipated like a flat tyre. It was still going to be like finding matching needles in a very large haystack.

I gritted my teeth and turned to the first record. It involved the murder three years ago of Charlotte Walsh, aged twenty-two. She was a dental receptionist in Primrose Hill and was suffocated in her flat with a pillow.

There were chic ante-mortem photographs on the file and what struck me immediately was the similarity between Charlotte and Hazel. Both had been dazzlingly pretty and had unusually long hair, both down to their waist. The one difference was that she was dark-haired, not blonde.

The photo of Charlotte given to the media showed it tied into a ponytail, but there was a mortuary photograph that sent an icy chill down my spine. It wasn't just the sight of this young woman's corpse, lying blotchy and purple on the steel table.

Charlotte's hair was much shorter in the picture.

The post-mortem didn't mention it, but a witness statement revealed she'd had a dramatic haircut only days before she was killed. Just like Hazel.

I barely noticed when Prue left the room to go to a meeting. By then I was hooked.

Although Claussen had warned me the files were 'read only', I tried to print the full report. Sure enough I was forbidden access. The same happened when I put in my USB stick in order to copy it. Blocked. Fair enough, I thought. You'd expect confidential details such as this to be protected to prevent it getting into the wrong hands.

What Claussen hadn't mentioned, however, was making handwritten notes. If I didn't want to stay cooped up in this stuffy office all day, that was what I needed to do. Then I could mull things over and reflect on what I'd found, away from this soulless setting. That was how I'd work best.

So, with Prue still away from her desk, and after checking that no one was looking my way, I surreptitiously pulled out my notebook. Omitting key names, so it wouldn't make sense to anyone out of context, I scribbled down the main details.

There was another case flagged up from my search, but I'd done enough for now. I was aching for fresh air and to stretch my legs, so I got up and left.

11

Three years earlier

As I step off the bus a few stops before I need to, it starts to sleet, icy fragments biting into my cheeks. I'm glad. It *should* be snowing at this time of year. The earth needs to freeze away all the bacteria so nature can start afresh.

I look up and watch as the tiny slices of ice fill the black sky with wet confetti. I've always loved winter and even wanted to get married in the snow, but that won't be happening any time soon. Not now I've given back the ring.

The film doesn't start for forty minutes, so I break away from the main road and stroll through back streets, past red-brick apartment blocks, then into a secluded area which would have been one of London's original villages.

It's refreshing to be away from the bustle of commuters and tourists. The further I drift from the main road, the fewer people are about and I'm aware of the intermittent crackle as leftover autumn leaves are tossed by the breeze into doorways. The only other sound is the lonely clomp of my boots on the pavement. They're tatty these days, but I can't afford new ones. I tried stitching the hole in the side, but I broke two needles in the process. Maybe I'll get to a charity shop at the weekend to see if they've got anything my size.

I'm drawn under an archway into one of the quiet cobbled mews. The courtyard cottages look homely and cosy, painted in shades of pastel pinks and pale blues. They remind me of cupcakes.

Lantern-style streetlamps, straight from a Dickensian Christmas card, are few and far between, creating ethereal pools of light on the melting sleet. I feel the woodsmoke in the air tickle my lungs. Blinds are down and shutters are closed. It seems like everyone in South Kensington has turned in for the night.

I slow down and daydream, picturing myself living in the luxurious interior behind one of these doors. This one, perhaps, painted glossy cobalt blue with a golden ring door knocker. Wearing satin pyjamas and mohair slippers, I'd loll in front of a real log fire. Make that fake mohair, now I'm vegan. I do a little twirl at the notion of it. Fantasies are my escape. With my job at the dentist under threat and an ex-fiancé who can't seem to grasp we're over, it feels like my dreams are all I've got. I'm going to have to cut back on food and clothes, give up my poetry class and probably move to a cheaper bedsit, but I can't bear to think of that now.

Even though it's pure make-believe, I want to create a blissful existence in my mind, full of beauty and magic. Dad says I spend too much time looking for escapism instead of getting on with important stuff like finding a better job and settling down. He says I'm always away with the fairies, but the real world is too hostile and tough for a 'delicate soul' like me. They were the words the new vicar at the church used to describe me last week and I think they're spot on.

I've spent hours on the net looking up properties for sale in places like this, admiring the décor, the furnishings and accessories. I've scoured magazines on home makeovers in the library – because I can't even afford to buy the publications. I've fantasised about bumping into film stars who carry me off to their private islands, being hailed as the next poet laureate, being left a huge inheritance by a long-lost relative. I know it's all in my head, but at least it gives me some form of comfort.

I reach the end of the mews, thinking it joins a larger road, but it continues round the corner and gets narrower. On one side is an ominous tall building with no windows, on the other is a railing with a gate, overhung with leggy branches. It looks like a scene from a gothic horror movie. As I look up ahead, it's a dead end.

It's then I know someone's behind me.

12

―――――

SAM

The Present

Miranda grunted when she opened her front door.

'You made it then,' she sniffed, about to turn away. Determined to break the stalemate between us, I grabbed her before she could move off and wrapped my arms around her in a firm hug. Then noticed she held a wet paint brush in one hand and an oily rag in the other.

'Careful...' She stepped back without looking at me.

I sighed under my breath. 'I'm sorry I missed the planning meeting last night. I was... there was something else I had to do.'

'Something more important, you mean.'

Her eyes smouldered with rage and she refused to look at me.

I'd spent my life walking the finest line with my sister – one drawn with an exceedingly thin nib. And I invariably got it wrong. Many were the times she accused me of interfering, smothering her, bullying even. Often, she misinterpreted what I said or did; regarding my actions as a threat to take away her freedom and stop her from being herself.

Yet I was only ever trying to keep her safe.

She left me, so I hung up my coat, then followed her.

'Mind where you walk,' she said to the space in front of her, weaving her way barefoot into the main room. 'Nearly everything has wet paint on it.'

Miranda's flat was entirely different to mine: open-plan with bare floorboards and scarcely any furniture. Perfect for an artist. She didn't even have curtains. Oil canvases lined the room, leaning in stacks against every wall and a black iron staircase spiralled up to the floor above from the corner by the kitchen. She owned the place, but only because Dad had stepped in. Working less than ten hours a week at the art project café, she'd never have been able to afford it. I often wondered how her bills were paid, but got my head snapped off whenever I even tiptoed in that direction.

'Coffee, I suppose?' she said, leaving the brush and cloth on a table cluttered with paint paraphernalia.

Miranda had spiky cropped hair, dyed blonde so severely it was now alabaster-white. She was taller than me with chiselled features and could disappear behind a drainpipe she was so skinny, even though she didn't seem to do any exercise. Much to my annoyance.

'New rugs?' I queried, noticing the threadbare Persian-style carpets lying piecemeal across the floor. They looked like they'd come straight out of a skip, but I hadn't seen them before. Miranda adored items that were 'pre-loved'. She said she could relate to 'damaged goods' – objects that had been disparaged at some stage, but which were now rightly treasured for what they were.

'You like them?' she responded, her tone mocking.

'They're very... you,' I said, thinking fast.

Wearing a fluffy jumper over baggy dungarees, she was going through a *hygge* phase inspired by the Danish craze. It was all about putting comfort and the simple things in life first. Her outfit was at least two sizes too big, but anything looked good on her.

I traipsed after her into the kitchen. It was chilly, with a draft wheezing under the back door, and I shivered. Unlike me, Miranda wasn't a great believer in keeping the place warm.

'How's the prep going?' I asked.

Miranda had been awarded a special grant to show her paintings outside the Camden Community Art Project for the very first time. Her maiden voyage into the mainstream limelight – and a big deal for her.

'Pretty cool actually,' she said, sounding upbeat although her flinty eyes were still steered away from mine. She scooted old wrappers and takeaway cartons from the draining board into the pedal bin. 'I've decided to hold the exhibition here.'

'What, here in your flat?'

'Sure, why not? It's on-trend for up and coming artists to showcase their work in their own studios.' She threw out her arm as if showing me the place for the first time. 'Just because I live here doesn't mean we can't open it to the public.' Words like insurance and damages came to mind, but I had to trust she knew what she was doing. 'Zoe's getting leaflets printed and I'm putting together a competition for Facebook to drum up interest.'

'Anything I can do to help?'

I wanted to do what normal sisters did: help her out, share life events, have a laugh, confide in one another, but it never seemed to work out that way.

She blew a dead fly off the top of the tea caddy. 'I think I'm covered now. Thanks. I've got friends lined up to help me hang everything on the day. I've got someone doing the drinks and social media is covered.'

It sounded, as usual, like she didn't need me.

I turned my attention back to the main room. 'Have you done any new pictures I can see?'

She marched ahead of me and pulled one out of a pile, then leant it against the table leg. I'd never been fond of Miranda's paintings. This one appeared to be large smears of sludge-brown and bruise-purple, resembling shapes from a landscape. It was only when I took a step back and pieced the contours together that it took on a different perspective. The intimate parts of a woman's body. Torn and violated.

A glutinous ball formed in my throat. I didn't dare ask who the woman was meant to be.

'It's definitely got something,' I said, cautiously, taking further steps back to see if it improved. It was garish and grotesque. Being offered to a prospective buyer for £250, according to the sticker on the edge of the frame.

'My tutor said it marks the start of a new stage – more earthy,' she explained. 'She said it was a real statement piece.'

I nodded, faking an air of favourable appraisal, hoping Miranda wouldn't see through me. My sister's artwork had a deep meaning for her and I could never bring myself to say what I really thought. It was too important to her; a crucial form of expressive therapy that kept her demons at bay.

'What about you? What are you doing with the police?' She handed me a steaming mug – the handle had broken off some time ago – and led the way to the beaten-up old sofa. She pointed to a shabby low armchair beside it, covered in newspaper. 'It's clean,' she insisted.

'I've been reading up on Jack the Ripper,' I said.

'What? Why?' She sat on the arm of the sofa, swinging one leg.

Instantly, I knew I'd said too much.

13

'Well?' she nudged.

It was too late to backtrack. Doing so would have made an even bigger thing of it and I knew only too well that my sister hated being kept in the dark. 'I'm... helping the police with something. That's all.'

Miranda scrunched up her nose. 'What? To find Jack the Ripper?'

I laughed. 'Not sure that would be the best use of police resources a hundred and thirty years too late.' I supped the hot drink; if Miranda had one saving grace it was that she made a good coffee. 'I'm not supposed to mention what I'm doing. Sorry.'

She tutted and looked at me askance. 'Mmm. You're reading up on Jack the Ripper and you're helping the police.' She tapped her lip repeatedly with paint-encrusted fingers. 'Let's get this straight, you're a psychologist and you've just been on a course about delusional behaviour. So that means...' The light went on behind her eyes and she leapt up. 'You're looking for a serial killer, right?'

I ground my teeth. 'It's not... I can't...'

She looked aghast. 'Shit – you are! You're tracking down a modern-day Jack the Ripper!' She stared at me as if she'd just heard I had weeks to live. 'Oh, God, you're not are you? It sounds really dangerous…'

'Not by myself,' I said with a soft smile. I was touched that she actually seemed concerned for me. 'I'll just be looking at the files, finding any connections and handing over any new information back to the force to see if it's worth following up.'

She shrugged. 'Oh…' Her animation dissipated instantly. 'Sounds a bit boring.'

'It's only for a couple of weeks. Maybe less, if it's a dead end. Pardon the pun.' I cradled my mug, grateful for the warmth. 'Thing is, I won't be able to tell you any details. I'm sorry.'

'I know the rules,' she said stiffly.

She sidled over to the window and looked down as if she was expecting someone. There was a prolonged silence where neither of us seemed to know what to say next. I was certain then that Miranda was hiding something. In a bid to turn the conversation towards the real reason I was there, I mentioned seeing Terry.

'Are you and he an item yet?' she asked, leaving the window and sitting down.

'No. But we had a kind of "moment" – I'm not sure it'll go anywhere.'

'When?' She was perky again.

'Yesterday evening. I needed to see him about… I needed to check something with him about this new role.'

'Oh, so that's where you were.' She flipped her bottom lip with a finger, looking coy. 'I always knew you fancied him. Only you've been in complete denial about it.'

I let out a long breath. She might have been right. 'What about you? Are you in complete denial about anything?'

My question caught her off guard. So much so that she didn't snap. She didn't even accuse me of prying or dismiss me. She went quiet and dropped her head. I reached over and lifted her chin with my finger.

'Is it the exhibition?'

She gave a nervy twitch of the head in response. 'No...'

I believed her.

Within seconds she restored her composure and got up, snatching away my mug even though I hadn't finished the drink.

She waltzed off into the kitchen without any further explanation. I heard water running in the sink, then the clatter of tins being rearranged in one of the cupboards. There was definitely something wrong and I wasn't leaving until I knew what it was.

There'd always been unspoken issues between the two of us. In the past, her secrets had led to devastating repercussions, so we'd made a pact not long ago to be more open with one another. No more lies, no more secrets, no more hiding things.

I took off towards the kitchen, blocking the door, not allowing her to escape. 'Is it money?' I asked gently.

'No!' She spun round. 'It's nothing. I'm just a bit tired, that's all.' It came out too fast. Too rehearsed.

I stood my ground and waited. I took my mind back to Terry. He had a what-you-see-is-what-you-get approach with people. No game playing. It was refreshing and the total opposite to Miranda.

She sank her weight to one hip. 'Listen, thanks for coming over and everything, but I need to finish a painting.'

There was no point in banging on at her. In spite of my resolve not to leave until I knew the truth, I backed off and went in search of my coat. My sister thought I was a control freak and party-pooper. She wasn't going to tell me anything unless she wanted to. If I hung around, it would only make her more determined to shut me out.

One thing was certain, Miranda was being mysterious. Evasive. After all our promises about not keeping secrets, she was definitely hiding something.

14

CHARLOTTE

Three years earlier

I stop dead, my back to you, listening. The only way out of this cul-de-sac is to turn round and retrace my steps. But then I'd have to walk right past you.

I'm probably being stupid, paranoid. My overactive imagination making up stories. It's just someone who lives here, maybe locked out or waiting for someone, or innocently out for a stroll, like me. But, if that's the case, why did your footsteps stop exactly when mine did. What are you doing?

The branch above the gate comes alive with a gust of wind; it creaks and moans, and I feel a claustrophobic rush of panic. I have to get out of here.

I count to five and spin round, my eyes like night cameras tracking every movement. I know I'm not going crazy when I see a figure in a khaki jacket lurking behind a potted bay tree on the far side.

Who are you? There are too many shadows and you've made doubly sure I can't see your face by keeping your hood up.

For three days I've had this eerie feeling. A faint niggle that someone's been creeping into the spaces around me, slipping in and out of my peripheral vision. What do you want from me?

It seems so much darker now, as though a vital light has gone out. I can't stay stuck to the spot, I need to get to the cinema.

I start moving again. I pick up speed and dart past the bay tree, then immediately skid on the cobbles coated with sleet like icing sugar. The next moment, I stumble and fall to my knees.

The world spins as I scrabble to my feet, but I get going again, aware that the shape behind me is on the move too. I break into a run, back on the street, but I don't know how far I'll get. Everywhere is so slippery and the soles of these Doc Martens have no tread anymore. I didn't know I was going to have to leg it at this kind of speed.

I daren't look round, but I don't need to. I can tell from the regular thud-thud of your clompy boots that you're within inches of me. My scalp prickles and I hear my own breathing swell to gasps. The worst nightmares flash through my mind: are you going to mug me, stab me, rape me?

There's a kerfuffle and thud behind me and the footsteps stop for a second. I think you've slipped and fallen too, in the skating rink that has become the pavement.

I cower behind a telephone box and take a quick look back. You're on your feet again, but limping a little. How can I shake you off? If I rush into an alleyway, I'll make myself more vulnerable. I need people.

I look ahead for someone to run towards, someone I can latch onto, but there are so few people about. A boy in the distance walking a dog, a man delivering pizzas, a woman jogging – all going in the other direction.

Who *are* you? A random stalker who's spotted my profile online? Someone connected to work? Then I think of Chris and how furious he is with me for calling off the engagement. But

Chris is far chunkier; it can't be him. Are you Darren, his best mate? Or one of his friends from work? You're not the right build to be any of them. Someone else from Chris's family perhaps, who thinks I've betrayed him?

Without looking behind, I manage to get my legs going again. I cut through back roads and a warren of narrow side streets and now I don't know where I am. I need to get to a busy road.

I can hear heavier traffic and head towards it. More lights, a bus going past.

Finally, I reach the main road and dive into a shop. It sells groceries. There are people. I rush to the checkout, unable to stop myself elbowing my way through customers.

'Someone's after me!' I yell to anyone who'll listen. 'Someone's chasing me.'

I have to stop and bend double, completely winded. My mouth gapes wide open as I make ghastly wheezing sounds, trying to snatch breaths. I'm sweating like a pig and my cheeks are on fire.

A woman with a young boy pulls him to her side, as if I'm the person they should be worried about. I stay bent over, my hands on my knees. 'Out there,' I rasp.

A man strides to the entrance and peers out. He turns round shaking his head. 'Can't see nothin'.'

Everyone seems wary of me, keeping their distance and pretending I'm invisible. One woman abandons her overflowing basket on the floor and rapidly slips out of the shop. An elderly man follows her. I feel as though I've a bomb strapped to my chest.

Finally, a young woman wearing an overall rests her hand on my back. 'You okay?' She looks Chinese. 'You need police?'

I consider what would happen if the police turn up. If you haven't fled already, you'll soon disappear into the night when you hear a siren. I don't have a description of you. I don't know where you've gone. I glance down at my shabby but clean unspoilt coat. My undamaged gloves over my hands. Nothing's happened. I could be making the whole thing up. It would be a complete waste of everybody's time.

I think of Wendy waiting for me at the cinema.

I gradually straighten up and walk gingerly towards the shop window, keeping away from the entrance. My breathing is still noisy and fast. I cup my hand over my eyes against the glass and stare out into the road. I can't see you. There's no one hanging around in either direction, on either side of the road. Everyone is on the move.

I spot one of the buses I could catch, trundling along the road in my direction.

'Thank you,' I call out to the assistant, turning back, but she's already moved on, carrying a box of baked beans towards an empty shelf.

I decide to chance it and make a dash for the bus as it heads towards me.

Seeing Wendy waiting for me, rubbing her bare hands together in the cold, calms my nerves. I let out the choked breath I've been holding and grip her arms.

'What's happened? Are you hurt?' she cries.

'Some lunatic's been after me.' I flip up my collar and pull it close around my neck to curb my shivering. 'Scaring me to death.'

'After you? What do you mean?' I can see her checking me up and down, looking for injuries or rips in my coat.

'I've had this creepy feeling since Wednesday. Like someone's been watching me.' My eyes well up, but I nip the skin hard above my lip to distract myself, refusing to break down.

'Who is it? What do they want?'

'I've no idea. I didn't see his face. He didn't confront me or anything, just lurked about then came after me. Followed me for ages. I thought he was going to... It was awful.'

She looks up sharply, scanning the environment. 'Is he here now?'

I follow her gaze, but everything looks reassuringly normal.

'I don't think so.' I turn full circle to check again. 'I think I lost him.'

She curls her arm around me. 'Do we need to call the police? Do you want a coffee? Shall I take you home?'

'No. I don't want him to spoil this.' I make a move towards the steps of the cinema. 'I'll decide what to do after the film. I'm okay for now.'

The film's in Greek with subtitles and whilst the images are beautiful, I haven't a clue what's going on. But it does the trick nevertheless. It transports me to a place where little boys run into waves the colour of sapphires and weddings take place on a glittering white beach. I can dream again and imagine that's me; my bare sun-kissed feet sinking into sparkling grains of sand. I hardly notice when someone in the row behind drops something in my hair – popcorn, maybe. I'm so caught up in my own secret world, I ignore it.

When the film's over, Wendy follows me into the foyer under the main lights. Without warning, she tugs hard on my sleeve, spinning me round. She gawps at me in horror, her hand over her mouth.

'What's the matter?' I shriek.

'Oh, God, Charlie. Your hair – someone's cut half of it off at the back!'

15

SAM

The Present

I could barely contain my amazement when Terry sent a text inviting me out for dinner. After an initial happy dance in my kitchen, I came to my senses. He'd probably invited Claussen along too – it would be a work thing. Then my insides turned to liquid at another thought. He was bringing along a 'new girlfriend' to introduce her to me. Penance for invading his privacy with the laptop.

Serves me right.

I'd accepted his offer by then, so it was too late to back out.

It wasn't long before I came up against another problem. One located in the wardrobe. I couldn't get any of my jeans to zip up. In fact, I couldn't get them over my hips. When had this happened? I couldn't believe it. I must have put on pounds during the last few months slouching around at lectures. I needed to kick-start my fitness campaign pronto.

Terry was alone at the table when I walked into Le Joyeux Panais, twenty minutes late. A waiter appeared at my elbow as I unbuttoned my coat and handed it over. After ransacking my entire wardrobe, I'd managed to find the one item that looked good on me. A lacy red dress with blacklining to highlight the design. Although that hadn't brought my woes to an end. The zip of the dress had got stuck and I'd been forced to perform ludicrous wriggling postures Houdini would no doubt have been proud of. It took me ten minutes to free the zip and start over.

I glanced around nervously for Claussen, or anyone else heading in Terry's direction, but when I reached his table there was only one other place set. It was just going to be the two of us. My shoulders sank with relief.

For once, I couldn't resist a pair of lethal stilettos, worn at a wedding two years ago before they went back into the box, wrapped in tissue paper, and were forgotten. I was taken aback when I sensed Terry's eyes tracking the lines of my figure as I approached the empty chair.

'Sorry I'm late,' I said. 'Wardrobe malfunction.'

He stood formally and welcomed me, clasping my hand. 'Looks good to me.' He was pretending to flirt. Nice touch.

In turn, he wore a slim-fitting suit in navy with a slight sheen. It looked expensive and smacked of having made an effort.

The place he'd chosen was just off Oxford Street, with walls painted charcoal grey. Candles on the tables kept the lighting subdued. Between the salt and pepper pots was a red rose and a Chopin nocturne was lulling diners towards relaxation. A bit more romantic than I was expecting.

He held out a bottle of wine. 'Is Chablis okay?'

He'd remembered from last summer.

'Lovely, thank you.'

After he'd filled my glass, he looked up and I caught his eyes as they flashed down to my cleavage. I blushed as a shimmer of desire caught me unawares. What was going on? This was Terry, my rough-and-tumble old buddie. Why after knowing each other so long were we acting like we'd barely met?

He put on a pair of black-rimmed specs to read the menu.

'My contact lenses are giving me jip,' he said, looking embarrassed. 'My niece says I look terrible in glasses.'

'She's wrong,' I replied.

The table was small, in a tight corner at the back, forcing us to sit close together. Terry looked down at the menu, then back up to my eyes, refocussing, bringing a shiver of incandescence as he kept them trained on me.

'What do you fancy?' he asked.

I barely heard his words; I was too busy staring at his mouth. For some reason, since our meeting the previous day, I was regarding him in an entirely fresh light.

16

I'd been holding the menu, not reading a word. I tried to apply myself to the job in hand, aware the waiter had been loitering at our table long enough. 'I'll have… the Norfolk quail, hazelnut and beetroots,' I said blankly, reading out the first starter I came across.

When the waiter left, I was acutely aware of the sound of Terry's breathing. It seemed to reverberate through my chair.

He asked what my sister was up to, so I explained about her exhibition. He mentioned he'd been hang-gliding in Austria and I wished I had tales of fascinating expeditions to Nepal or China, or a cruise around the Caribbean to regale him with. I cringed inwardly. I hadn't even spent a night away from my flat since I'd seen him the year before.

'I haven't been hang-gliding,' I said feebly. 'Between lectures, I've been… busy… reading, eating, playing Scrabble, that kind of thing.'

Without a doubt, I came across as deeply uninteresting, but he didn't appear to mind. He smiled a lot, chuckled in all the right places, and made me feel at home. Silences hung between our exchanges and I felt no pressure to fill the spaces. He didn't seem to be in a rush to keep the chit-chat going either. A true indication that we were both at ease. Time and motion slowed down and it was as if nothing could touch us; two butterflies flitting above a whirlpool.

The starter arrived and I wished I could concentrate more on the flavours igniting my tongue, instead of the electricity surrounding our table.

'Divine,' he said, dabbing his lips with his napkin.

Terry's hair had grown since last summer. There's something sexy about a man whose thick hair is swept back from his forehead so it reveals his hairline. It certainly sent my heart rate shooting up.

'I've started on the cold cases,' I said, keen to pull myself back down to earth before I turned into a giddy teenager.

His eyebrows shot up. 'Already?'

'You know me. I like to roll up my sleeves and get cracking.'

'A dog with a bone, you mean?' he teased with a grin.

I wrinkled my nose in response.

'Found anything interesting?'

'Too soon to say.' I put down my fork. 'But if I do come across something, can I talk to you about it?'

'Is that allowed, you mean?' His long unfashionable sideburns made me think of the leading men in Poldark, the TV drama series. The ones every self-respecting female had a crush on.

I clarified my question. 'Am I allowed to share details with you, but also – are you up for it? This crime malarkey is pretty new to me and I don't want to end up barking up the wrong tree – me being a dog with a bone, and all.'

He laughed, then looked serious. 'Please do. I'd be honoured. Interested, obviously.'

I went on to ask about his family as we tucked into the main course.

'Dad is still into thatching cottage roofs and Mum runs classes in confidence-building at the community centre,' he said, 'I don't see them much now they're retired. They're always gallivanting off somewhere to see landscaped gardens or take photos of exotic birds. I see more of my brother and his family, but even then, we get together only a few times a year. They live in Yorkshire. Not exactly round the corner.'

I'd met his parents a long time ago. They were chatty and easy-going, unlike mine.

'The niece who hates me in specs,' he went on, 'asked for a telescope for her latest birthday. She's thirteen and loves stargazing. I took her to Greenwich Observatory a while back. She was in seventh heaven.' He smiled as a memory touched him and I wondered if he'd ever wanted children of his own. It was the kind of intimate landscape we'd never ventured into.

'You wish they were closer?'

He nodded and dropped his gaze. 'As long as they're happy... and safe. That's all that matters.'

And safe. As a dedicated police officer, keeping people safe was Terry's raison d'être. Always had been. He never referred to it, but he'd been awarded some kind of commendation for his heroism the day he'd responded to the emergency call-out at the bank that ended with him being shot in the knee. I couldn't imagine the degree of courage it must have taken to challenge a masked man wielding a sawn-off shotgun.

'None of us are ever truly safe, are we?' I said, thinking about Charlotte, one of the women I'd come across in the cold case files.

He sighed. 'I'd like to think family is the safest place to be, but having worked in the force, I know – like you do – that family is sometimes the last place you should run to.'

I nodded gravely.

Terry wasn't just referring to my work as a therapist. He

knew about my tough upbringing. Born to two fiercely ambitious parents and sent away to boarding school at the first opportunity, I'd walked on eggshells most of my childhood. Without encouragement or support, I'd had to fight to follow my chosen career path. My father wanted Miranda and I to be clones of them; Dad was a barrister, my mother a history professor. In their eyes, a meagre psychologist with the NHS, I could only ever be regarded as a disappointment.

'You see much of your parents?' Terry asked tentatively.

I shook my head in such a way that he'd realise this particular subject was closed.

When I turned my attention to tasting it, the main dish was superb and only when I carefully scoured the dessert menu did the penny drop that the restaurant was Michelin starred. This was no run-of-the-mill night out; Terry meant this to be special.

Once the waiter had taken our order for pudding, I deliberately sat back to look at him.

'Okay, what's this all about?'

His eyes grew wide with innocence. 'What's all what about?'

'This. A fantastic meal together in an exquisite French restaurant. What am I missing?'

He laughed. 'You're always so suspicious.'

I tipped my head to one side. 'Well?'

He focussed intently on my eyes, roaming from one to the other. 'I made you a promise last summer – don't you remember?'

I blinked fast, not knowing what he meant.

'I dumped you in deep water with the Regent's Canal case. It was my fault you got involved and I told you at the time I'd take you to the Dorchester – or somewhere posh – as penance.' He tapped the edge of his wine glass with his nail. 'And I never did.'

'It was a joke! I never expected you to actually do it.'

'It was a genuine promise given in good faith.' He leaned

forward, looking earnest. 'I couldn't get us into the Dorchester – it was fully booked, so...' He glanced up at the surroundings, looking vaguely guilty.

I felt my face grow hot. 'Now I feel really bad.'

He straightened up sharply. 'Whatever for?'

'About what happened at your flat.' I toyed with the corner of the table mat, unable to meet his eye.

'What? Enjoying yourself and having a bit too much to drink?'

'No. Snooping at what was on your laptop. Seriously, that was out of order and frankly, I'm surprised you're even speaking to me. Let alone... all this.'

He reached out and covered my hand with his. 'So, maybe we're quits then.'

17

It took considerable effort, but I made an early-morning detour to the local gym before heading over to Camden. It had been some time since lycra and I had been on good terms, so I'd opted for a baggy tracksuit instead.

Beginning with a warm-up on the rowing machine, I jogged for ten minutes on the treadmill, avoiding the annoying cartoons flashing across the overhead TV screen. So far, so boring. Weights next. Bracing myself for the trails of glistening sweat left behind on the seats, I tried to tune out the grunting, but there was no doubt about it. I was surrounded by buffalos.

The bench press, dip station and leg extension machines were the only ones without a queue, so my circuits were restricted. At this rate I was going to end up with biceps and calves the size of watermelons with the rest of me resembling putty. Returning to the main room to use a bike, I found them all occupied by riders who looked like they'd settled in for the London to Brighton race. It was starting to come back to me why I hadn't stuck with this in the past.

I skipped the cross-trainers; they always made me feel like I was being hung, drawn and quartered. On returning to the rowing machines for my final burst of activity, a small but fierce-looking woman stepped into my path.

'You've been on this one already. It's my turn,' she snapped.

I wasn't geared up for hostility quite so early in the morning. I turned to look for the gym assistant so we could establish what the 'rules' were.

He sauntered over. 'Sorry, she's right. Once you've used the equipment there's no return within an hour.'

'Like parking?' I said, tongue-in-cheek.

No trace of amusement brushed his features, he simply looked confused. 'It's how we operate. Sorry.' His accent was Australian. Maybe he hadn't come across UK parking restrictions.

I showered and left with a heavy heart. This wasn't going to work on a regular basis. My route to fitness wasn't going to involve the gym. I was going to have to find something else.

Prue was nowhere to be seen when I strode into the admin office. With further disappointment, I noticed the desk I'd used the first time was occupied. I found an empty one beside the water dispenser and soon discovered why it was free. The vent in the ceiling above me was working twice as hard as all the others, and apart from making me feel like I was in the Arctic, it rattled like a pneumatic drill. In addition, the dispenser gurgled with an intensity not unlike vigorous burping, creating an irregular rhythm all of its own.

I hated this hot-desking concept. Had I worked here permanently, it would have infuriated me. I liked the idea of setting up my workstation exactly how I wanted it. I dreaded the thought of having to play musical chairs each time I came in; there was always a chance of being the one standing when the music stopped.

I left my coat and briefcase clearly visible by the keyboard to secure my place and made myself a coffee. No one appeared to take any notice of me. Everyone had their heads down, perusing files, scrutinising CCTV footage or inputting data.

With no faffing about this time, I flung myself into my search with gusto. By now, I knew what I was doing. Getting into the system without a hitch, I pulled up the file on Charlotte I'd identified last time. Underneath it, also brought up with the term 'haircut', was a record of another young woman. I scrolled down. A second unsolved murder.

This one had taken place nine years ago. The deceased had been hit by a train on a stretch of track between stations in South London. At first, detectives had suspected the death was an accident or suicide, but the post-mortem found otherwise. There was a head wound, consistent with being whacked on the crown with a branch of a tree. That changed everything, especially once the improvised weapon was found with bloodstains near the scene.

I read on.

As the details filled out, a nauseous sinking feeling of déjà vu came over me. The victim was named as Lorna Sullivan, aged nineteen, from Parson's Green. A former model, she'd been studying fashion design at Westminster School of Arts. Once I saw the photograph, I was positive. I knew her. Lorna had been a patient of mine; she'd been for a number of sessions at St Luke's Hospital.

My heart missed a beat. I remembered her clearly even though it was nearly a decade ago since I'd seen her. She was lovely; vivacious, insightful and full of plucky resilience. I checked the dates and snatched a sharp breath. Lorna died in

November 2010. Surely that couldn't have been long after our final session together.

I remembered her long flowing hair; it was the first thing anyone would notice about her. Caramel blonde with kinks all the way down from tying small ribbons in it when it was wet.

A sinking feeling gripped me as I read on. The report stated that she'd had a haircut in the final days before she was killed. It didn't sound like Lorna at all; she loved her long hair, it was her pride and joy. I pulled up the last photograph of her and shuddered. All that luscious hair had been cropped into a short pixie cut.

I stopped there. I couldn't bear to look at the shots from the crime scene.

I got to my feet. There was a clear link here. Three deaths: Lorna, nine years ago, Charlotte, three years ago, and Hazel, just last week. Three attractive young women with long hair who'd had drastic haircuts literally days before they were found dead.

It was too much of a coincidence, surely.

I sat down again and checked to see if anyone in the office was milling around. I waited for a man to close a filing cabinet and return to his seat, then I quickly took out my phone. I snapped screenshots of all three women, taken from the smiley photos their distraught families had provided.

Then I rang DCS Claussen's number, but reached her PA. I explained who I was.

'Oh, DCS Claussen said you need to report to DI Fenway in the first instance,' she said. Of course. My mind had managed to block out that particular part of the instructions I'd been given only days ago.

'*Everything* has to go through him?' I asked on the off-chance.

'That's right. He's leading the Serious Crime Analysis Unit.' She gave me his number. I recognised the final few digits from our exchanges last summer. 'As I've got you on the line I'll put you through,' she said, helpfully.

I jumped in straight away. 'No, no...! It's okay I'll–' If I was going to have to speak to Jeremy Fenway, I needed to gather my thoughts first. I wasn't quick enough. After a click and brief hiatus, he was on the line.

'You're with us again, I hear,' he said tartly. No warm welcome or attempt at courtesy, not even a *Hello*.

'It appears so,' I said, in the same scathing vein. Suddenly the idea of revealing what I'd come across felt ill-judged and downright naive. *Where was the evidence of delusional behaviour?* I'd latched onto the first intriguing connection I'd come across in the cold case files and hadn't thought it through. So horrified was I to find out that Lorna, someone I knew, had been murdered that I'd jumped the gun.

I sank back in the seat. That was invariably my problem. Often acting on impulse, grabbing at a chance to make a differ-ence before I'd given any real consideration to what it might involve. I cringed. This was exactly what DI Fenway had accused me of during the Aiden Blake case. Damn and blast. I should have run it past Terry first instead of charging ahead.

I changed tack completely.

'I'm touching base,' I said breezily. 'I've started checking the cold case files and I'll get in touch as soon as I find anything of interest.'

'Right...'

'Okay then. Thank you.'

'Is that it?'

'Yup...' I had to clear my throat. 'Just making contact.'

I ended the call and let my tongue hang out. That was close.

18

———

Terry was working late, but suggested we meet at 9pm. With the rest of the day to fill, I carried on trawling through report after report in the cold case database, using different search terms to try to trace any other unsolved murders that could be linked. Nothing else was shouting out at me like the haircut cases.

I had no idea whether the killer behind those three deaths had been suffering grandiose delusions, but the more I considered it, the more I thought he could have been. Delusions often originate from fairy tales or myths and hair regularly features in such folklore. Stories such as *Rapunzel* and *The Goose Girl*, for instance. Could some such tale have triggered a delusion? Certainly, there was a link between these three cases that no one else had spotted.

My first problem, of course, was the incident involving Hazel Hart. Although interviews with witnesses were still in progress, her death was being treated as a tragic accident. From what I could remember from taking a sneaky look at Terry's laptop, Hazel had been hosting a party in her flat, but had been alone on the balcony when she fell attempting to take a selfie. Horror-stricken onlookers all said the same thing. No one pushed her. No one was anywhere near her. It wasn't a homicide. I needed to prove otherwise for my theory to hang together.

I distinctly recalled, from the report, that the post-mortem hadn't made any mention of Hazel's hair. That had to be the place to start. I needed more information from the pathologists. That was when I came up against my second problem. I was meant to be examining only cold cases; current investigations were off-limits.

An idea came to me in seconds. I raised my arms above my head in a big stretch and let out an unequivocal groan. It was designed to check out who, in my vicinity, was immersed in their work and who could be easily sidetracked.

A face looked up. A man with hair the colour of pumpernickel bread raised his eyebrows, a smirk on his face.

'Fancy a hot drink?' I offered in a whisper, getting to my feet.

He nodded, pulling a hangdog face and got up. He rolled his shoulders. 'I'm going to turn to stone if I sit here much longer.'

'I'm Dr Willerby, by the way.' I turned on a big show-host smile, holding out my hand. 'Sam is better.'

'Kevin Ormerod,' responded the officer. I judged him to be in his late thirties, with chubby rosy cheeks that made me instantly think of a ventriloquist's dummy. 'Wouldn't mind a herbal, if there are any bags left.'

I boiled the kettle and rooted around in the cupboard for the mint tea I'd spotted on Saturday. I brought over the hot mug and put it on the coaster by his phone.

'Cheers,' he said, holding up the mug. Then he turned away to get on with his work. I dug into my handbag and furtively pulled out a packet of ginger snaps.

'Take a couple,' I whispered, glancing around as though we were doing something wrong. His face was consumed with a gleeful expression on a par with me having saved his life. It created an immediate bond between us, whether Kevin knew it or not. Basic psychology. The simple tricks are often the best.

'Are you working on cold cases, too?' I asked casually, as he dunked his biscuit.

'No. I'm helping the exhibits officer. Logging evidence connected with a burglary.'

'I don't suppose you know who did the post-mortem on the Hazel Hart case?'

'Not offhand, but I can find out.'

'Only if it's easy,' I insisted, deliberately not looking at his computer as he typed.

He clicked on a folder and scrolled down. 'Dr Anna Shaw.'

'Brilliant. Thank you.' I gave him a friendly parting pat on the shoulder as he chomped his way through his remaining biscuit.

As soon as I returned to my desk, I called reception and asked to be put through to Dr Shaw. Once connected, I told the pathologist who I was and where I was calling from, without mentioning that my remit was restricted to cold cases.

'I'm calling about the recent PM on Hazel Hart. I understand you carried this out?'

'Hold on,' Dr Shaw said, 'let me get the details up on screen.' The faint clatter of computer keys followed. It didn't take her long. 'Hazel Hart – yes, that's right.'

'Could I check if you examined her hair at all?'

'Er...' Dr Shaw stalled, presumably reading the report. 'Routine checks for head injuries, disturbance to the hair, any foreign matter in the hair... that kind of thing?'

'Yes.'

Another wait. 'Okay, scissors were found on the body, so we did look in detail at her hair and scalp, but aside from debris from the pavement and residue from hair products, there was nothing unusual.'

'Her hair had been much longer until very recently, judging by the photos on her report,' I said.

'Yes, one of the investigators noted that, but I'm not sure how relevant it is.'

'Are you able to say approximately how long before her death Hazel's hair was cut?'

'Hmm... it can only be approximate,' Dr Shaw told me, 'but based on the average length a person's hair grows in a month, I'd say that Hazel's hair had been cut very recently. A matter of days. Hair never grows uniformly and the longer it gets the more uneven it becomes. We're talking tiny amounts here. The ends start to split over time too. In Hazel's case, due to the sharpness of the cut, I'd say around three to seven days before her death.'

I made a note of that on my notepad and underlined it. 'Was there anything unusual about the haircut?' I persisted.

'What do you mean, exactly?'

'Would you say it was done professionally or did it look like an amateur job, like she'd done it herself or got a friend to do it?'

'Er... it was very neat. Nothing to suggest a slapdash job, but it wasn't an area I was looking into particularly.' A weighty silence followed. 'If you want us to take another look at her with this in mind, you'll need to submit the usual request through the SIO.'

'No, no. That's fine,' I said, keen to end the call and avoid being caught straying into forbidden territory. 'That's really helpful. Thank you.'

19

LORNA

Nine years earlier

It's raining when I leave the library, but my visit's been worthwhile. Their equestrian section is the best I've found, and it's much nicer to browse photos in a book than on a screen. I could have spent hours longer in there, but I mustn't miss the concert.

I get moving at what my mum would call a 'brisk pace', my soft shoes making a splat as they hit the pavement. I can't wait to tell everyone about my new idea. It came to me this morning after my tutorial at college. Designing stylish outfits for horse riders, whether they're competing or simply looking for country fashion. It's totally brilliant! My tutor said I should get in touch with *Horse and Hound* magazine, but I need to get together some sketches first.

The rain patters onto my umbrella and drips in a dancing circle of beads around me. Ahead, a woman stops abruptly and fiddles with her bag. I look briefly behind me to make sure I don't bump into anyone as I skirt past her. That's when I see you.

It's the khaki combat jacket I recognise; one with lots of

pockets. You're shrouded in a bulky hood covering most of your face. Still, I know from the way you hold yourself that you're the same person I saw yesterday. It's spooking me. Mum says you should always be on the lookout for lads just hanging around. *Always up to no good,* she says. *They prey on pretty young ladies like you.* She thinks they're about to grab my shopping or my purse. Or push me into an alleyway. In fact, she's mentioned it so often, it's made me nervous. But she could be right this time. What are you up to? Are you following me?

A man with a poodle walks past, muttering something about what a terrible night it is, but doesn't seem to expect a response. The dog tries to pee at the next lamp post, but the man tugs him on, not allowing him to stop.

I can hear Mum's voice in my head saying *Don't take any chances*, so I hurry to catch a group ahead of me taking the shortcut through the park. They sound Italian; excited teenagers with identical yellow rucksacks. Off the main road it's darker, with widely-spaced lamp posts no match for the earlier shopfronts and headlights. Have I put myself at more risk here? I stay glued to the oblivious guys in front, not daring to look back.

Adrenaline skitters across my chest as the tube entrance comes into view. Once I reach it, I'll mingle with commuters and shake you off.

Through the main gate, across the road, and I'm inside the ticket hall. I glance back, but I don't see you anywhere. No need to tell Mum about any of this. No point in worrying her. You must have found someone else to bother.

Nine years earlier

Hammersmith is jam-packed when I emerge from the underground. For once I embrace the crowds. I can hide under the wings of the masses. *Massive Attack* logos and slogans are everywhere. Mum thinks the band's dire, but the place is buzzing and I can't wait.

I join the long curling queue and for about five minutes I'm swept up in the frenzy of fandom and anticipation and forget the scare you've just put me through. Groups are breaking into tunes from the band's hits, swinging their arms around, ignoring the bad weather.

When it stops raining, everyone starts folding up their umbrellas and I feel less protected, more out in the open. That's when a shiver catches the back of my neck. It makes me look around. My heart is thudding like a herd of stampeding wildebeests, but I can't see you. There's only a woman bending down behind me tying her laces and a man on his mobile. Nevertheless, I don't trust my sweeping inspection – there are so many people around, you could easily weave in and out.

A text comes in from Mum asking if I've got here okay. I punch a quick one back, all cheery and light-hearted. Don't want her getting anxious.

Julia is late. She should be here by now. My phone pings with another message. She's stuck in traffic, literally metres away. I'm jittery on my own, so I find a friendly face in the queue and we chat mindlessly about the band. She spots the badge on my lapel and asks which riding school I go to. Turns out she's obsessed with horses, perhaps even more than I am, and I tell her about my shiny new plan to design riding gear.

'OMG,' she cries, as though the letters don't need filling out, 'how sick is that? You could do loads of like, funky stable wear and fashion jodhpurs and, like, breeches and stuff for every day.' She whips out her phone to show me her Instagram feed, swiping through post after post. Each one features her cheery face alongside a myriad of different horses. 'We must "follow" each other,' she squeals. 'I'll buy something once your range is released.'

I raise my eyebrows. Her frenzied enthusiasm is overpowering. Almost as intense as her garlicy breath. I take a subtle half step back, hoping she won't think I'm rude. 'I think it'll be a while yet.'

When Julia finally arrives, I fling my arms around her and she looks at me like I'm on something. 'You okay?' she asks, 'you look a bit shell-shocked.'

'I'm fine.'

As the doors open, the girl who loves horses waves manically at me, even though she's less than a metre in front of us. I give her a weak smile and she moves off.

'You don't look fine, what's going on?' Julia knows I had a rough time a few months ago and had to see a therapist.

'I'm not sure. Just some guy.'

'Some guy?' She looks up. 'Which guy? Doing what?'

'That's the thing, I don't know. I can never see his face. Keeps showing up, like he's watching me, tailing me.'

She wraps her arm around me protectively as the queue moves forward. 'I've had that before – a couple of times, but nothing's happened. It's probably just a guy who fancies you, waiting for you to make eye contact or plucking up the courage to ask you out. That's all. If you ignore him, he'll eventually get bored and move on to someone else.'

'What if he doesn't?'

'Get someone to have a word with him or call the police. Come on...'

As the queue shuffles towards the entrance, a surge of electricity zaps through me, gearing me up for the imminent performance. At last, I can leave all thoughts of you in the gutter.

It's only when we've taken our places and I bend forward to push my bag under my seat that my world falls apart again.

Julia is yelling into my face above the racket of the warm-up band.

'Shit, Lorna – what have you done to your hair?'

21

———————

SAM

The Present

DCS Claussen had made it clear I wasn't allowed to interview anyone connected with the cold cases on my own. As I left the admin office and walked to the tube, I could hear her voice from our earlier conversations grating in my ear.

'You can visit public crime scenes, you'll have a certain amount of access to forensic details, you can speak to pathologists and team officers as long as you don't pester them, but if you want to speak to anyone connected to the victims – you ask first, okay?'

'Right.'

'No tapping on people's doors without our say so, got it?'

'Loud and clear...' I just managed to stop myself from saying 'Ma'am'.

'And never claim to be a police officer or allow persons of interest to make that assumption. You're a civilian helping the police with their enquiries. That's all. No pulling the wool over people's eyes as leverage to get more information.'

My reputation, it seemed, had gone before me – ringing loud alarm bells.

I'd dutifully told her I understood exactly what she was saying. Understood it, yes. Perfectly. Intended to obey her every word? Personally, I was a bit fuzzy on that part.

In fact, it so happened I was already one step ahead of the game. Having worked with Lorna in therapy, I had a record of her close friends. All procured before I was assigned to this role. With several hours remaining before I was due to meet Terry, it was time to get the show on the road.

Once I got home, I flung my coat on the sofa and went straight to my bedroom, taking my laptop with me. I got down on the carpet on all fours and peered into the stacks of locked metal boxes that made up the dusty world under my bed. Nine years ago, all my notes were handwritten. Because my office at St Luke's was small and space was at a premium, I kept old records at home. Erring on the side of caution, I always used initials instead of patients' full names.

Luckily, I'm meticulous and take notes after every session. Detailed notes. It's important to remember the small things when someone's putting their complete trust in you. There's nothing more frustrating for a patient than the therapist forgetting a significant name or getting part of their story wrong. I'm paid to listen. It's the bedrock of my job.

It didn't take long to find Lorna's notes. I removed them from the filing system and laid them out on top of the duvet, then flicked through to the final page. I was right about one thing. Our last session took place less than a month before she was killed.

I didn't read any of the content. At this stage I was looking for only one thing: the name of Lorna's best friend.

It was near the top on the first page. Julia Mendrick. Opening my laptop, I ran a search for her on social media. I knew Julia had been interested in horses nine years ago; it was how she and Lorna had met, so I flicked through several profiles with that name, checking the posted photographs. It didn't take long to track down the right person. Her profile picture showed a woman in wellington boots, her arm wrapped around the head of a chestnut-coloured pony.

As luck would have it, Julia posted regularly, so ignoring Claussen's warning, I sent her a private message explaining who I was.

Within twenty minutes, Julia had spotted it and we were chatting on Skype.

'Lorna mentioned you,' she said. 'I remember she said how useful it was being able to offload to someone after the collision at the bank. It really messed her up.'

Julia had curly black hair and a bright girlish smile.

'I know this must be distressing, but is it okay to ask you a few questions about her?'

'Sure.' Her eyes flashed wide. 'What do you want to know?'

'I'm working with the police and...' I paused. I had to be very careful about what I revealed to her, especially as I shouldn't have been making contact with her in the first place. 'I'm sorry to bring all this back up for you, but I've only just found out she died.'

'Oh. Yeah. It was awful...' Her words fizzled out. She looked down, her hand reaching up to stroke her neck.

I gave her a moment. 'Did you know her killer was never found?' I said, as sensitively as I could.

She let out a little moan. 'Yeah. That bastard is still out there somewhere. It scares the shit out of me.'

'As I said, I'm doing some work with the police and I'm hoping to get them to look into the case again.'

Her head jerked up. 'Really? Wow, that would be amazing.'

The picture broke up for a second, then re-established.

'It's not official yet and you mustn't mention this to anyone. Not a soul, you understand?'

'Yeah, of course.'

'If it goes ahead, I might need to get back to you – would that be okay?'

'Absolutely. I'll do whatever I can to help. Anything. She was such an amazing girl. I still think about her. We have a memorial bench at the stables for her.'

'You were her best friend at the time, is that right?'

'Yeah. We spent a lot of time taking care of the horses over at our riding school.'

'I remember Lorna had gorgeous long blonde hair. She died a few weeks after I last saw her, but her hair was much shorter by then. Do you know anything about that?'

'Oh, God. It was such a shame.'

'I know it was a long time ago, but do you know where she got it cut?'

'It was a place in Chelsea. I think it's still there. Giovanni's. On the Fulham Road.'

'I remember how much she loved her hair and I was shocked, to see she'd had it all taken off.'

'Me too. A pixie cut suited her – I mean anything would because she was so pretty, but...' I waited, but she couldn't end her sentence.

'Do you know *when* she had it cut?'

Julia blew out a breath and took her time. 'I remember we met two days before she died and it was short then. She was at college Monday to Friday, so she would probably have had it cut the Saturday before.'

I blinked fast, grabbing a pen for my notepad. 'Hold on...' I was working it through as I jotted down the details. 'So, she had her hair cut on the Saturday – only six days before she died. Is that right?'

'Yeah.' Julia came to a halt. 'Why – is that important?'

'I'm not sure yet,' I said guardedly, 'but this could be very helpful. Was that her regular hairdresser?'

'Yes. She'd been seeing Giovanni himself at the salon for ages. He was very good. A bit too expensive for me, but Lorna's hair was really important to her.' Julia's voice cracked and she dropped her head again, rubbing her forehead. 'Sorry...' she sniffled, as her voice disintegrated into tears.

'Don't be. What happened to Lorna was terrible.' The stark description I'd read on Lorna's police file had left me sickened: *struck unconscious with the branch of a tree... parallel grooves in the gravel indicating the body was dragged to the railway line... hit by a train... dead on impact...*

I snapped back to the present. 'Thank you for your time, Julia. I'm sorry it's upsetting for you.'

She wiped the heels of her hand into her tearful eyes. 'I don't care – if it gets her case reopened.'

'I hope it will. I'll let you know.'

I was about to end the call, when Julia spoke again. 'She didn't *want* to get her hair cut – you do know that?'

Her words took my breath away. 'No, I didn't.'

'She had no choice. Someone had hacked a chunk of it off at the back.'

A band of heat closed around my throat. 'Really? What happened?'

'I was the one who noticed it. It was an awful mess. A gap in the top layer where someone had just snipped it off.'

'When? Can you remember?'

'Oh, I spotted it at a pop concert at the Hammersmith

Apollo. I remember the date because it was my mum's birthday. November twelfth.'

Exactly a week before Lorna was killed.

I kept Julia talking. This was important. 'Did you see it happen?'

'No. It was dark inside the venue, obviously, and really crowded. But Lorna did mention it might have happened in the queue outside.'

'Did she see who did it?'

'No. She thought she felt something on the back of her neck, but she'd put it down to raindrops falling from an umbrella or someone's hood. Like I say, there were loads of people around.' Julia stared intently through the screen at me. 'Having said that, she did say she thought someone had been following her.'

There'd been no mention of this on Lorna's police file.

'Did she tell the police she was being followed? Did she report it to anyone?'

'I don't think so. I reckon she didn't think there was much point. She mentioned it briefly to me before the concert, but said she didn't know who it was – she never saw his face.' Julia hesitated, her finger trailing back and forth over her chin. 'Come to think of it, I remember she told me it stopped after her hair was chopped off. I thought it was either someone who'd briefly taken a shine to her or was part of some stupid prank.'

22

Terry was on time, as ever, waiting outside the Victoria Arms. There were too many staff involved with HOLMES 2 to accommodate them at the Stanhope Street police station, so he worked at an annex near Camden Road train station, half a mile away.

He was looking in the other direction, so I spotted him before he saw me. Drawing closer, it was as if I'd never seen him before. I took in the debonair way he held himself; his chest lifted, the powerful ridges of his shoulders shaping his jacket and his lean long legs. An intense anticipation, a longing I'd rarely felt before, almost got the better of me and my legs threatened to buckle.

'You look flustered,' he said, rather too observantly. 'Tough day?' He held open the pub door for me and I grabbed hold of it gratefully.

'No. Quite the opposite, actually.' Inside, the bar was dimly lit and I almost tripped headlong over the rug laid just inside the door. 'I've had a very productive day and I'm going to tell you all about it. What are you drinking?'

'Thank goodness someone has some energy,' he said with a wry smile. 'I need a pint of IPA, whatever type they've got.'

I nudged him towards the lounge and stood at the bar to get the drinks, adding a bag of nuts in case he hadn't eaten.

The place was hectic, but in a high-spirited rather than volatile way and we were squashed together at the end of a table near the doors to the kitchen. Wafts of fatty chips and a rich meaty aroma smothered us every time a bell sounded. It reminded me I hadn't, in fact, had anything to eat myself.

It was like being in a Wild West movie; the saloon doors beside us swishing back and forth whenever a staff member shot through. Each waiter carried more crockery than seemed feasible, like they were part of a circus trick, except the plates were piled high with steaming cabbage, pie and mash, rather than spinning.

I turned to Terry as he took a long first sip and I launched straight in, keeping my voice low. 'Okay, I know you're not going to like this, but I think the police should look into Hazel Hart's death more closely.'

He made a low grumbling sound.

I went on. 'I've found two other cases where attractive women with very long hair had radical haircuts before their deaths. Just like Hazel.'

He hunched forward, cradling his glass. 'Wait up, can we go a bit slower, please.'

I glanced around to make sure no one was listening. A group of three men at the far side were waving their arms at a TV screen, discussing VAR, the controversial video referee system, and the couple nearest to us seemed to be embroiled in an argument. I dropped my hands into my lap and took a deep breath. 'Hazel Hart had waist-length hair. It was stunning – have you seen the photographs?'

He nodded, taking a handful of peanuts from the packet.

'According to the pathologist, her hair was cut much shorter three to seven days before she died.'

'According to the pathologist?' he queried, his mouth crammed with nuts.

I took my eyes away from his. 'That's right, we had a quick chat.'

'Did you now?' He narrowed his eyes, his tone almost scathing.

I ploughed on. 'Anyway, I found two other unsolved murder cases from 2010 and 2016 with considerable similarities.'

He sat up straight. 'Falls from a high-rise balcony?'

'No. The methods were entirely different, but all three women had very long hair and had radical haircuts during the last days before they died.'

'O-kay,' he said, taking the pitch up at the end.

I pressed closer to him, forcing myself to keep my voice down in my excitement. 'One of the women, Lorna Sullivan, was being followed shortly before she died. Someone hacked at the back of her hair – took out a chunk in the top layer without her knowledge. It was exactly a week before she was killed. That's why she needed the haircut. She didn't *want* to have all her hair cut off – she was forced into it.'

He plucked another nut from the packet and nodded, his eyelashes fluttering in the way they did when he was thinking.

'Hazel had a dramatic haircut in her last week,' I said, 'and a witness said Charlotte had too. During the final week before she died. It's a bit weird, don't you think? Surely it's something?'

He tilted his head from side to side, weighing it up. 'It's certainly odd.'

I went on, desperate to convince him. 'So, the haircuts themselves are definitely a pattern with each of these three women, but what if there's more than that?'

He turned to face me and studied each of my eyes in turn so

deeply, it felt like he was climbing inside me. It knocked me off balance. I'd never before been faced with a conflict between the determination to get my point across and the desire to simply sink into a man's arms. It was disconcerting to say the least.

I decided to own up. 'I knew Lorna. She was a patient of mine nearly ten years ago.' In an instant I wished I hadn't. I gripped his arm. 'Don't say it's a conflict of interest. I really want to get to the bottom of this. I owe it to her. She was such a sweet innocent girl. Only nineteen when someone dragged her to a railway line and stood by as a train came and...' I couldn't go on.

He raised his other arm as if he was about to comfort me, then picked up his glass. 'It would be a conflict of interest if you were a detective investigating this case. But you're not. You're gathering ideas together to put forward to the cold case team.' He said it with gravitas, as much to remind me of the confines of my role as to reassure me.

I let go of his arm. 'And Hazel's case? It's making me think Hazel's death wasn't an accident.'

'We'd need evidence to show it wasn't. I've been updating her file, so I'm pretty clear on the details. Hazel was definitely alone on the balcony according to the report. She had a history of risk-taking, snapping daredevil selfies. People do these stunts for social media fame, then they lose their balance or the wind blows and – poof – they're gone.'

'What if the killer knew Hazel took dangerous selfies and crashed her party, then pushed her?'

'Evidence,' he said.

That word again.

He went on. 'Every witness said there was no one else with her on the balcony. The people at her party stood and watched from the inner door. It was windy. She fell off. End of.'

A twitchy silence hung between us.

His voice softened. 'What else have you found?' He reached

out for another handful of nuts and realised I'd scoffed the last one. He dusted the salt off his hands.

'Nothing really. I can't get beyond these three cases. They've got under my skin. The thought of dropping this and moving on to something else doesn't feel right. At all. I *know* there's something here. I just know it.' I felt my shoulders droop, defeat making my limbs like lead.

'And you'd feel like you were letting Lorna down if you didn't follow this up?'

'Yes!' I said, gazing deeply into his infinity-pool eyes. 'I want to see her killer brought to justice. I knew you'd understand.'

'I do, but I also know about the limitations. You can't step in and turn this into your own private investigation. You've been given privileged information that has to be dealt with in the right way. You're not the person to be investigating it. You have no authority to–'

I drew back, closing my eyes. 'I know, I know. Claussen made it all very clear.'

'You need to start with evidence of delusional behaviour and find cases you think could be linked. Not one where you have personal involvement with one of the victims and where one of the deaths isn't even on the cards for murder.'

I stopped and took a long slug of wine. 'Perhaps I should call it a day and go back to my patients at the hospital.'

He jerked back his chin. 'That doesn't sound like the Sam Willerby I know.'

I sighed without a smile and sank back wearily in the seat. 'But, I'm not going to get anywhere.'

'Isn't today officially only day one of your assignment?'

It already seemed like an age since I'd first embarked on this task. That's what emotional involvement did to you.

I wrinkled my nose. 'I suppose it is.'

He scooped his wayward hair away from his forehead in a

broad stroke. 'I've never known anyone like you, Sam. The way you think, the way you notice things no one else ever sees.'

I savoured his words, wanting to believe them.

'You've got one of the sharpest minds I've come across,' he went on, 'and normally you have the tenacity of a camel.'

'Shouldn't that be donkey?' I queried with a grin.

'Don't interrupt.' He took in my face, then looked away, shaking his head wearily. 'I don't know what it is about you, but after all these years, you still manage to take my breath away...' His words petered out.

A tingle scampered down the back of my neck. He'd never said anything remotely like this to me before. My eyes shot down to the table.

'I think you might have gone a bit off-topic,' I said, taking a sudden interest in the beer coaster under my glass.

He shrugged. 'Yeah, well a bloke is allowed to get sidetracked now and again.'

He was watching me, his head slightly tipped on one side. I wanted to go back to the bit about taking his breath away. Had I misheard him?

'I know you too well to say "don't give up",' he said tenderly. 'You'll find a way through this. You'll discover something else you can get your teeth into. I know you will.'

I kept my gaze in my lap. I didn't want something else. I wanted to pursue what I'd already unearthed. He leant over and planted a moist kiss on my cheek. 'Just be careful, that's all.'

I opened my mouth to respond, but he'd turned away and was reaching for his wallet.

'Another drink?' he asked, and the moment was broken.

23

―――――

I didn't waste any time the following morning, joining the early-bird flush of yawning commuters on their way to north London.

When Terry had come back from the bar with the second round, we'd dropped the subject of the cold cases. Our conversation took a detour down memory lane instead, and he challenged me to remember the last time I'd used a payphone in the street. That took a while to figure out. After that, we ended up talking about our first Sony Walkman and travelled even further back to Etch a Sketch. But, hidden to the outside world, the haircut cases continued to put down hefty roots in my mind, like those of a giant sequoia. Not for one moment did I consider giving up and starting again.

Once inside the office, I honed in on Kevin, hoping the desks either side of him would be unoccupied at this early hour. I was lucky and bagged the one to his left.

'Hi,' I said. 'When did you get in?'

'Only a few minutes ago. Piles to get through today.' He pulled a face and turned back to his screen.

I logged on and got to work, examining Lorna and Char-

95

lotte's files in detail, searching for any other common threads between them. The methods, locations, occupations and backgrounds of the women. The more information I found, however, the more everything seemed poles apart.

Hazel worked as an estate agent in Dulwich, Charlotte was a dental receptionist in Primrose Hill and Lorna had been a fashion student, studying at Westminster College. The one and only link I could see was the haircut shortly before they died. I knew Terry was right when he said it wasn't enough to reinvestigate.

It was frustrating not having access to Hazel's file, but there was a reason I chose this particular workstation. After a stretch and a yawn, Kevin left his desk, dutifully logging out of the system before he went. When he returned a few moments later, I got up and discretely made sure I was directly behind his chair when he logged back in.

Trombones76

I sauntered over to the water cooler and brought back two plastic cups full, as if that was my sole reason for getting to my feet. I plonked one on his drinks mat. This shameful behaviour was new to me. I'd rarely been one to break the rules – bend them a little for very good reason perhaps, but not deliberately flout them. And only ever those within my own profession. The stakes within law enforcement were higher, but if bringing Lorna's killer to justice meant stepping over the line here and there, I was on board one hundred per cent.

'You're definitely spoiling me,' Kevin said with a chuckle.

I gave him as broad a smile as I could manage at that time in the morning and settled down to resume my endless trawling of the files, focussing on Lorna's this time.

She'd come for therapy in 2010 after a van had crashed into a queue of people standing with her at a cash machine. Lorna wasn't injured, but others were seriously hurt, one of whom later died in hospital.

Kevin made me a coffee mid-morning. 'No biscuits, I'm afraid. Sorry.' He tapped his rotund belly. 'Post-Christmas resolution. Boring, I know.'

He checked his watch and threw his eyes up. 'Bollocks. Got a meeting five minutes ago.'

I felt a sweat break out on my palms. 'Must be annoying if you're in the middle of something,' I said, playing it cool. 'Will it last long?'

He tutted, grabbing his bag. 'The DI usually drags on. Could be an hour. Who knows?'

Once he'd gone, I waited a few minutes, observing the comings and goings in the office. If I shuffled to the next seat along would anyone notice?

Before I could change my mind, my trembling fingers were hovering over Kevin's keyboard. I typed in his password and was in without a hitch. It didn't take long to pull up Hazel Hart's incident report. I jotted down what I needed, closed the file and logged out.

Only seconds later, Kevin was back, striding towards me. I was still perching on his seat. Thinking fast, I crouched down and came up waving my pen in the air. 'Sorry. Knocked it off my desk,' I said, getting up.

He barely registered what I was doing. 'Meeting was cancelled,' he chuckled with a grin, reclaiming his seat. 'Made my day.'

24

Tamsin Jones lived next door to Hazel on the nineteenth floor of Ledwick Tower, near Kings Cross. It only took me twenty minutes to get there on foot from the office.

'I've already had visits from the police,' she said, opening the door wide enough to allow a visitor only the size of a cockroach inside. She was chewing, half a banana in her hand. 'I'm surprised there are more questions.'

I'd told her I was a psychologist working with the police. 'People remember things a few days later... know what I mean?' A pang of guilt caught in my throat. I wasn't meant to be interviewing anyone. I knew that.

She sighed and stood back from the door, letting me in. 'I'm on my lunch break, so I can't be long.' She took another bite of the banana. 'And watch the toys – they're a death trap.'

Plastic trucks, dinosaurs, a ship, and half the cast from Toy Story were strewn across the carpet like there'd been an earthquake. 'My nephew,' she said, by way of explanation. 'Want a drink?'

I declined.

Tamsin looked in her forties but was dressed like a twenty-year-old, wearing a low-necked leopard-skin top, a short denim skirt, no tights and high summer sandals with cork platforms. She left me in the main room and wandered off to the adjoining kitchen. I saw her pour herself what looked like a can of lemonade, but could easily have been a ready-mixed gin and tonic.

'Shit morning at work,' she said, clinking the ice in her glass on her return. 'You sure you don't want something?'

I shook my head.

She pointed to a space on the sofa between newspapers and more toys. A lottery ticket fluttered to the floor as I took a seat. When I looked up, I noticed a photo of Hazel and Tamsin, their faces squashed together in a blown-up selfie. It sat on an electric keyboard in the corner in a bright pink frame. A cherished picture judging by the size of it.

'How well did you know Hazel?' I asked.

'We were really good mates,' Tamsin said, dropping her chin. She stared at her nails. Half were long and painted, the others chipped or broken. She swiftly put down her glass and hid them inside the pockets of her skirt.

I pointed to the photo. 'When was this taken, can you remember?'

'Oh... about two years ago. A few months after she moved in. She threw a party for her twenty-first.'

'Did Hazel throw a lot of parties?'

Tamsin coughed out a laugh. 'You kidding me?' Her smile was tainted with nostalgia. 'All the time. She knew loads of people and was the biggest party animal ever.' Her voice broke. 'Happy Hazel we used to call her.'

'Do you have more pictures of her?'

Tamsin reached over to her phone, also pink, face down on the coffee table. 'Hundreds on here,' she said, snivelling. 'I can't bear to look at them.'

She let me glance through them. I soon realised Tamsin's

youthful outfit was an exact copy of one that Hazel featured in several times. I wondered if they could even be Hazel's own clothes.

I handed back her phone. 'You seemed to be having a lot of fun together.'

'God, yes! She was a laugh. Game for anything.' Tamsin's face fell as she no doubt recalled what had brought Hazel's life to an end.

'Were you at the party the day she died?'

'Of course.' Tamsin reached over for a packet of cigarettes, slid one out and lit up, not offering me one. 'She liked to have all-day parties now and again. Lots of our friends are freelancers or arty types who don't have nine to five jobs.'

'The police said around fifty people were there. Did you know them all?'

She mulled it over. 'Pretty much.'

'Anyone you didn't recognise or were surprised to see?'

'They asked me that. No, I can't think of anyone who wasn't meant to be there.' Tamsin hesitated, looking down sheepishly. 'Although I did tell them I wasn't wearing my contact lenses.'

'Right...'

'Yeah, they play up when it's windy sometimes – you know, grit and stuff – so I took them out.'

'So, you couldn't be certain who was there?'

She thought about it. 'Hazel said she knew everyone. All part of our usual crowd, although even with my lenses in I couldn't tell you all their names.'

'Did you open up this flat too, or just use Hazel's?'

'Mainly next door. She's got better speakers for the music, but we did spill over into the corridor and in here as well.'

I stood up, mainly to distance myself from the clouds of cigarette smoke about to envelope me. Tamsin took it to mean something else.

'Did you want to see it? Hazel and I shared keys, so I can let you in, if you like...'

25

Hazel's flat bore a strong resemblance to her neighbour's in terms of décor, soft furnishings and accessories. There was an identical fluffy throw over the sofa, a similar Hollywood-style tripod lamp and faux zebra-skin rug in front of the sofa. In fact, almost a carbon copy of the flat next door. Or most likely, it was the other way around, given that everything here had an air of authentic luxury absent in Tamsin's flat. The biggest difference, however, was how uncluttered it was: no toys, no newspapers, no ashtrays.

'I tidied up after the party,' Tamsin told me, 'once the police said it was okay. Couldn't bear to see a reminder of that day.'

She'd certainly done a good job of clearing up; there was little evidence of the last event in Hazel's life.

'Hazel lived in America, went to Africa, went everywhere,' Tamsin said, as I adjusted my stride to avoid standing on the zebra's back. 'Loved travelling. She sold properties abroad. Homes in the sun, that type of thing, as well as standard property here.'

I remembered from the police report that Hazel had worked in an estate agents in upmarket Dulwich Village.

Neon pink was definitely a prominent feature; in the frame around the mirror, the wall clock, the huge framed picture of a lipstick pout on the wall. I stood by the sliding door to the balcony and Tamsin opened it for me.

'This is where it happened,' she said, her hand over her mouth, not able to look.

It was a small area lined with plants. I walked up to the protective barrier to see how high it was. It came just above my waist. According to the post-mortem report, Hazel had been five feet eight; three inches taller than me.

Floating heart balloons, sprays of cut flowers and cards had turned the space into a little shrine. The sun glinted between clumps of puffy cloud and sent warming rays directly onto it, like a blessing.

'What was the weather like on Thursday?' I asked, having to shade my eyes.

'It was like this, I suppose, but it was quite windy. No one was using the balcony much.'

'Do you mind if I take a few pictures?'

'Absolutely, go ahead. What are you looking for?'

'I'm not sure.' I clicked away from as many angles as I could. 'Can you remember what was going on just before it happened?'

'Everyone was milling around. Drinking, smoking, chatting, dancing. The usual.'

'Did Hazel have any love interest in her life?'

'She'd seen this bloke, Ivan, a few times, but she said she wasn't interested. Quite happy on her own.'

'Who's Ivan?'

'A guy in a local band. I don't know his surname. Plays the drums. He's been into her for ages. Keeps hanging around, but like I said, she insisted she wasn't into him.'

'Did anything odd happen at the party? Anything at all?'

Tamsin glanced down at the acid-green toenails poking out

of her sandals. 'No. Not that I can think off. I mean the police asked me about her mental state, you know,' she tapped her temple, 'but Hazel was great. Her job was going well, she was planning another trip, she was happy as Larry.'

I paused, choosing my words carefully, so as not to upset Tamsin. 'Did you see it happen?'

'Yeah.' She slapped her hands over her ears at the memory. 'She lost her balance. Then we heard this most blood-curling cry...' Tamsin doubled over, melting into sobs.

I reached down and rested my hand on her back as she straightened up. She leant her weight against me, so I wrapped my arms around her.

'I still can't believe it,' she blubbered, pain cracking her voice. 'I don't know what happened. She'd taken loads of shots like that before.'

'From up here?'

Tamsin nodded. 'She took a selfie out there in every season and on special occasions. She'd been on tower blocks in New York, hanging off cliffs in Switzerland, mountain ranges in India. She was a pro. Why she fell, I'll never know.'

I waited as Tamsin wept into my collar.

She finally straightened up, smudging her mascara into sooty smears as she wiped her eyes. I led her to the sofa and she sat hunching forward, her elbows on her knees.

'I have to go back to work,' she said, looking lost. 'I need to clean myself up.'

I couldn't let her disappear just yet. 'Can I ask if you have the selfies she took from here?'

'Sure, I've got them all. On my phone.'

'If I give you my email address, could you send me them?'

She shrugged, like a disgruntled teenager. 'Okay. I suppose.' Her lips tightened. 'I thought the police were moving on. I mean... everyone knows it was an accident.'

'I know this is unpleasant, but do you know if anyone had a grudge against Hazel? Was there anyone she'd fallen out with or had upset at all?'

Tamsin's face crumpled into a deep frown. 'No way. Everyone loved her. I mean, she was amazing; generous, warm, bright – lived life to the full.'

I'd had a feeling she'd say something like that. Tamsin was probably Hazel's number one fan.

She rounded on me. 'Are you saying someone pushed her? Is that what you mean? Who told you that?'

'No,' I said, flapping my hand. 'No one has suggested anything like that. Honestly. I'm just checking things out, that's all.'

Tamsin turned her back on me and moved briskly towards the front door.

I changed tack as I felt my remaining moments running out. 'Hazel had hairdressing scissors on her when she fell. It's a strange thing to keep in your pocket. Do you know why?'

Tamsin stopped and turned around with a groan. 'Oh, God. She loved her hair, didn't she? I mean, if you've got golden locks like that why wouldn't you be vain about it.' Tamsin stepped ahead of me into the corridor. 'She had them on her after it happened. Kept checking in the mirror to see if it needed tidying up.'

She waited for me to join her, then locked the flat door.

'After *what* happened?'

She stood facing me outside her own flat door, her back to it like a sentry. 'She was devastated, kind of ashamed, as well. She cursed herself for letting it happen. Didn't tell anyone about it except me.' She hesitated, looking uncomfortable.

'Letting what happen?' I whispered as gently as I could.

I sensed her sizing me up, considering how much to tell me. 'Letting someone hack at her lovely hair.' Tamsin's eyes flicked briefly to mine. 'Some bastard snipped off a big piece at the back. Two days after New Year. She had a scarf around her neck so she didn't feel the scissors. That's why she had to get it all cut off.'

26

———

Instead of charging straight back to the office, I returned home to take stock. I'd learnt my lesson. Nothing would happen with Hazel's police investigation unless there was concrete new evidence. In their eyes I had nothing.

I was putting together a late lunch of Marmite on low-calorie crispbread – a modest alternative to the buttered muffins I would have preferred – when my phone pinged. True to her word, Tamsin had sent over the photos I'd asked for – Hazel's selfies taken from her balcony. A message came with them:

There are over a hundred shots, so I'm only sending twenty. I laid awake last night thinking about our discussion and for what it's worth, I think you're wrong. No one would want to harm Hazel. She just lost her balance.

The selfies had been taken in all seasons, at different times of the day: during thunderstorms, with snow drifting down in the background, with planes flying past. The latest one, taken at New Year, had a backdrop of fireworks bursting open in the night sky. It showed Hazel perched on the top of the balcony barrier looking victorious, her hair floating out behind her like a magical aura. Certainly striking.

I'd made a note of the time of death recorded on Hazel's post-mortem. It had been 2.03pm when pedestrians on the pavement below had seen her fall. Only an hour later than the corresponding time of my visit to Tamsin this lunchtime, when the sun had broken through in short bursts. Did the police believe that had been a contributing factor? Maybe it shone straight into Hazel's eyes and blinded her momentarily.

In every shot, Hazel was holding more or less the same position. Perched in a sophisticated pose in the manner of Jackie Onassis or Lady Gaga, lounging on yachts for magazine shots.

I found the highest sturdy surface I could find in my flat; the chest of drawers in my bedroom, and hitched myself into the same position to try it for myself. Holding up my phone, I put my other hand beside me. I was sitting kind of side-saddle, my feet dangling off the floor.

I closed my eyes. Even centimetres from the carpet, I felt myself wobble at the thought of being nineteen floors up and vulnerable to the winter elements. What was Hazel thinking? Perhaps the police were right.

I clambered off, my heart racing.

Nevertheless, Hazel had done this time and time again. She'd captured at least a hundred such occasions on her phone. The toxicology report I'd glimpsed that morning stated there were no traces of drugs and only small amounts of alcohol in her system. That made it even less likely that she'd misjudged the situation and had fallen of her own accord.

I was torn.

Had Hazel told anyone of her intention to take a selfie from the balcony? I immediately chased that thought away. Surely, anyone who knew Hazel must have known it was likely. Had someone therefore planned for 'an accident', in some way?

What about Ivan, the guy interested in her – had the police spoken to him?

I dabbed at the crumbs of dry crispbread on my plate with my finger and sighed. All I knew for certain was that Hazel's hair was hacked off without her consent. I reflected on Tamsin's exact words. Two days after New Year.

My stomach churned. Exactly a week before her death.

Just like Lorna.

27

HAZEL

Five days earlier

That numpty Tamsin is getting on my nerves. She's been fussing and faffing all morning. Have we got enough glasses? Have we got the right playlist ready? Should she put out another bowl of crisps? Chill your butt, woman! It's a party – we're meant to be having fun.

She keeps asking how things are going with Ivan all the time too – it's driving me nuts. I'm sick of telling her he's wasting his time. I think she's jealous that I've got an admirer. No, not jealous – envious. She's been in step with me ever since I moved in; buying the same clothes, going on the same diets, getting the same stuff for her flat. It was flattering to start with, but now it's doing my friggin' head in. I'm going to tell her to get her own poxy life if she doesn't pack it in.

'Machi's here!' Tamsin shouts from the corridor. She's waiting for people by the lift, it's embarrassing.

Machi comes in with a gang from Dentworths behind her.

'Help yourselves, guys. You know the ropes.' I indicate the table stacked with glasses, most already filled with wine. 'You can't all be here!' I call over to my mates from work, my eyes wide. 'Who's holding the fort?'

'No idea,' Carol says, dipping her hand into a bowl of cheese puffs. 'I'm on legitimate annual leave.'

'So am I,' one of the blokes from reception butts in, a bottle of lager already in his hand.

Machi sits on the edge of the sofa.

'You okay, hun?' I ask her.

'Sure.' Her bottom lip quivers a fraction.

'Is your boyfriend coming?' She wrinkles her nose. 'You two fallen out again?' I slip my arm around her. Her hair smells of candyfloss.

'Sort of. I hope he doesn't turn up, if I'm honest. I can't bear another round of the blame game.'

'Listen, before it gets noisy, I want to talk to you about my trip to Japan in the spring. I've only got ten days over there and I want to know if I should spend more time in Kyoto or Nara.'

Her face lights up. She's keen to talk about home, although it seems that any subject other than her on-off boyfriend will do. She rattles through a list of bamboo forests, shrines and temples, raked Zen gardens and the best places for tea cere-monies – all with strange Japanese names – none of which I'll remember. 'I'll send you the links,' she says.

Ten more people arrive at once, so I turn up the music. Let's get this party rockin'!

28

SAM

The Present

I spent the next morning chasing from one area of London to another, speaking to hairdressers.

I started with the salon Lorna had used before she died in 2010; the one Julia had mentioned. On the way, I got back to Tamsin, thanking her for the photos and to ask who had restyled Hazel's hair shortly before her death. Given how close the pair were, I was sure she'd know. She responded straight away; a place called Clippers in Kings Cross.

I'd already made a note of the salon Charlotte had visited from her file – The Cut Above, near her home, in Primrose Hill. Three different salons, miles apart.

It was a while since I'd been to Chelsea and new gelato parlours and boutiques had sprouted up at every turn. I wandered along the Fulham Road as shop owners threw open their rattling metal shutters and set out sandwich boards on the pavement. It was all so reassuringly normal.

I'd got an early start, driven by the urge to find out more, but the aroma as I passed the first coffee shop grabbed me and practically bundled me inside, all by itself. Not having had breakfast, it seemed negligent to have an expresso without involving an oven-crisp croissant, so I treated myself. Then immediately regretted it. I patted my not-so-flat stomach on the way out. Those extra pounds weren't going to disappear on their own, I really did need to make a move towards shifting them.

I crossed the road into the morning sun. According to the map on my phone, Giovanni's was further down.

There were two customers already there when I walked in. One with her head decorated in silver foil, the other leaning back over a sink. Both in their twenties, I'd guess. Promotion posters for techniques such as *balayage* and *strand-lighting* hung on wires from the ceiling as if it were an art gallery. I could see from the price list that this wasn't the place for a traditional pensioner's 'shampoo and set'.

A man with blond highlights and black roots glided towards me with short dainty steps, holding a hairpiece. He was barely taller than me and about half as wide. 'Are you here for highlights?'

I couldn't help noticing the block heels on his shoes. 'No. Actually, I wanted to get some information.' I flashed my NHS identity card and told him I was working with the police on an old murder case.

It was a long shot speaking to stylists about clients going back so many years, but I had little else to go on. Nevertheless, when I held out my phone and showed Giovanni the screenshot of Lorna I'd taken from the cold case file, he blinked fast and drew up tall.

'Ages ago, wasn't eet? Even so, she stuck in my mind,' he said in a flamboyant Italian accent that didn't quite ring true. 'She was in a terrible state – I do remember that.'

'She'd had a chunk of hair cut off at the back,' I reminded him.

He narrowed his eyes, his delicate fingers playing a tune on his lips.

'Did she mention that at all?' I knew as the words came out of my mouth I was clutching at straws. A thousand clients must have passed through his doors in nine years.

He shook his head. 'I just remember eet was a mess.'

'You mind if I check with the others?'

'They've not been here long, but you can try.'

He picked up a long soft brush and swept scatterings of hair towards a pile in the corner.

Both the other stylists had still been at school at the time I was referring to. Once out of earshot however, I had a slightly different question for each of them. I wanted to know what they thought of Giovanni. The general consensus was that he was fair, good-humoured and a first-rate hairdresser.

'He's from Peckham – did you realise?' whispered the first one, wearing black jeans so 'distressed' they displayed more bare skin than fabric. 'His real name is Joe Topping, but he prefers to be known as Giovanni from Naples.'

Other than this harmless attempt at subterfuge, neither had any reason to question his character.

It was a similar story at Clippers at Kings Cross. They all remembered Hazel clearly, as she'd been there less than two weeks earlier. None of them knew why she'd had her hair hacked off at the back.

'She was really upset. Said she didn't want to talk about it, so I didn't push,' said the senior stylist.

At my final stop, The Cut Above, more detail emerged. An assistant found a battered card for Charlotte in an old client file box left in the broom cupboard. An industrious stylist had scribbled the following note:

19/10/2016: Client needs restyle – hair spoilt at back; about 10cm snipped at collar on 16 Oct. Remaining hair collected for wig as very long. Client signed consent form. Sent to Flynn 21/10/2016.

I froze, my mouth gaping open. This was the final piece of confirmation I needed. I took a photo of the card and asked the assistant to take good care of it in case it was needed by the police.

I hastened back along the main road, my head buried in my notebook, unaware of everything around me. I nearly charged straight into a letterbox and missed barging into a traffic warden by a couple of centimetres. I was comparing dates, trying to work out exactly what the pattern was.

The salon visits didn't tally: Hazel had a professional cut five days before she died, Charlotte four, and Lorna six days before. Situated in disparate locations in London, there didn't seem to be any shadows lurking over the stylists who'd tidied up the victims' hair.

Giovanni was the only one who'd been a hairdresser in 2010 and I couldn't imagine him exerting brute force against anyone. He probably weighed less than me with celery-thin arms – not the type to pump iron at the gym. I couldn't see him pinning Charlotte down with a pillow or dragging Lorna's body onto a train track.

But there was another pattern: not only was the hair of the three women secretly snipped off at the back, but it took place exactly seven days before they were each murdered. If that wasn't the signature of a serial killer, I didn't know what was!

I stabbed Fenway's number into my phone straight away, but reached only his voicemail. I drew in a breath, then snapped my mouth shut and let the air go. In my fizzing state, my thoughts batting around like a pinball, I couldn't trust myself to leave him a clear and concise message. It would merely come out garbled and hysterical, no doubt reinforcing how misguided Claussen had been to get me onboard in the first place.

I put my phone away and strode on in the direction of the park at Primrose Hill. After a few strides, my elation waned even further. All I had was a pattern of dates and an unknown stalker who had hacked off the victims' hair. Someone who had remained off the police radar for nearly ten years. How the hell was I going to find out who that person was?

29

I had ground to make up with Miranda after letting her down on Friday night, so I texted from a bench halfway up the grassy slope on Primrose Hill to say I was on my way to see her. I could get there on foot in under thirty minutes. She got back to me explaining she was busy at CCAP and instructed me in capital letters not to turn up before three.

With time to kill, I decided to try Fenway again, only this time I'd put my thoughts down in an email with exactly what I wanted to say.

It took three goes to put together a sensible and dispassionate message outlining what I'd uncovered, namely two cold murder cases with unmistakeable similarities; that of Lorna Sullivan and Charlotte Walsh. I ended with the slightly more contentious part:

> *I think I've found evidence that a hair fetish could be involved and that there are distinct signs of the same pattern in the recent death of Hazel Hart.*

I pressed send before I could change my mind and my message disappeared from the screen.

My heart was pattering when I got to my feet. The ball was in his court. Now things might actually start to shift.

I headed towards the edge of the park, kicking the potpourri of long-fallen leaves strewn under every tree. Periodically the sun broke open the molten sky, highlighting the muted colours below, from amber to muddy brown. There was a mournful fragility about the scene; dead leaves, the light vacillating before it darted for cover behind the next cloud.

I was surprised when another officer, DI Lynda McBride, got back to me on Fenway's behalf. She explained he was heavily involved in an internal investigation and advised me to keep him updated with any breakthroughs.

'This is a breakthrough,' I insisted.

'Right...'

'When will he be available?' I asked, not unreasonably.

'It won't be today. He's snowed under.'

'Is there anyone else I can speak to about this?'

'No, it should be him. He's the only person dealing with it at the moment.'

The conversation was beginning to take on a resounding similarity to countless other fruitless calls I'd made recently to my bank about an overpayment drawn on my account.

'Oh, wait,' she added, 'he did have a message for you.'

At last, something concrete.

'It says here you mustn't interview anyone involved without his prior consent and must always be accompanied.'

'Okay. Yes. I knew that. Thank you.'

I felt my hackles rise. The sun had gone for good and the sky was a restless and chalky grey. A brutal wind clawed at the flaps of my coat and I was glad I hadn't ventured onto the exposed higher ground.

How was I meant to get anywhere with these cases if Fenway was the only person I was meant to liaise with and he was tied up with something else?

I strode on towards Miranda's neck of the woods, the clamour of stop-start traffic and exhaust fumes resuming centre stage in my awareness. I inwardly cringed at the growing list of individuals I'd already spoken to, using my involvement with the police as leverage. In my bid to make headway, I'd already stepped over the mark. Then I let myself off the hook. I was trying to get to the truth. The police were involving me because they thought I had something to contribute. In any case, I wasn't, in fact, 'interviewing' anyone; we were simply having a chat.

Even so, I kept my fingers crossed no one found me out.

30

I tracked down Miranda in the café at CCAP. I was a few minutes earlier than her immutable appointment time and dallied at the door in two minds over nipping to the ladies' toilets first. In that split second, I noticed she wasn't alone. A man with his back to me was chatting to her. In fact, the pair were looking very cosy.

I observed for a while, until Miranda looked at her watch and sat back. The man nodded and stood up, then planted a lingering kiss on her upturned lips. I shrank away from the door, taking a detour to the loo after all. I needed a moment to gather my thoughts.

When I joined her, Miranda was tapping her fingers on the table and the mystery man had gone. It was then I realised there was something familiar about him.

'Who was that?' I asked, taking his seat. The residual heat of his backside left me unaccountably uncomfortable.

She blinked fast, manufacturing surprise. 'Who was who?'

'The guy you were chatting to.'

'Oh, just someone who comes in from time to time.' She pushed her empty cup and saucer away. 'He likes my work.'

I knew her too well to keep pushing. She'd closed down like a clam and no amount of force would get her to open up.

'Look, you wanted to help with my exhibition,' she said, deftly changing the subject. 'So I've found you a job. Interested?'

'You'd better tell me what it is first.'

'Okay. I want to get fliers and posters up everywhere we can in the area. I've got five hundred printed. You up for it, Sammie?'

Five hundred... It sounded like a mammoth task.

She went on. 'You can't stick them on fences or street lamps – that's flyposting and it's illegal, but you can go into shops and cafés and ask if they'll display them in the window.'

She can't have missed the look of sheer horror on my face. 'You don't have to do it on your own,' she added. 'In fact, here she is...' Miranda stood up and welcomed a woman to our table with a big hug. 'This is Emily Chambers. She's new here. She's helping with the posters. This is Sam, my sister.'

'Hi.' Emily remained standing. Taller than me and super-slim, she wore nifty trainers and all-over lycra that accentuated the compact muscles in her thighs and calves. 'So, what are you having, Sam?' Emily asked. 'Tea, coffee, something stronger?'

I was struck by her self-assurance.

'Er, coffee, please.'

Miranda asked for an orange juice.

I watched Emily's sleek black hair fan out behind her as she strode over to the counter. She looked slightly younger than me; early thirties, perhaps.

'Emily's only been coming here for a few days,' Miranda whispered, leaning towards me. 'She's the new self-defence tutor. We've been asking for one for months. Doing it for free too.' Miranda was smiling and animated, the chattiest I'd witnessed in ages.

Emily came back with the drinks.

'You got the posters?' Miranda asked her, once she'd got settled.

'Absolutely.' Emily patted her rucksack.

A voice from the door called out Miranda's name and she apologised to us both before leaving the table.

'Your sister says you're a clinical psychologist... did I get that right?' Emily was supping one of those gloopy green concoctions that was meant to be good for you, but wouldn't have looked out of place on the floor of a cowshed.

'Spot on. I work at a hospital near London Bridge.'

'Tough, I should think. Miranda said you do a lot of trauma work and help people who've lost their memory.' Emily sighed, stirring the thick liquid with a wooden spoon. 'People who've lost their way, I guess. Emotionally draining work, I imagine. I admire you.'

I raised my eyebrows. Most people nodded politely and changed the subject when they found out what I did. 'You sound like you know something about it.'

'I haven't had therapy myself, if that's what you mean, but I've got friends who have. Really helped them. In one instance, I'd say it probably saved his life.'

I gave her a sad smile. We sipped our drinks in unison.

'Is teaching self-defence your main job?' I asked.

'Not quite. I'm a gym instructor. I work in a few places in south London. I used to be a cyclist for a courier company, but I was knocked off too many times. Broke two ribs last time, so I decided to call it a day.' She looked me up and down. 'You're in good shape. Do you go to the gym?'

I snorted. 'Funny you should say that. I used to do spinning classes and yoga, but I've been useless lately.' I tapped my belly. 'Too much sitting down and giving in to snacks between meals. I gave my local gym a go this week, but I can't kid myself – I hated it.'

She shrugged. 'It's not for everyone. These days, instead of using the bike so much, I go running. At night. It's amazing. Best thing I've ever done. You should try it.'

I wrinkled up my nose. 'I used to get roped into the 400 metres at school. Mainly because no one else would do it. I remember throwing up after a race once. I don't think running is for me.'

'The longer sprint races are killers,' she replied, pulling a face. 'I don't blame you for being put off. But *long-distance* running, if you learn the right technique and the best way to regulate your breathing – it's like meditation. It's freedom, it's empowering, you lose weight and get fit – and it doesn't cost you a penny.'

'Hmm...' I wasn't convinced.

'Okay.' She put her hands flat on the table. 'You look like a woman who doesn't shy away from a challenge, so how about this? I'll teach you to love running in four weeks for free, if you give me the chance.'

A flicker of astonishment sent my eyebrows up. 'Where do you live?' I asked, before we went any further.

'Putney Bridge.'

'Really?' She must have wondered why I sounded so surprised. The fact that it was one of my favourite spots felt oddly encouraging, like an omen.

She carried on. 'I rent a rundown one-bed flat. I wouldn't be able to afford if it wasn't due for demolition.'

'I'm not that far away. Clapham Junction. Five minutes' walk from the station.'

'Perfect!' said Emily, as Miranda came back to our table. 'And like I said, there's no charge. It's just a great excuse for me to get a few more miles under my belt.'

'Thank you. I appreciate it.'

'What are you talking about?' Miranda asked, looking

bemused. No doubt she was expecting us to be discussing the itinerary for distributing her posters.

Emily gave me a conspiratorial look. 'Ready to start tonight? How about we make it this area to begin with. We can put up the posters and get fit at the same time.'

I was sold. 'You're on.'

31

———————

HAZEL

Five days earlier

I spot you – you nasty piece of shit – but it's already too late. You're entrenched in a group by the bookshelf; chatting, laughing, looking like you're one of us. I don't want to create a scene by getting someone to throw you out. But I'm damned if you're going to ruin the afternoon. I glare at you, like you're the devil. It's designed to send you a message in no uncertain terms: *keep your effing distance, you lowlife, and don't expect me to utter one word to you.*

Someone taps me on the shoulder. I spin round and my heart flips as though I've been handed first prize in a competition. 'Flavia! Thank God you're here.' I fling my arms around her.

She looks disconcerted. 'Why, what's happened?'

'Nothing.' I slip my arm around her. 'Glad you made it, that's all. Red, white or fizzy?'

I love Flavia. She's been my best friend since primary school. Brutal honesty is one of her traits and unlike a number of my mates, she never plays stupid mind games. Her dirty laugh goes hand in hand with her gross sense of humour. My kinda gal.

I go with her to the table, but don't take a glass myself. I need to keep a cool head for later.

When I glance up, Tamsin has a look on her face that could curdle milk. She's twigged Flavia's arrival. She hates the place Flavia holds in my life, but never says a thing. Just stares, sucking in her cheeks, letting the occasional bitchy comment slip out when she's had too much to drink.

My eyes slide back to the corner by the bookshelf. You know I'm not happy you're here, so you raise your glass at me with a smirk. I pretend I don't see your fuckwit gesture and look straight past you, but not before I've noticed you're wearing a white ruffle shirt, like Prince, with unusual silver cufflinks that twinkle like midnight stars. As though you've been looking forward to this occasion and have dressed up specially. *Who the hell told you about it?*

I find my hand reaching subconsciously up to my cheek. The spot where you left your mark. I was only trying to help. Especially given that she insisted she'd always wanted to sell up and relocate to Spain one day.

Then you came out with all that other bollocks. That was nothing to do with me – I wasn't even out of my cot, for crying out loud. In any case, there was nothing illegal, no wheeling and dealing – I don't know why you were so friggin' uptight about it. My parents set up a legitimate business on the high street, that's all. Tough shit. It's a competitive world out there in case you hadn't noticed. Our family made a better go of it than yours, that's all.

I turn away. So you know, I'm not giving up. I told your mother I'll be back and my promise still stands. I'm taking more brochures with me next time, so she can choose exactly what she wants. Just you see!

I take a swig of wine from a glass someone has left on my coffee table. I'm angry now. I wish I'd taken my selfie earlier. I don't want you to be part of my special moment. It's like a ritual to me; stepping out alone onto the balcony and doing what no one else here would dare to do. Ever.

'So, are you ready?' It's Flavia's voice beside me in a whisper.

I nod. 'Soon.'

'You sure? It's bloody windy.'

I put the glass down, disowning it. 'I'll be fine.'

I've got plenty of online 'friends' who get what I do, but only a couple of real ones who truly understand. Flavia is one of them. Her brother took up cave diving in his teens and she's always been his prime cheerleader. She made it her mission to be the first to greet him when he clambered out onto the rocky surface, primed with a hot flask and energy bar. Flavia knows the thrill that consumes me. The same way her brother feels when he finds a phosphorescent underground lagoon or an echo chamber he can howl into like a wolf. She knows balancing with no hands on the railing of the nineteenth floor is incredible, even though I've done it many times before.

Unlike Tamsin, I don't need drugs to pep me up or to take life into the fast lane. This is my high. Literally. The anticipation, the build-up; my heart galloping with a cocktail of terror and exhilaration. There's nothing like it. It might not be as impressive as a magnificent dive into a canyon or a quadruple lutz on the ice, but it's dynamite to me.

'I'm thinking of setting up a world record for the number of daredevil selfies,' I tell Flavia. She's seen my selfie from Niagara Falls, one on a crane above a skyscraper in Manhattan, shots on London high-rise rooftops.

'Wow – what a fabulous idea.'

'I need to look it up online and see how many I need to aim for.' I stretch out my arms, watch my quivering fingers jittery with nerves. I feel like an athlete getting ready for a race.

'Go to the loo and psyche yourself up,' she says. She knows my routine inside out.

No one notices when I disappear. The music pounds on and friends dance and mingle. I haven't told anyone except for Flavia what I intend to do, but I'm sure it won't come as a surprise. She'll announce it just before I go out to make sure no one does anything stupid to startle me. Thankfully, there are no balloons that could burst.

I lock the bathroom door and take a deep breath in front of the mirror. I still get a shock every time I look at myself since it happened. My beautiful hair all gone. Taking my identity with it. Savagely stolen from me by some idiot who didn't even have the guts to show his face. This will be the first selfie I've taken with my hair cut short. I hope it's not a bad omen. Samson and all that.

I stood out there earlier, before people arrived and I know what I'm up against. A tugging breeze, sunshine, nothing I've not handled before. With my eyes closed, I run through my warm-up once more in slow motion.

My balcony is hardly the Empire State Building, but it's still over two hundred feet above the ground. When I tell people to imagine standing on the roof of a double-decker bus, they think it sounds high. But their jaws drop when I say: 'Now imagine *fifteen* double-decker buses on top of each other and then you've got the measure of it...'

I unlock the bathroom door and stand in the doorway to my living room. I give Flavia the nod. I'm ready.

Flavia makes her announcement. '...and don't forget, everyone, no photos. Hazel doesn't want to have to deal with any flashes or phone screens catching the light. She's got enough to concentrate on without any distractions.'

An uncomfortable flutter of laughter follows. There a deathly hush as I slide open the door to the balcony and step outside. An immediate roar of traffic from below hits my ears. I take three steps, then with extreme care, I hitch up onto the barrier, digging my heels against the glass once I'm sitting on the top. Facing inwards and keeping my weight forward, my abs tight against the gusts of wind, I hold out my phone. The sunlight is dazzling, but I don't want to hide my face with sunglasses.

It's only once I'm in position, about to line up my phone when an uneasiness crawls over my skin. I remember you've gatecrashed my party and my mind buzzes with questions again. Why did you turn up? What did you hope to gain from sneaking in? What have you been telling my friends?

I see my image in the screen – and freeze, hit again by that pang of horror at what someone has done to my hair. I judder as if a mild earthquake is shaking the railing beneath me.

Don't lose it. It's okay. You can do this.

Suddenly a fresh thought occurs to me. It can't be, can it? Could you and that maniac who sat behind me on the bus be one and the same person?

A film of sweat coats my hands and the phone almost slips through my fingers. It hadn't occurred to me, because I never saw your face. And the military-look clothes you wore; they aren't your style at all. But now it makes sense. You wanted to scare me with your sick stalking, didn't you? Wanted to make me pay – and all because I tried to help your mother find happiness.

I make a decision. You're not going to get away with this. As soon as I've taken this shot I'm calling the police. I just need to compose myself first. Plant a smile on my face; look on top of things. Get this done.

A flash from somewhere blinds me and I make the mistake of looking up for a fraction of a second. You're with a group of others in the doorway and you've slipped your hand out of your pocket. How clever of you. Your mirror cufflink is reflecting a pure beam of white sunlight straight into my eyes. I see red blotches and blink, but it's too late. Already my weight has swung back a fraction too far.

There's nothing I can do.

For an instant, I seem to stay where I am; the moment holding me in its arms one last time. Then the hungry breeze snatches at my chest and flings me over.

32

SAM

The Present

It was windy and threatening to chuck it down, a storm brewing with latent rage and hostility when I met Emily inside the ticket hall of Camden Town tube. Not the best evening to begin a running campaign, but I had a job to do and at least I wasn't on my own.

'Do you always go running this late?' I said, my teeth rattling. 'Most sensible people are snug in front of the fire at this time in the evening.'

She laughed, zipping up her tracksuit top. 'This is early for me. I usually start after midnight. That's when the night is just beginning.'

I slapped my gloved hands together to generate some heat.

'Glad to see you're wearing layers,' she said. 'You can strip off and tie your top round your waist as we warm up.'

'You're kidding me. I'm keeping everything on.' I was shivering and we weren't even exposed to the elements yet.

She pulled a sheet of paper from her pocket. 'Miranda gave me a list of places to try: pubs, clubs, restaurants. Some of the notices are fliers, so we can leave a pile each time, others are posters we want people to display.' Emily glanced down at her list. 'Let's do the places around here first as a warm-up, then we can run properly to the next ones.'

'Okay. I'm in your hands.'

Still undercover, she took me through a set of stretches. 'Got any injuries I should know about, or muscles that tweak if you run for a bus?'

'No, nothing I can think of. Just unfit.' I felt my bones creak as my arms flailed towards my shoelaces. I let out a telltale grunt and she laughed before hoisting her heavy rucksack onto her back.

'You need to give me half the posters to carry,' I said, 'you can't take all of them.'

'No way. This is your first time. What have you got in your backpack?'

'Water, purse, phone. That's all.'

'Good. Never more than that. Let's powerwalk to get going.' With that, she shot out ahead of me. The rain had broken through and was dancing off the pavement with a velocity that made me want to stay exactly where I was.

She turned. 'Let's go.'

Reluctantly, I joined her, striding out fast to keep up. Cars roared past us, their wheels making a sound like cymbals, as they crashed through the puddles already collecting at the side of the road.

We covered the first few venues on Emily's list: two delis, a cinema and a late-opening vegan café. Half seemed happy to help, the others muttered excuses. *I don't think the owner allows this… No room on the counter… Sorry, we're too busy…*

We ran between the next cluster of businesses: a library, two hotels, a community centre, more pubs and late-opening shops.

'How are you doing?' she asked, stopping to take a swig of water from her bottle.

'Not bad.' I was a bit out of breath, but not struggling. I bent over, holding my knees to ease my aching back. 'It's bitty though, isn't it?'

'I know. What if we take a good run without stopping. I can finish off the rest of the posters during the daytime tomorrow.'

'I can't let you do that. I'm supposed to be helping.'

'Don't worry. I'll do a good job, believe me. You won't find them stuffed in the bins! Then we can meet tomorrow night, if you're still keen – and run properly without the breaks. You'll ache, but we'll build up slowly.'

I straightened up, rolled my creaking neck. 'Let's see how I get on over a longer stretch first, before I sign on the dotted line.'

She laughed. 'Sure. You ready?'

Five minutes later and I had to stop. 'I've got a stitch,' I gasped, as I bent over, clutching my side. 'Not used to it.'

'You're doing really well. Don't get cold, just walk for a bit.'

We walked and talked, then broke into a gentle jog.

'You said you mainly run after midnight,' I said, as we turned into a quiet tree-lined avenue. 'Do you feel safe on your own?'

'Absolutely. I reckon it's probably safer in the small hours of the morning, than it is earlier. That's been my experience anyway. All the drunks have either gone home or passed out. But I know I can look after myself. I teach self-defence, remember!'

I liked her plucky spirit. In fact, I liked Emily – full stop. She was warm and generous with a no-nonsense approach I'd connected with straight away.

We crossed over the road and set up an easy jog along the back streets.

'For years, I've run at night,' she said. 'The later the better. That's when I come alive. Coursing through the streets, alone, when most people are asleep. There's nothing like it. So liberating...'

'I can see that.' I already felt a sense of other-worldliness; seeing a side to London I'd rarely witnessed, when blinds and curtains are drawn, TVs are on, children are in bed, and the grown-ups are winding down before they turn in for the night.

'I've never slept well too – that's part of it,' Emily went on, her regular steps breaking up her speech. 'I've never been able to stay still for long. I used to drive Mum mad as a child; I wouldn't sit and watch television or read a book. I was always doing handstands or had one leg up on the window ledge, prac- tising the splits instead.' She glanced over at me a smile on her lips. 'I'd never be any good at meditation.'

We crunched along a gravel track, between two detached houses. It led to a tall wooden gate and we cut through a small park which backed onto a cemetery. Between the grave stones, I spotted a motionless black shape. I grabbed Emily's arm, but she nodded nonchalantly. As we got closer, the figure shuffled to a bench and slumped down. I looked ahead, not wanting to stare. It gave me the creeps, but Emily was unfazed. 'Someone else who prefers to move around in the shadowlands,' she whispered.

Emerging on the other side, I was glad of the street lights again. Emily led me along winding lanes and narrow pathways, constantly aware of me, letting me dictate the pace.

'You're getting the hang of it...' she said, 'breathe in for four, then let it out for four... focus on your breathing.'

Before long, I found a rhythm. The rain stopped and we threw back our hoods in unison. Gradually our shoes and anoraks stopped glistening.

'I love laying down an invisible trail, like a cat's cradle, weaving back and forth,' she said. 'I never bring headphones when I'm on my own; for safety reasons, obviously, but also because I like to hear the sound of my own breathing.'

I grasped what she meant. There was something invigorating about hearing my own controlled breath. It made me feel strong.

She stopped talking for a while and we ran as one, both inside our own separate worlds. My mind drifted off to the three cases that had occupied every waking hour during the last few days. The tangled energy they brought fired me up, driving me on.

When we crossed the road after the next corner, I was surprised to find we were back at the tube station.

'You did it,' she said, slapping me on the back. We slowed to a stop inside the shelter of the ticket hall.

I leant over, getting my breath. 'That was brilliant,' I said, between gasps.

Emily was barely out of breath. She straightened up, jogging on the spot, lifting her knees high like a hurdler. 'You were amazing. A natural. So easy to run with. You're way fitter than you think you are!'

I broke into a smile. 'Thank you,' I said, holding onto her arm nevertheless.

Once we'd had a few glugs of water, we found our travel cards and headed down the escalator. On the platform, it was clear there'd been a series of train cancellations. We were both going south and had to squash our way through a crowd of late-evening revellers growing in numbers with every second.

'There are fewer people up this way,' I said, leading her to a spot that was less busy only for a moment, but which quickly filled up behind us as more people joined the crush. Before long, the display board showed the train was due and I felt the familiar distant rumble under my feet and suck of the air as it approached.

I wasn't sure what happened next.

I remember we were on the yellow line and the train was coming in from the left. There was a surge around us, hands and elbows near my face, people pushing. The next thing I knew, Emily wrenched my arm almost out of its socket, as I came within centimetres of toppling onto the track. She hauled me back from the platform edge with such force I was flung to the ground and she ended up on top of me.

'Oh my god, are you okay?' she shrieked, shoving legs and bags out of the way, so I wouldn't get trampled on.

I was lying flat out, shaking, trying to breathe, overheated from the run and the baking temperature underground. Everything was spinning.

Emily grabbed a pile of posters from her bag and wafted them in front of me. 'Someone tried to shove you in front of the train!' she shouted. She handed me her bottle of water and wrapped her arm behind my shoulder so I could sip.

The fleeting blurred image of a black and white stripe flashed into my head. I let out a little moan and blinked slowly, waiting for everything to stay still. By then, the train had gone and passengers had thinned out considerably. Only a small group had remained on the platform, gathering around us to see what had happened.

'I'm fine,' I mumbled, taking another swig of water. 'I'm sure it was an accident.'

A flash went off as one of the onlookers took a photo.

Emily shot to her feet. 'Show's over!' she shouted with authority as she shielded me. 'Nothing to see, ladies and gents.' She hurled out her arms to nudge people out of the way.

My legs were wobbly as she turned back to help me to my feet. 'Thank you,' I managed, still feeling woozy.

We stood facing each other, our arms entwined.

'Bloody hell, Emily – I think you just saved my life.'

33

'I'm fine, honestly.'

Terry wouldn't take no for an answer. He'd called on the pretext of enquiring about my progress on the cold cases and had asked why I sounded breathless.

'It's nothing.'

'Where are you?'

'Camden tube when I last checked...'

'You sound very odd – are you okay?'

'Bit of an incident on the platform,' I'd said vaguely. I'd given him a heavily edited version of events.

'Bloody hell! Someone actually *pushed* you?'

'Apparently, but I really don't think–'

'Stay where you are,' he'd instructed, 'I'm coming to get you.'

'No, don't worry, I'll be–' He'd cut me off before I could finish.

Emily had left me in Terry's hands when he arrived. 'You're not going to let this put you off, are you?' she whispered.

'No way.' It came out sounding braver than I felt.

She left with a wave. 'Tomorrow night then.'

Terry took over. 'Shouldn't we get you to A&E?' he queried, on the way to his car.

'I'm fine,' I said, drawing out a big smile. 'No bones broken. I'm just a bit shaken.'

'You're sure you don't have concussion?'

'No,' I said, emphatically. 'I didn't black out. I'm okay.'

Terry drove me back to my place and insisted on running me a bath. I hadn't been expecting visitors and was more concerned about my underwear drying in full view in the sitting room than the bruises that were blossoming like pansies on my limbs.

'I don't suppose you've eaten properly this evening, have you?' he chided, as I emerged from the bathroom, feeling wonderfully sleepy.

I didn't catch his eye, fiddled instead with the belt of my bathrobe.

'I *know* you, Willerby. For a health professional, you're useless at looking after yourself.'

'It's too late now for steak and chips,' I said churlishly. In spite of his nannying, it was delightful to be fussed over for once.

'Why not have a bit of porridge? You haven't tried my new recipe, have you?'

It was after eleven. Not only had Emily and I been required to hang around while we recounted the incident to the transport police, but they'd asked us to wait while they took a look at the CCTV footage.

'In cases like this where there's a big crowd, it's hard to see exactly what happened,' Sergeant Downie had explained, stating the obvious. 'Did you see who pushed you?'

I'd glanced at Emily. 'I'm not sure it was deliberate,' I said, tentatively, not wishing to contradict her.

'Did you see anyone?' the officer reiterated.

'No. I remember a black and white stripe near my face. I don't know what that was; a football scarf, a collar, a furry hat?' I shook my head, knowing I had nothing more to tell him.

He made a note. 'Is there anyone you know who might wish you any harm?'

'Me? No. Not at all.'

'Anything unusual happened lately? Or any reason anyone might target you? You say you work with people with mental problems, could there be a patient you've upset?'

I considered it, then shook my head again. 'I don't think so. I'm sure it was an accident. Too many people pushing and shoving to get close to the doors. There hadn't been a train for fifteen minutes. Near misses like this must happen a fair bit, don't they?'

Sergeant Downie put his hands on his hips. 'A couple of witnesses, including your friend, made it clear they thought someone was trying to get to you. They all said someone lunged forward with considerable force before the train actually reached the platform.'

'They did?'

I looked at Emily who was nodding.

'Maybe whoever it was mistook me for someone else. Or perhaps they were angry about something and lashed out at the first person who caught their eye.'

'Commuter rage?' he suggested.

I shrugged. 'Or a disturbed individual. Unstable, drunk, on drugs, not well…' I'd had enough experience with mental illness to know random acts of violence happened all the time.

Terry brought in the bowl of steaming porridge and snapped me out of my reverie. He sat beside me on the sofa, watching while I took each spoonful. It was warming, tasty and creamy; pure comfort food.

'Yummy. This is exactly what I need.'

'Cocoa coming up. Still your favourite nightcap?'

'Yes, but I can get it.' I set the dish aside and shuffled forward, but he put out his hand like he was stopping traffic. I felt like an invalid.

When he returned, he grilled me in the same way the transport police had done, but I kept coming back to the same conclusion. 'It can't have been deliberate. Why would anyone want to target me? It must have been an idiot who'd had too much to drink.'

34

───────

I cradled the hot cocoa, burying my face in the steam as I took a sip. I was hoping we'd reached the end of the matter. Surely Terry could see that what happened in the underground was indiscriminate jostling. Thankfully, my explanation seemed to do the trick and he dropped the subject.

I sank back into a nest of soft cushions and updated him on my new findings with the cold cases.

'All three had a salon restyle after someone snipped off their hair at the back.'

'It certainly puts a different slant on someone being "hacked",' he said, unable to hide a chuckle.

My foot, clad in a fluffy pink bedsock, shot over and gave his shin a sharp kick. 'This is serious!'

'Sorry, I couldn't resist.'

'The problem I have is that most of the police evidence in each case relates to the days the murders were committed, not the week before. That's the key bit – the women having their hair cut off in the first place. That's the pattern.'

'And you reckon the same person went on to kill the victims, exactly seven days after the assaults?'

'It's precisely the same time frame in each of these three cases. Otherwise, it's one hell of a coincidence.'

'So we're also talking about Hazel Hart. You think her death wasn't an accident?'

'The pattern's there. Exactly the same. Someone may not have been physically on the balcony with her, but–'

'The interviews are still ongoing with Hazel's case, so it's not cut and dried by any means. I'll have a word with the SIO first thing tomorrow as well. Make sure they follow up the hair-cutting angle.'

'Thank you.' I curled up into a foetal position, facing Terry.

'You think a grandiose delusion could be behind their deaths?'

'It's only one possible explanation. But it's where I've got the new skills so that's where I'm focussing. I've got a feeling about it too. Delusions can stem from rituals and hair plays a big part in folklore and certain pagan ceremonies. In myths and fairy tales too.'

'Like Samson, you mean – he lost all his strength when his hair was cut, didn't he?'

I nodded. 'And like plenty of other legends throughout the world. I came across one from Russia about a woman with hair made of pure gold, too heavy to carry.' I nipped my lips together. 'Even if it does come from some story or other, I'm struggling to figure out how these particular women are chosen and why there are big gaps in the time frame.'

Terry had no response.

I carried on. 'Or maybe there is no myth and the killer randomly targets lots of attractive women with long hair, then goes on to kill whoever he manages to assault.'

He grunted. 'That doesn't narrow it down much.'

'I know – there are hundreds of thousands of pretty women with long hair,' I said with a sigh. 'And if that's the only connection then it's going to make it almost impossible to pinpoint the killer.'

'What happens to the hair?' he asked, sinking into the cushions, sounding sleepy. 'After it's hacked, I mean. Is it a trophy for the killer? Are there any patterns there?'

'Good question – I don't know where it goes. According to the crime scene data, it's not left with the bodies. But, of course, the hacking happens a week before the murders themselves.'

'Do you think the killer gets rid of it?'

'Hard to know. It depends on whether, in itself, the hair has value or meaning for the killer. Or it could be more like a signal of intent. Like that particular victim has been selected.

Terry's face stiffened. 'Like being branded?'

I gave him a grim nod.

Even though I wasn't finding any answers, a surreal sense of serenity washed over me as I snuggled so close to Terry. We weren't touching, but I could feel the heat of his arm as it almost brushed my bent leg. There was nothing awkward; it felt the most natural thing in the world.

'You'll find something. You always do.' He held out his mug of cocoa and clinked it against mine.

I yawned, aware of the time. I needed to sleep, but my brain was still hurtling round and round like a Formula One racing car.

'I can stay if you like,' he suggested innocently. 'If you're still a bit jumpy?'

I wasn't, but I didn't want him to leave.

'On the sofa, obviously,' he said pointedly.

I knew this wasn't the time to suggest my bed had plenty of room for two. The moment wasn't sizzling enough and he was only there because of the incident. If we were ever to take a definitive step in that direction, I wanted it to be as the result of a spine-tingling passionate clinch between us. Not with me in my baggy pyjamas, my hair dragged back under an Alice band, smears of dried chocolate around my mouth. Besides, Terry was too much of a gentleman to use the situation to his own ends. He would never do anything that could be construed as 'taking advantage'. It was likely to be pure wishful thinking on my part, in any case. He was probably just being 'a good mate'.

'I'd like that,' I said, heading for the linen cupboard.

It was only once I'd snuggled under my duvet and turned out the light that I began to see flashes of the incident on the underground in my mind. I'd convinced myself that it had been a random lashing out or an accident, but now darker thoughts crept inside my head to torment me.

What if someone had targeted me deliberately?

35

'You did an amazing job with the posters.' Miranda had rung as I was tying the laces of my trainers, about to hit the streets again with my new running partner. 'I've seen them everywhere. Flyers too. How did you manage to get them in The Crosskeys? The landlord is a tyrant. And the cinema?'

I paused, my mind a blank. The venues didn't ring a bell. 'Ah. That must have been Emily,' I said. 'She did most of them on her own.'

'Never mind who did what – she said you were great. So, thank you.'

There was no irony in her voice, no grating edge, merely lustrous gratitude. It wasn't like Miranda to be so effusive. Certainly not with me. I was touched, even though I didn't fully deserve her appreciation. Emily had done the lion's share.

'How are you doing after last night?' Emily asked, as I joined her by the flower stall at Clapham Junction.

'The running or the fun and games in the underground?'

She laughed. 'Both!'

'I'm fine. A bit stiff from the run and pummelled after the fall, but no harm done.'

'You'll feel better after this.'

After powerwalking for a couple of blocks, we broke into a run and I found a solid rhythm straight away. This time, I had no stitches, no discomfort, not even a blister. According to Emily's tracker, we covered two kilometres before we stopped for a water break.

'Woah, that was exhilarating,' she exclaimed. 'You okay?'

Now we'd stopped, I realised how out of breath I was. 'Not bad. Aware I'm holding you back. You'd go a lot faster – and much further, without me.'

She batted my comment away. 'Na, I love running whatever speed we go. It makes a nice change to have a partner.' The smile slipped from her features as we kept warm, jogging on the spot. She looked like she was about to say something important. 'I was geared up to be an elite cyclist when I was younger. My coach had even talked about the Commonwealth Games, but I had a bad crash and my chances of contending at that level went up in smoke.'

The catch in her throat didn't pass me by. 'I'm so sorry. What happened?'

In the inky shadows away from the street lights, her expression became increasingly sombre. 'I caught someone's wheel during a race. It was a tight bend and there was oil on the road. The surgeon knew straight away my shoulder would never be the same again.' She was close to tears, but didn't hide them or apologise. 'I'm not quite over it – as you can see.'

She let out a loud sigh, sending out a foggy cloud of breath. 'Come on, slacker,' she said, setting her app to zero. 'Another burst?'

36

I was in the shower after our run when an idea came to me. Like I'd told Terry, it was proving almost impossible to make progress on the two cold cases as the police investigations focussed on the deaths of the victims, not on the period beforehand. But I'd overlooked one vital resource I had of my own.

Lorna Sullivan's therapy tapes. Of course.

Perhaps there'd be a clue hidden amongst her words, some forewarning as to the appalling events that were to follow.

Hurriedly, I'd dried myself off. It was late, but I knew I wouldn't sleep until I'd at least got my hands on the cassettes. Back in 2010, it wasn't yet standard procedure to use a phone or laptop.

By law, there's no need to keep any details dating back longer than five years after a patient's visit. But, because I only taped occasional sessions to discuss in supervision, I always kept everything. I'm not sure why. Maybe it was because I thought one day a patient might come back. It would save us a lot of time to have their details already to hand. And sometimes patients did return. I felt a sinking feeling. Lorna would never be one of them.

I tipped out an entire box of tapes over the rug beside my bed before I found them. There were six in all. I stood up, clutching the plastic boxes, wondering where I'd left my old Walkman. That's if I'd kept it at all. The tapes were useless without it; my hi-fi system had long since been replaced with a CD player.

~

It was after midnight by the time I found it in the hall cupboard, stuffed inside a bag beside a hideous brown vase my mother gave me one Christmas. Both intended for a charity shop. One of those tasks that luckily I'd never got around to.

I returned to my bedroom, slipped the first tape into the machine and pressed play, hoping the batteries were still working.

I inwardly crumpled at the sound of Lorna's voice. It took me straight back to the first time she came into my office. Tall, immaculately dressed in slinky white trousers and a cropped top revealing her belly button. Her long flowing hair the colour of golden syrup.

Before starting a course in fashion design, she'd been a child model and it was easy to see why. I remembered being struck by how beautiful she was; how elegant and poised, the moment she greeted me like a dancer entering stage right.

She had a tinkling voice that was easy to listen to – refined, feminine, chatty. As the tape played on, the lemony-jasmine fragrance that had wafted into my office with her that day seemed to drift across my bedroom. I'd always meant to ask her what perfume it was.

At nineteen, her life was only beginning to unfold; the first steps on a yellow brick road that could have taken her anywhere she wanted. I listened as Lorna described the incident which traumatised her that springtime: the van mounting the pavement, just missing her, and one of the injured subsequently dying.

I propped my pillows up behind my back and slid my feet under the duvet. As the tape carried on, Lorna spoke about flashbacks and nightmares she'd been having. How she'd wake up gasping for breath, reliving the accident.

'Every night, I'm back in that queue seeing it happen over and over again in slow motion. People are checking their phones or looking in their bags. They don't see the van as it bumps off the road and careers straight for us. I didn't even scream. I mean, how stupid was that?'

She told me about the hardest part.

'I just stood there as this old woman beside me went down. I watched her go under the wheels. She kind of reached out like she thought I could help her. She's the one who died later in intensive care. Then there was a woman with a child in a buggy. She didn't have time to push the buggy away. She froze, shielding her child.' She whimpered. 'They all went down like skittles. I watched them. I didn't know what to do. It was awful.'

Lorna told me how, soon after, she'd picked out the man she thought was behind the wheel, in a police line-up. A local man called Neville Larch. It turned out she'd got it wrong and he was soon released, but not before the details had leaked to local press and he'd been hounded. I remembered she was almost as traumatised by her mistake as she was by the incident itself.

The temperature around me seemed to drop and I tugged the duvet up over my knees. As our conversation played out, it soon became clear that Lorna didn't speak much about the rest of her life. The odd reference to her mum – they seemed close – but no mention of boyfriends, nothing about college. I sank lower on the pillows. It wasn't adding a lot to what I already knew. After my late night last night, I was struggling to keep my eyes open. In the end, I drifted off to sleep with Lorna's voice still speaking softly in my ears.

Over breakfast the next morning, I listened to the rest of Lorna's first tape. Then I referred to the notes I'd taken about the suspects in her murder enquiry.

One of the men interviewed was Neville Larch. He was brought in when Lorna's family drew their attention to a spate of recent incidents designed to taunt her. They'd started after the line-up. And after local papers had done a fine job of smearing Neville Larch's name.

Her tape revealed that Larch had turned up at her flat once in Parson's Green, shouting and swearing at her. Other 'odd' things had happened at that time too: a padded envelope containing chicken bones had been posted through her letterbox and a tin of red paint poured through onto the carpet. She also mentioned that a voodoo doll complete with pins had been left on her windowsill. She'd even brought it in to show me.

'Have you been to the police with these things?' came my voice on the tape.

'There's no point really. I threw out the envelope with the bones without thinking and there was no tin with the paint for fingerprints. The doll with the pins, well, it's just silly. There's no proof. Mum said we should tell the police, but it's only my word against his and I've put him through enough already. I should never have picked him out in the line-up, but... I was so certain at the time.'

I remember suggesting she had every right to report him, but then I backed off. I was her therapist. There was no actual crime. It wasn't my job to force her into anything.

Another van driver was charged soon after the collision and the bottom line was that Neville Larch was in the clear right across the board. With an alibi for the day Lorna was killed and no DNA at the crime scene to contradict it, he'd walked free.

37

After our next run that evening, I suggested to Emily that we go for a drink. 'Unless you think it spoils the hearty workout we've just had?'

'No way. I'd love to,' she said, flicking back her long raisin-black hair. 'I'm not a health freak, just love being fit.'

'Good. I need something to take my mind off the aches and pains.' I rolled my tight shoulders. 'I knew my body would make a fuss after a day or two.'

'You're not going soft on me, are you?' she said with a grin, nudging my arm.

'No way.'

I suggested a small pub off the main high street, only a few minutes from my flat. It was less rowdy than many in my area and the bar staff let you taste their guest beers before buying. Emily had mentioned she had a weakness for real ales, so it seemed ideal.

We stood at the bar when we arrived and tested a selection of brews with names like Malten Lava and Ray of Hop. Surprisingly, we were unanimous in our choices and carried away four half-pint glasses on a sticky black tray.

'Fancy table football?' Emily asked as we trawled the place for a seat.

'I'm not very good.'

'Neither am I. But it's fun.'

In fact, Emily should have said, *I'm an expert – and I'll beat you hands down*, because as soon as we started, her competitive streak came to the fore. Eleven-nil. I should have seen it coming.

Mercifully, she called it a day before it got too embarrassing and we grabbed a couple of stray stools in the main bar.

'How are you getting on at the art project?' I asked. 'Given any self-defence classes yet?'

'Just one. It was full, so it's a great start.' She glanced down, looking a little self-conscious. 'It's a wonderful place. I keep popping in whenever I get the chance, if only to chat with people.'

I nodded. 'Lovely atmosphere. They're open and welcoming.'

'A really nice bunch turned up to my class. Your sister was there – she was probably the most advanced.'

'That doesn't surprise me,' I said with a wry smile. 'She's got a feisty streak and hates being taken advantage of.'

'I like her. She doesn't look as though she gives up easily.' Emily took a sip of ale, then set down the glass and watched the orange dregs slide to the bottom. 'Same as you, actually.'

I let her see my smile, but didn't pursue what she said. 'How's she getting on with the exhibition? Do you know?'

'Yeah – it's going great, so far. I seem to be heavily involved,' she said with a chuckle. 'Helping with admin, but I said I'd be there on the day as well. Ralph's on the scene a lot, but I expect you know all about him.'

Ralph? Was that the guy Miranda had been cagey about at the café?

'Her boyfriend?' I said neutrally, taking a chance.

'Hmm.' Emily nodded.

'Actually, Miranda's been a bit cloak and dagger about him. With me, at least. I haven't even been introduced.'

'Really? Everyone seems to know about him at the project. They seem very pashy. I keep catching them snogging.'

I folded my arms. 'Miranda isn't always forthcoming about her love life. Even though I'm the younger sister, she demonises me as some kind of wicked stepmother out to spoil her fun.'

Emily was about to laugh, then realised I was being serious. 'Oh, that's rotten. Bit like me and Kipper, my older brother. Utterly clueless. Used to get into a complete fluster whenever there was a problem. No ideas or initiative of his own.'

Emily stared down at her twitching fingers, as if she was turning pages in a photograph album of her life. She looked at her glass then directly at me. 'I've only just met her, but your sister seems like she's had a tough life one way or another.' Her eyes stayed on me. 'And you too. But in a very different way. And I imagine you don't talk about it much.'

I laughed awkwardly. 'You're very astute. Ever thought of becoming a psychotherapist?'

She laughed for real this time.

'Seriously,' I added.

She cleared her throat. 'I'll think about it. Maybe. When my body gives out and I can't teach sports anymore.' She grinned. 'Thanks for the vote of confidence. It means a lot, although I think I'm a bit too messed up to be any use to anyone.'

I shook my head. 'Ah, that's not how it works. You need to have struggled yourself in order to help others. You need to know from experience the savage clutches of pain and suffering. Otherwise, you can't feel your way into someone else's misery.'

She nodded slowly. 'I suppose so.' She appeared to chew it over, then dropped her head. 'It's my dad's birthday today, or would have been.' She sniffed and wiped her nose with a tissue from her sleeve.

I put my arm around her. 'Want to talk about it?'

'Not much to say, really. He was wonderful. Had a heart attack when I was eight.' Her words fell heavily in the air between us. 'I was the one who found him.'

I let out a sympathetic whimper.

She tugged a strand of hair from her mouth. 'I heard a crash and found him in a heap beside the toilet.' A faraway look claimed her face. 'Mum was out at a Tupperware party with her girlfriends. My brother was fast asleep.' Emily threw a glance at me. 'That's it. Except I still miss Dad like crazy.' She lifted her head, her eyes moist. 'Have you lost loved ones in your life?'

'No one close – no family or friends, but there have been patients who've died. Some on my watch. Always tragically.'

She winced. 'That must be tough. You must feel responsible.'

'A troubled kind of grief, certainly.'

Something jabbed inside my heart at the thought of Lorna. I cleared my throat and sent the focus back on Emily. 'Did your father get to see you shine at sport?'

Emily shifted her gaze into the distance. 'No. He died before I showed any talent. Such a shame. He never saw me do well. Probably my greatest regret.'

A tear dribbled down her cheek, catching the light. Emily looked up suddenly as if she'd forgotten I was there. 'Sorry. This must be a busman's holiday for you.'

I smiled. 'I'm on a break from the hospital, so I'm kind of missing my fix of listening to people.'

She chuckled. 'Don't you get fed up with them getting upset or moaning all the time?'

'It's not like that. There's something about a person telling the truth about themselves, digging deep to reveal what is most painful or secret or shameful inside them that's very special. It's more rewarding than you might think.'

She stared at the stray beer mat on the table, her features perfectly still.

I broke the fleeting silence between us. 'You don't need to stop. I'm not going to analyse you or anything.'

'Oh, I'm not bothered about that. If anything, you're too easy to talk to. I can see why you're good at your job. Miranda said you were absolutely first-rate.'

I felt a glow burst open inside me. 'Did she?'

Emily nodded and turned towards the clock behind the bar. 'One more half before we go?'

'Sure.' I was settled, pleasantly tired after the run and in no rush to get home.

38

———

I watched Emily as she strolled, head high, to the bar and waited to be served, chatting with ease to the woman beside her, nodding and smiling. The main door opened and a crowd of men burst in, rapidly swelling around her, wanting drinks. I lost sight of her until she weaved her way out holding two glasses.

There was something different about her. A deep frown carved furrows into her forehead and she looked flushed.

'You okay?' I glanced back to where she'd been standing.

'Just some guy.' She plonked the glasses down and flopped into the seat looking rattled. 'I think he's gone.' She took a long swig of ale, looking pensive. 'This is going to sound crazy, but there's been this bloke hanging around the last couple of days. I'm sure that was him. He tried to grab my hair at the bar.'

'He what?!' As her final words hit me, I shot to my feet. 'Stand up!'

She stared at me. 'Why?' Reluctantly, she stood and faced me.

'Turn round,' I instructed.

'Why? What are you doing?' Her voice was trembling.

'It's okay,' I said, examining her shoulder-length hair. 'He hasn't done anything to you. Did you see who it was?'

'No – a bunch of them were jostling, trying to get served – you know what it's like. A bit of a bun fight.'

'Like in the tube?' I said, my mind flashing back.

Her eyebrows shot up. 'Yeah, like that. Then I felt an arm... and someone behind me pulling my hair at the back... I couldn't turn round fully, but I caught sight of his jacket.'

I dropped back into my seat, my brain spinning into overdrive. I hadn't told Emily anything about the murder cases I was looking into. I hadn't mentioned the hair-cutting to anyone except Terry. Not even Miranda.

'And this has happened before?'

'Not exactly.' She rested her elbows on the table between our drinks. 'I think he might have been following me, hanging around outside my flat. It's the third time I've seen someone in the last few days. Same jacket.'

'Can you describe him?'

She chewed mindlessly at her thumbnail, something I'd not seen her do before. 'Around five feet ten. On the slim side, trim-looking, fit. He wears a kind of green military jacket with a big hood, so I haven't seen his face properly.' She paused to think. 'Possibly mid-brown hair?' She wrinkled her nose. 'Maybe dark brown... I'm not sure.' She stared at me, open-mouthed. 'Should I be scared? Should I tell the police?'

'I think you should tell the police,' I said, not wishing to scare her by mentioning anything more. 'I also think you shouldn't be doing any running on your own, and definitely not after dark.'

'Oh, come on.' She pulled back, looking askance.

'I'm serious. It's not worth it.'

A little huff escaped her lips. 'But we can go together, right?'

I had the feeling Emily might continue to head out alone, if she had no alternative. 'Only if we're really careful.'

'You think this is linked to what happened in the underground?'

'I don't know... but it's a bit of a coincidence, don't you think?'

Emily looked confused, then defiant. 'Cheeky bastard.'

We stood, leaving the drinks.

'What the hell's going on?' she asked, as we stepped outside and the chilly air sought out our exposed flesh.

I shivered, pulling on my jacket, tugging the zip right up under my chin. The temperature had dropped since our run and I could have done with an extra layer. 'If you see him again,' I said, stuffing my hands into my pockets, 'try to take a photo without him knowing.'

She pulled a face in response to my suggestion, which was undoubtedly easier said than done.

It took me in the wrong direction, but I insisted on walking her back to Clapham Junction. We checked behind us every few steps, on the lookout.

She turned to me as she was about to go through the ticket barrier. 'Promise me you'll run back to your flat.'

I pressed her hand. 'I will. And text me when you get home, okay?' She nodded, assuring me she'd call in at the police station on her way. 'There's one at the end of my road.'

I jogged back home myself, as much to get warm as anything.

My communal front entrance had an intercom system that was frequently on the blink, but I checked and doubled-checked the lock until I was satisfied it was secure. Once inside my flat, I locked and bolted the door. Nevertheless, I knew I couldn't relax until I heard from Emily.

I sat on the bed and flicked off my trainers. Phone in hand, waiting for it to come to life, I was mulling over the description Emily had given me. Could her stalker be the phantom haircutting killer?

I glanced down at the screen and flicked through the photos from the cold case files I'd secretly taken at the police station. The details Emily gave me could fit Neville Larch, but equally half the male population of London.

I was on edge until finally my phone lit up and Emily texted to say she was home safely. Only then did I let out a full breath. I got back to her, agreeing to her request to meet again the next day for a run.

Does it have to be evening?

I asked as an afterthought.

Sorry, working until 19.00. We'll stay in well-lit areas. See you at the station at 20.00.

I sent back the single word 'okay', but not without a degree of unease.

I took a quick shower and tumbled into bed, but in spite of my all-consuming exhaustion, I couldn't switch off my brain. Between snatches of light dozes and disquieting dreams, my consciousness broke through with fresh perspectives on the incident when I was almost pushed onto the tracks.

Maybe Emily had got it wrong. Perhaps I hadn't been the target that night. What if Emily was the one meant to end up under the train?

39

———

I couldn't put it off any longer. With a week of my allocated period on the cold cases already gone, it was time.

Once again, Fenway was hard to get hold of, but I persisted. After all, no one else would do.

Finally, I reached him through the switchboard.

'So, what have you got?' he asked, out of breath. 'I read your email – perhaps you could give me the details.'

I explained: three dead women; all around twenty and beautiful, linked by an ante-mortem assault on their hair. I gave him the file reference numbers. I had indisputable evidence of connections between the cases now. He had to take me seriously.

When I heard no response, I went on. 'After their hair was snipped, each woman was forced to get a professional haircut.' I snatched a breath. 'The key factor is that each of the victims was stalked shortly before they had their hair hacked off. And here's the thing – they were each killed *exactly seven days* after the attacks.' I let my final words ring loud and clear as though I was filling a lecture hall. Those were the facts that held the key.

'Hmm,' he muttered. He was actually listening. I did my best to rein in my excitement.

'There are no apparent links between the salons the victims used,' I punched out at him, 'and the victims all lived in different areas of London.'

'What about any connections between their places of birth or upbringing?'

I'd thought of that. 'I can't find any overlaps there. They didn't appear to know, or have any link, with each other.'

'Okay...' He sniffed. 'And you believe Hazel Hart's death fits this very same pattern?'

Good. Aside from my email, Terry must have got through to him.

'To the letter. Yes.'

I hung on, twitchy for his response. I knew, had we been face to face, he would have not been looking me in the eye. He had an annoying habit of looking over my shoulder, checking his watch or staring into the distance, as if he was itching to be somewhere else.

'As it happens, our ongoing enquiries have turned up something interesting about Hazel's fall,' he said, the strain in his voice giving away his reluctance to admit this.

'Really?'

'We've found three witnesses to her balcony stunt who confirmed she seemed distracted by something just before she toppled over.'

I punched the air. 'Wow. What was it? What distracted her?'

'No one seems sure. Two witnesses said it was as if someone had taken a photo with a flash, but no one owned up to doing so and no one was seen with a camera or a phone during those crucial moments. Another witness said the flicker of light wasn't as bright as a camera flash...'

'So it was some kind of light that disturbed her – a flash of some sort…' I muttered, mulling it over out loud.

'Hmm.'

I heard myself utter the words I'd been bursting to let loose. 'So you're treating it as a suspicious death now?'

He wouldn't be drawn. 'We are looking into it very closely. As we would be doing anyway.'

I was glad he wasn't in front of me. I would have given him a glare sufficiently scorching to set fire to his lapels.

He went on. 'Using your new-found knowledge on grandiose delusions, what can you tell us?' The hint of sarcasm in his voice didn't go unnoticed.

'In spite of the broad time frame, these murders look like the same person to me. The signature method is identical – around five or six centimetres of hair cut off at neck level each time.'

'The police don't like serial killers,' he grumbled. 'We avoid going down that route at all costs. It causes public panic, speculation, hoaxes, false leads. You name it. It's a minefield.'

I didn't mention Emily's stalker. I didn't want to cloud things. Besides, it may not have been the same man in the pub. It wasn't enough.

'What's the hair-cutting about, do you think?' Fenway asked, sounding genuinely intrigued. 'Is it purely to spoil the women's looks? Is it to perform some deeper ritual?'

'I'm not sure yet. It could be linked to some religious belief or a myth that already exists or is created by the killer.'

'Okay. So you have no leads on that yet.'

'No.' I wanted to consider a different angle. 'From the case files it looks like there's no sexual interference. Am I right?'

There was a hiatus while he looked up the records.

'I agree. No sexual overtones at all.' He took a breath. 'How come these women didn't know someone was cutting their hair? Wouldn't you feel it?'

'I think whoever did it knew what they were doing.' I knew from Tamsin that Hazel had worn a thick scarf, pulled tight around her neck, on the bus when she thought she'd been targeted. It must have been something similar with Charlotte and Lorna. 'In each case, the killer must have made sure there was some reason they wouldn't feel it.'

'Hmm. They'd have made a fuss straight away if they had, I suppose.'

I sent my eyes to the ceiling, glad he couldn't see me. 'I think hair colour is irrelevant,' I added. 'Two of the women, including Hazel, were blonde, Charlotte was dark. The hair lengths and type are different too: sleek, curly and kinked. For me, this removes a "lookalike" scenario. As in, I don't think the killer is finding women who remind him of someone from his past – such as his mother.'

'So, just a bloke obsessed with hair?'

'No. More than that. We need to look at the difference between obsession and delusion. The Yorkshire Ripper, Peter Sutcliffe, killed thirteen women, claiming the voice of God had sent him on a mission to kill prostitutes. Many believed he was responding to a grandiose delusion.'

I could imagine Fenway scratching his head, trying to figure out what I was talking about. I put him out of his misery. 'Okay, briefly: delusions are imaginary, unshakeable beliefs, that persist regardless of how illogical they are or how much evidence there is to the contrary. They can manifest in patterns of behaviour, such as this ritual of haircutting. Obsessions are similar on the surface. The difference is with an obsession you have some level of awareness that you're doing it.'

'Like obsessive tidying or cleaning, you mean – you're aware of it? But a delusion is ingrained and subconscious?'

'Good way of putting it.' I tried not to sound patronising.

'And a *grandiose* delusion involves power; it includes the impulse to act in some way to take control over another person.'

'How do people get grandiose delusions? What causes them?'

'They're often developed after a deep-rooted trauma compounded by emotional instability, stress, insomnia, isolation.'

'Sounds like me,' he said dryly.

I rolled my eyes again.

He muttered something I didn't catch. '... so, what's next?'

'Access to Hazel's file?'

'No way,' he said instantly. I knew he'd refuse.

I huffed into the phone. 'I feel like I'm doing half of this blind, without full details of the investigation.'

'What do you need to know?'

I didn't mention my conversation with Tamsin; it didn't seem a positive move. 'Did anyone know Hazel was being followed, for instance? Did she know who that person was?'

Tamsin claimed Hazel didn't know, but I wondered if she'd confided in anyone else. 'There could be a boyfriend. Or someone in plain sight who was interested in her.' I didn't dare let Fenway know I knew about Ivan, the drummer keen on Hazel. It would definitely have let the cat out of the bag.

'We'll check on that,' Fenway said. I heard the sound of a pen hitting a wad of paper in the background.

'I read in Charlotte Walsh's file that she was due to marry a man called Chris Pitlock, but she'd called it off and was seeing someone else. Did anyone find out who the new boyfriend was?'

'Hold on, let me look that one up.'

Another short interlude of tipperty-tap on a keyboard.

'No. That was a major line of enquiry in 2016 and we didn't identify the new mystery man in her life. Family, friends – no one had a clue.'

'Mr Pitlock was the prime suspect, but had been at work when the murder was committed, is that right?'

'Yup – solid alibi across the board.'

'What about Neville Larch, can you speak to him again?'

Silence.

I was getting impatient. 'It looks like he harassed Lorna Sullivan in the months before she was killed.'

'I know who he is,' Fenway said with clipped finality. 'And no. He was thoroughly interviewed as a suspect at the time. Very picky solicitor. No one is going to reinterview him without fresh evidence. You see my point?'

'How about casually, off the record?'

He laughed. 'Don't even think about it.'

The brick wall I was banging my head against was getting thicker and thicker. I was getting nowhere like this.

40

CHARLOTTE

Three years earlier

There's been an accident on the high street when I leave the dental surgery. I can see a bicycle wheel sticking out from under a coach, but I can't bear to let my eyes find anything else. I flip my gaze towards the patterns in the rug shop, then watch the glum technicians in the empty nail bar as they wait for customers. It's been chucking it down all afternoon and everyone's driving too fast. I left without my gloves and umbrella this morning, but I don't have enough money for a taxi, so I slip and slide my way home to Primrose Hill, as the rain turns to sleet.

Once inside, I get the gas fire on in the sitting room and strip off my wet things, hanging them near the sputtering flames on a broken wooden clothes horse I found behind the fridge the day I moved in.

It's a dingy basement flat, but it's cheap. Mainly because the foundations are dodgy and there's damp everywhere. Nearly every wall looks like a bad replica of a Jackson Pollock canvas. It smells like a graveyard. One of these days I'll catch some terrible disease from it and die a grim death.

I pull on my pyjamas and a thick dressing gown and sink into the sofa. It's too early for bed, but I've dragged in my bedding for an extra layer. I need to conjure up as much cosiness as I can in this place.

All the time, I'm thinking.

I'm not in a great headspace just now. Chris is still really upset. I could do without his best mate calling me every five minutes. True to form, just as I'm getting settled, the phone rings. It's Darren again, telling me my fiancé's going to jump off a bridge and it's all my fault.

'It's *ex*-fiancé,' I say, correcting him. 'And tell Chris he's going to have to pull himself together. People split up all the time. Obviously, I'm sorry he's so gutted about it, but telling me he's going to end it all is... it's more or less blackmail.'

Darren chunters on. What am I supposed to do? I thought I loved Chris, but I made a terrible mistake. I didn't mean to hurt him. I didn't want it to end like this, but Chris isn't the one for me and I'm glad I saw sense before I ended up walking down the aisle.

While Darren's on the line, I ask if he's been following me. 'Did you cut off my hair at the cinema last week? The Gate in Notting Hill?'

'What are you on about?' His voice rises to a squeak. 'You're nuts.'

'So, where were you exactly a week ago today? At about eight o'clock.'

'If you must know, I was at the greyhound track. In Romford. I didn't go anywhere near Notting bloody Hill. I was with Chris, as it happens, so don't start accusing him while you're at it.'

It rang true. It wasn't the first time Chris had been to the racetrack. I'd come to discover he was a gambler, one with a serious habit who'd managed to keep it from me, until I came across his credit card bill when I opened his mail once, by accident. It turned out he put bets on anything that moved: dogs, horses, racing cars, football teams. Unfortunately, it wasn't his only nasty habit. Alongside a penchant for peeping through keyholes, I caught him carrying cocaine once, for a mate at work. When I challenged him about it, he claimed it was a bag of baking powder for his gran. He changed his tune when I asked him to tip some out into a cup so I could make a vegan chocolate cake. He'd had to own up, although I knew for a fact he'd kept on doing it.

'Please leave me alone, Darren. Stop calling me. What happened between Chris and me is our business. And it's over.'

'I'm ringing because he's in a bad way, Charlie. Honestly. He needs you. He's a broken man.'

'I'm sorry, Darren. I've made up my mind and there's no going back. I've moved on. I suggest you tell Chris to do the same.'

Chris's big problem is he's got no backbone; he gets sucked into things and can't stand up for himself. As well as taking on the super-risky job of being a runner between drug dealers, getting his mates to beg on his behalf like this, is a case in point. Trying to be a man and falling short from every angle. I can't believe I got as far as setting a date with him.

I tell Darren I'm putting down the phone before I get angry.

It wasn't just Chris's personality that caused issues between us. Sex with him started to get a bit embarrassing too. He had no imagination. Once we were engaged, the romance dried up and he stopped making an effort. I got to the stage where I was dreading the idea that marriage meant I'd lose the chance of sex with anyone else. I'm not a girl who sleeps around and I don't like cheats, so the thought of being stuck with him in the bedroom was starting to panic me.

That's why I had to end it when I did.

And who would have thought it? Meeting someone else so soon afterwards wasn't on the cards at all, but it has certainly helped clarify everything. My eyes have been well and truly opened. And the sex is amazing...

But now my period's late and my head is a mishmash of babbling deliberations. Is it too soon to take a test? What will I do if it's positive? It can't be Chris's, that's for sure.

I shiver, then feel a pounding headache brewing behind my eyes. I think I'm coming down with something.

There's a faint tap at the door. So faint, I stay still, thinking I must be mistaken. No doubt slobs on the street flinging rubbish down into the alcove at my front door. It happens all the time. Sleazebags even shuffle down my steps to throw up or take a pee. A nice present for me when I leave for work the next morning.

The tap again. My doorbell broke three months ago and it's been the last thing on my mind. The wage packet for a dental receptionist isn't great and I still haven't heard if my job's being axed.

'Oh, it's you.' I hear my voice drop at the end. You've got your hood up, pulled tight around your ears and I can see the ribbing of a woolly hat on underneath. All trussed up, I barely recognise you.

'Can I come in?'

I pull the dressing gown tight around me, feeling vulnerable. I half-close the door as the wind whips the persistent rain into my face. I'm not in the mood for company.

'It's not a good time,' I say. 'I'm going to bed. Not feeling too well.'

Your clumpy wet boot is on the threshold. 'It won't take long. I'm not here to give you a hard time. Quite the opposite. I've got something for you.'

You glance down at the plastic bag in your hand.

I stand still, wondering what you could possibly have brought that I'd want and you mistake my hesitation for an invitation. You're brushing past me into the sitting room before I know it.

I stand with my hands on my hips. 'As I said, I'm just off to bed.'

You hand me the plastic bag. There's a bunch of pert yellow roses inside. My favourite.

'Let's put some music on, shall we?' you announce, striding into the area my landlord calls the kitchen, but which is really only a plyboard partition, hiding a mini-oven under a two-ringed hob.

I fold my arms, watching you. What's going on?

You switch on my ancient CD player and the baseline thud of my favourite band, The Sky Lighters, bursts into the room. It's the last thing I need right now. I hold my head, a wave of nausea claiming me. You perch on the edge of the sofa, looking up at me with a smile.

'Sit down and relax,' you instruct, patting the cushion beside you. 'You look tired.'

I sit reluctantly, crushing my pillow behind me. I point to the bag. 'Why have you brought me flowers?'

'Because you deserve them.'

You turn and slide the pillow out from behind my back. You start plumping it up, with little punches. 'Because I know things have been difficult lately. Everyone's been having a go at you about calling off the wedding and I just wanted you to know that, well...'

Before I know it, the world goes grey. It happens so fast, I think the lights have blown. But it's the pillow that's blocking out the light and air. It's against my face, your weight forcing it down.

I fight back, struggling to sit up, but you pin my arms under your knees, straddling on top of me. I hear my nose snap as you throw all your weight onto my face and keep it there. I try to grab the edges of your jacket to drag you off me, but I claw uselessly, unable to grip anything.

I try to buck with my legs, but you're too strong. I can't shake you off. I can't breathe. I suck the cotton pillowcase into my mouth as one song ends and another begins.

Stop! You've got to stop!

I'm frantic. Jerking my body up in wild attempts to throw you off. But you're steadfast. I can't believe you're so strong. I didn't see this coming for one second. The song keeps going and you keep pressing. You're not going to stop, are you?

My nose throbs with pain and the blood is blocking my nostrils, getting into my mouth. I'm choking. I battle to twist my head from side to side, aching to find the tiniest gap, so air can reach me.

But there is no gap. No air. Instead, a thick black fog soaks into my mouth and fills up all the spaces. The last thing I'm aware of is the music:

Ba-by, you should have kept me in your heart…

41

SAM

The Present

Miranda invited me over for lunch at the CCAP, so I turned up early. I was hoping, on the off-chance, to spot her with Ralph, the new mystery man of hers. The one I wasn't supposed to know about.

She wasn't in the café when I arrived, so I drifted into the gallery to see if she was giving anyone an impromptu tour. I saw her gesticulating in front of a large oil canvas, speaking to a woman dressed all in black. I didn't want to eavesdrop, so I backed off and sat on one of the padded benches by the broad window.

A text came in. From Terry. Inviting me over to his place that evening:

Trying out a new dish: a Pakistani Bhuna Gosht. Need a willing guinea pig who won't sue me. Any chance? X

The kiss at the end took me by surprise. He'd never done that before. I would have remembered.

174

I sent a reply back:

Only if you make my favourite dessert – and you have to remember what it is first… No cheating by using your 'phone a friend' option. X

A reply came back straight away:

Life is just one big challenge to you, isn't it, Willerby! Good job I've never forgotten the incident at the Uni summer ball with the plate of stolen profiteroles. I assume they're still your number one? X

I sent back a smiley-face emoji. He'd got it spot on.

When I looked up, the woman in black had walked away and the man I'd seen in the café once before was standing close to Miranda. She rose onto her tiptoes to kiss his cheek and he pulled her hard against him in an ardent embrace. As she untangled herself and stepped back, I saw his face.

What the f–

I launched to my feet as if a gun had gone off. Then darted behind the nearest partition, blocking their view of me. I needed to buy myself some time to process what I'd just seen.

It was definitely him. Ralph Stone, an ex-patient of mine. He'd been to see me the previous year. I hadn't recognised him from behind. A sly unforthcoming man who'd had complicated and unresolved sexual issues. I fought the rising bile in my throat. He was dating my sister.

My first instinct was to storm over to the pair of them and warn her off him, but I knew that was out of the question. Not only would I completely humiliate and alienate Miranda, but it would be a major breach of confidentiality. No one could know he'd ever been a patient of mine, let alone why.

The exit was about ten strides to my right. I needed to get out without Miranda seeing me. Then get to the café and pretend nothing had happened. Give myself time to work out what I was going to do.

～

Miranda joined me in the café shortly afterwards, all jaunty steps and smiles.

'So, what've you been up to?' I said lightly, looking up, a menu in my hand.

We exchanged a brief hug.

'Let's order first,' she said. 'Then I'll fill you in.'

'I'll get them,' I said, reaching for my bag.

'I fancy beans on toast.'

I came back with a table number painted on a big wooden spoon.

'So?' I nudged.

She squealed. 'Ticket sales are going better than we hoped. Online and at the desk.'

Her exhibition was the following week.

She went on. 'I can't believe I'm actually showing my work to the big wide world. People here have always been supportive, but to get my work on an even playing field with *real* artists...' She shook her head. 'It's... it's...'

'It's incredible,' I said. 'It really is.' Only then did the real reason Miranda wanted to show her artwork in her own flat occur to me. The ethos openly underpinning CCAP was recovery. Everyone involved in the project had a history of addiction, abuse or mental health issues. Although Miranda loved the place, she'd got to the stage when she wanted people to regard her simply as an artist. Without having the label around her neck that read 'damaged' pointed out to them. 'You've worked so hard and put so much of yourself into your pictures. You really deserve this. A proper public platform.'

She reached over and squeezed my hand. 'Thank you, Sammie. That means a lot.'

The food arrived, but I barely touched my salmon salad. I was still feeling queasy after the shock in the gallery.

Miranda nattered on about which paintings she'd chosen and the order in which she was going to lay them out around her flat. I nodded and smiled and let her revel in her excitement. I couldn't bring myself to mention Ralph. I didn't want to burst her bubble and ruin her day with a confrontation. She wouldn't listen to me anyway. I'd have to find another way to deal with it.

The biggest problem was that I couldn't tell Miranda *why* she and Ralph being an item worried me so much. What he'd revealed to me, in confidence, in therapy, had turned my stomach.

His relationships with women started with misleading and lying to them, claiming he was looking for 'commitment' with a soulmate. He would ooze charm, be attentive and generous. He went on to have sex for a few weeks as normal, fussing over his chosen prey and showing how keen he was on them. He called this his 'adoration' phase.

Then things changed. During that first period he'd 'find' a second woman. Someone who would join them in bed. Because ultimately, Ralph could only enjoy sex properly in a threesome. And a threesome that involved sadistic techniques to boot. As soon as that dynamic was established, he dropped the first woman (if they hadn't already run a mile) and started the process all over again.

It wasn't what any self-respecting woman needed, let alone one with schizophrenia. He'd frankly admitted he'd had umpteen partners and hurt countless women over the years. Left them outraged and devastated. Miranda, more than anyone, needed to be with someone emotionally and mentally available. Someone honest, for a start. Caring and reliable. As far as I could tell, not one bone in Ralph's body contained those qualities.

Certainly, therapy didn't seem to be what Ralph had been looking for and our sessions dried up pretty quickly. He confessed his cruel patterns in considerable detail, relishing the impact they had on me and showing no remorse. In the end I started to think his sole motive had been to shock me – another way of getting his kicks. He certainly wasn't ready to change.

On the contrary, it was almost as though he wanted me to condone his behaviours and to reinforce the fact that he wasn't breaking any law.

'...so, he's going to try to get to the opening,' Miranda said, snapping me out of my train of thought.

'Sorry, who?'

'The guy I mentioned.' She rolled her eyes. 'For a therapist, you don't make a very good listener.'

I laughed and gave her a mock punch on the arm.

By then, I'd decided what I needed to do. I was going to have to take matters into my own hands.

42

I left Miranda still enthusing about her exhibition and made my way back home.

When I walked in it was as though I'd caught a rock band about to trash a hotel room. Clothes were strewn everywhere, wet towels slung over the sofa, laundry spewing out of the Ali Baba basket, a pile of unpacked tins and cartons on the kitchen table. Dead flowers in a vase in the hall. Not like me at all. Events had caught up with me. Too many evenings taken up with running, time out with Terry and a total dawn-till-dusk preoccupation with the police murder cases.

In a flurry of domestic activity, I did a cursory once-round; clearing, tidying, putting everything in its place. That still left unwashed laundry, ironing, hoovering and dusting, but at least I could walk around without tripping over something.

All the while, I was fuming about Ralph. How dare he lure my sister into his sleazy lair? What the hell was he playing at?

But, before dealing with Ralph, there was one other matter I wanted to address first.

During the enquiry, three key individuals had provided most information about Charlotte, but none of them were able to shed light on the mystery boyfriend the police had tried to track down. It was a lost piece of the puzzle that could be extremely helpful.

I was lucky. I looked up the name Charlotte Walsh on Facebook and by a process of elimination, found her old profile page. It had been left up as a tribute to her. Many of the names tallied with friends and family from the case files, but the difference was the online details were up to date.

Charlotte's pal, Wendy, was the one who posted most vociferously, probably over-revealing personal and detailed information: trips to the hospital with her mother, intimate holiday snaps, photos of her spaniel, books she'd reviewed. I took a chance and sent her a message on Facebook, not overly confident of a response.

In the meantime, I hurried to my wardrobe and flicked through the hangers, working out what I should wear for my evening at Terry's. Cool and casual? Classy and hot? I wanted to look my best without making it seem as if I was trying too hard. It wasn't really a date, after all, or was it? More a meal with a mate? I wasn't sure.

In the past, Terry had often remarked on how assured and self-reliant I was. Did he think I was so self-contained I didn't want a relationship?

My laptop pinged with a message and I was surprised to see, so soon, that it was from Wendy.

Glad the police haven't given up on Charlie. We all loved her. I'm going to Crete on Monday, but I'm around today if you can meet for coffee. Can you get to Charing Cross by 4pm?

I'd be cutting it fine to get back, changed and over to Terry's by seven, but I didn't feel I had a choice.

43

Wendy was late. I waited almost half an hour outside the café she'd chosen before she came tottering towards me in platform heels, looking frozen in a thin bomber jacket and short skirt.

'Sorry,' she said, her nose running. 'Mum felt dizzy and I couldn't leave her.'

Wendy's yellowy-white blonde hair was stripped of every shred of natural colour and looked brittle, hanging around her face like drying spaghetti.

'Thank you for making it,' I said, wrenching open the stiff door. As we entered, globules of fat floated towards us, suspended in the air ready to envelope our clothes and settle in our hair. It wasn't a place I would have picked.

I hesitated, but Wendy seemed at home, heading straight for the counter to order. I caught up with her, insisting I pay. She ordered a diet Coke and pointed to a salad.

'Sorry, I missed lunch. Is this okay?'

'Sure. Absolutely.' It was the least I could offer, given her rapid response in meeting me.

Wendy picked up a plate with a dry slab of ham and two

sprigs of gem lettuce. I took a bottle of mineral water; I didn't trust anything else.

Wendy pulled out a chair at a table where plates of congealed chips in gravy had been left by the previous customers, stacked on top of each other. She found a space for her own plate, then shifted the used crockery to a table already occupied with diners. Not surprisingly, they gave her an affronted stare in return. I tried not to catch their eye.

'So you're working with the police?' Wendy said, as I joined her.

I explained my position.

'You were lucky to catch me. I've not been well,' she said, rubbing her forehead. 'Mum's been in and out of hospital and it's taken its toll on the rest of us.' Wendy spoke with overfamiliarity, as if we were old school friends. 'And now you're bringing it all up again.' She sniffed. 'I hope it's worth it.'

It was only when Wendy started on her lunch that I saw the size of the fork she'd been given. She could have harpooned a whale with it. She snorted and put it down, tearing a piece of lettuce from the plate directly with her fingers instead. She nibbled it, then pushed the plate to one side, not having touched the meat.

'I hope so. Anything you can tell me, anything you might have overlooked during the initial interviews, could be really helpful.'

She dropped her head. 'Poor Charlie. It was dreadful. She was so beautiful, had all these plans to go back to college to do English. She'd just got involved in a campaign against animal cruelty – she hated all that. Did you know she wrote amazing poems and took great wildlife photos too? I've never known anyone like her.' A grave shadow claimed Wendy's face. 'Did you know I was the one who found her?'

I shook my head. I must have missed that in the file. One of the problems with not having access to the records outside the admin office.

'I barely recognised her.' Wendy drew a shuddering gasp and fussed with the loose cuffs of her corduroy jacket. 'I can't believe they never got the bastard.'

'Who let you in?'

'I had a key to her flat. We had a shared thing where if she went away, I could use her place and vice versa. She hadn't shown up for work and wasn't answering my calls, so I dropped round. I let myself in when she didn't answer the door.'

'I hate to take you back to that scene, but do you remember anything unusual when you went inside?'

Someone shouted out 'table nine' from behind the counter and Wendy flinched. She took a nervy sip of Coke. 'Charlie was in her pyjamas. She often did that in the evenings To keep warm before she went to bed. Her duvet was scrunched up on the floor beside the settee. There was no pillow though. The police said whoever killed her took it with them to avoid leaving DNA behind. They also think he wore gloves, because there were no fingerprints unaccounted for in the flat.'

I remembered those details from the file.

I nodded. 'They thought Charlotte must have known the killer, because there was no evidence of a break-in. Is that how you saw it?'

Wendy shrugged. 'There were no smashed windows, nothing at the front door to suggest it was forced. No mess, like there'd been a fight. Her gas fire was still switched on, the CD player too, and there was a bunch of flowers in a bag on the floor. So, she must have let him in.'

I recalled the police file. They had followed up the yellow roses they'd found on the floor. They'd been left in a used bag from WHSmith with no branded or distinctive wrapper. No till receipt or fingerprints either. The local florist had been checked out, but it went nowhere. The roses could have come from any store or market in London.

Wendy went on. 'We all wondered if it could have been Chris, her ex-fiancé, but he had an alibi.'

I knew Chris Pitlock had been cleared as a prime suspect. Apparently, he had a firm alibi, didn't have a police record and according to people who knew him, no history of violent outbursts.

Wendy hadn't finished. 'Although, I heard afterwards that someone else had borrowed his van that evening. So it might not have been Chris the police picked up on CCTV at the time of her murder.'

I grabbed my bag, delving inside for my notebook and pen. 'Did you tell the police this?' I asked, making a note.

'Someone did – Bernie Proud. He was the one who pointed it out. He worked with Chris, but the police never interviewed him. I don't think so, anyway.'

'Did Chris use the van for work?'

'Yeah. He's one of those guys who goes around fixing traffic lights. They get called out at all hours of the day or night.'

Wendy ran her jagged nails over her bare knees. Pale and bony, they were laced with a network of previous scratches. I guessed she might have a problem with anxiety, perhaps also anorexia, judging by her attitude to lunch.

'How well did you know Chris?'

'He socialised with us once he got together with Charlotte. Pestered her for months until she finally gave in and starting seeing him. He's quite a soft bloke, if you know what I mean. Really crazy about Charlie. But he was easy-led and inclined to get in with the wrong crowd. He was gutted when she finished with him.'

'And she met someone else, it seems?'

'That was the sense we all had. Not until they were over

though. Charlie wasn't like that. She'd never sneak behind a guy's back.' Wendy took her gaze away and fiddled absently with her earring. 'She was very secretive about the new bloke and I took that to mean he was married. No one knew who he was.'

'And you *still* have no idea?'

Wendy shook her head.

'Do you think they were serious?'

She stopped to think. 'Yeah – I think they were, actually. Charlie seemed different. On cloud nine. I'd never seen her like that with Chris.'

'Charlotte was being followed before she was killed,' I said. 'Did you know about that?'

'Oh, God, I'd forgotten about that. Someone cut off her hair, didn't they? And, yes, she said someone had been prowling around after her, on the streets.'

'Did she know who it was? Have any idea?'

'It wasn't Chris or any of his usual mates. I remember she was clear about that. I don't think she ever worked out who it was though.'

Our discussion drew to a close after that. Wendy sat back, staring out at the busy street. I imagined she was replaying in her head the store of treasured memories of someone she clearly missed. The only remaining souvenirs of a beloved friend who would forever be perfect, frozen in time.

I thanked her as we got up to leave. As I opened the door, she grabbed my wrist.

'You will get her killer, won't you?' She squeezed hard, her rough nails digging into my skin.

I assured her I'd do everything I could, handing her my business card. 'And if you remember anything – even if it seems really small, do let me know, okay?'

44

———

Wendy and I went in opposite directions once we'd left the café. I had no idea of the time by then and when I glanced down at my watch, I was horrified. Damn. No chance to grab a shower or change before seeing Terry. I'd have to rush straight over to Earl's Court or I'd be late.

I didn't need to look in a mirror to know I looked an utter mess. I'd intended to wash my hair before the evening, but I'd have to tie it back in a ponytail. The baggy linen trousers and baby-blue mohair jumper I'd had for years we're not the epitome of elegance I'd wanted to convey.

Terry opened the door red-faced, his hair in a tumble. 'Hi,' he grunted, smearing a streak of powdered spice across his nose. 'Oh dear, I'm not having a great day. It's all gone pear-shaped. Managed to forget the garlic, and the rice has burnt on the bottom of the pan.'

He stopped and took in my face. 'But, it's bloody good to see you.'

He wore a stripy chef's apron and the overall appearance of him – earnest, but also hot and bothered, made me smile.

'Smells amazing.' I stepped inside.

I peeled off my coat, feeling decidedly awkward under his scrutiny.

'Wow. I've always loved that jumper.' He reached aside to hang up my coat. 'You used to wear it in Manchester, remember? Really suits you.'

'Oh, thanks,' I said, somewhat startled.

His eyes seemed to glow as he looked at me and I blinked hard, feeling all of a fluster. He held my shoulders and I wasn't sure if he was going to stroke my face, touch my hair or wrap his arms around me. In the end, his mouth reached for my cheek, but I felt his lips linger longer than a simple peck. Long enough to taste my skin.

I drew in the intimate smell that the proximity of his body brought with it; the faint oiliness of his hair, the slight waft of warm caramel from beneath his collar.

He led me through to where more intense aromas, music and a cosy log burner were waiting for me. He poured a glass of Chablis, then handed it to me.

'Cheers,' he said heartily.

I took a sip. 'I can't wait to see what you've got to offer,' I said, raising an eyebrow.

He pulled a face. 'I hope it's edible. This might be the worst evening you've ever had.'

'I very much doubt that.' I gave him a coquettish grin. I took another sip and welcomed the burst of alcohol as it burned my chest. In that moment, I had a reckless desire to completely let go, tired of the limbo-land between us. A tiny flicker of prudence pulled me back into line. Perhaps I'd got the wrong end of the stick. Best to let things play out – wait and see.

I sat with him at the breakfast bar as he stirred and taste-tested the dishes. He asked me about Miranda's forthcoming exhibition and I told him how excited she was.

'Will you take me to it?' he asked.

I couldn't hide a grimace. 'Do you know the kind of pictures she paints?'

'No, but it would be good to support her.'

'She'll be chuffed. It's a long time since you've seen her, I imagine.'

He nodded, reaching for the oven gloves. 'It's ready,' he said, with trepidation. He pulled out a plumped-up naan bread and beckoned me over to the dining table. As well as several spotlights, there were candles twinkling on almost every flat surface, giving it the feel of a top-class restaurant.

The dishes were spicy, but not too hot. Rich with plenty of tomato and ginger. Just my kind of curry. He'd even added an aubergine dish.

'You're totally spoiling me,' I said.

'Mmm... not bad, is it?' He chewed, hiding a big grin.

I was glad I hadn't dressed up. It would have seemed presumptuous somehow. This way, I felt more relaxed. I told him I'd started running with a new friend. I didn't mention that Emily thought she was being followed. There was nothing he could do, in any case.

I had second helpings and after the last forkful of lemon rice, finally sat back. 'That was brilliant. Seriously.'

His eyes were shining. 'I'm thinking of doing the course on Lebanese cooking next. What do you think?'

I patted my stomach. 'Definitely. And whatever you try your hand at I'll be your chief taster and head dishwasher.'

He chuckled.

This time, I drank plenty of water alongside my wine to reduce the chances of making a fool of myself. I was glad he hadn't asked about the cold cases, even though my conversation with Wendy kept resurfacing in my mind. I didn't want to admit I'd spoken to her.

Eventually, we retired to the lounge area. Terry turned off the lights, so the candles dotted around the room took centre stage. As I leant forward to stand my glass on the coffee table, he came up behind me and smoothed my hair away from my neck. The next thing I knew he was planting a kiss just below my ear. It sent ten thousand volts right through me.

'Do you feel it too?' he said.

I turned to him, my jaw wide open.

'Something's changed between us,' he went on. 'Unless, I'm way off beam.'

I shook my head, still caught in headlights. 'You're spot on.'

He went on, his words brushing my earlobe. 'I don't know when or how or why things have taken a different turn, but they have, haven't they?'

I gazed into those fathomless lagoon-blue eyes. 'And there's no going back now, is there?' I replied, my voice a soft purr.

My lips met his and a cascade of fireworks exploded in my chest. It was one of those moments I wanted to trap in a bubble; one I was reluctant to step out of.

He pulled me down beside him on the sofa. 'I've wanted to do that for about a hundred years,' he said. I laughed and he stroked my face. Being this close to him, I saw his eyes were more complex than I'd thought. They were not simply blue. Layered with mystery and promise, they were silvery grey with flecks of sapphire, turning them almost purple in the dancing light.

He took my hand. 'Shall we go somewhere more comfortable?'

'Good idea,' I murmured, my voice trembling.

'Are you sure?'

I kicked off my shoes. 'I've never been more sure of anything in my entire life.'

As he led me to his bed, I expected to feel that bitter pinching in my stomach that had plagued me all week. *Would taking things further ruin our friendship? Would we regret it?* But it was blissfully absent. Instead, a flood of inner knowing took its place. I felt it in every sinew of my being. This was right.

Part of me expected us to tentatively fumble like awkward teenagers, apologising and giggling, killing the mood. But not a bit of it. My body responded to his touch like sorbet melting on the tongue on a scorching summer day. I gave myself up to him completely, oblivious to anything except the exquisite pulse of rising excitement.

My attraction to Terry had come out of left field, but I knew something for sure. My feelings for him ran deeper than friends with benefits. I wasn't reaching out to him through the gloom of loneliness or a dread that time was running out. I was ready for this; seeing him as though for the first time – as the wonderful and attractive being he truly was. Sincere, warm, steadfast, generous, humble – and very sexy. A cupid's arrow seemed to have stung me around the same time he was prepared to risk making the first move. What were the chances of that happening?

Afterwards, I couldn't get the smile off my face.

'What's going on?' he said warily, retrieving the duvet that had made its way to the floor.

'I'm the cat that got the cream, that's all,' I said, licking my lips.

'You're shameless, Dr Willerby,' he said, nibbling my bare shoulder.

45

The first sound I heard in the morning was the ping of my phone. In the throes of our ardour last night, I'd forgotten to switch it off. It was a text from Wendy:

Can you call me? I might have found something.

I slid out of bed naked, grabbing Terry's bathrobe from a hook on the door. He turned to watch me, resting his head in his hand.

'Sorry, I need to make a call.'

'The woman of mystery already...'

I threw my eyes up, padded into the kitchen, switched on the kettle, and rang Wendy back.

'Thanks for texting me. What have you found?'

'Our chat made me realise that after all this time, I still had the key to Charlie's old flat,' Wendy said, sounding morose. 'Last night, I decided to go back to Primrose Hill to hand it over. There are new tenants, of course, but the couple were nice and asked me in.'

I forgot about making the coffee and hoisted myself onto the breakfast stool.

'They'd had a leak in the bedroom radiator a few months back and had to take part of the floor up. They found a box tucked away with some of Charlie's poems and black and white photos in it. Ones she'd taken herself.'

'It'd been hidden all this time?'

'Looks that way. The tenants didn't know what to do with it. They didn't know who it belonged to. No one had told them who'd been in that flat before they moved in. I mean... you wouldn't, would you?'

'They'd kept them?'

'They said they meant to throw them out, but with all the upheaval of recarpeting after the leak, they'd forgotten about them.'

'Did you see the pictures?'

'Yeah. They let me have them when I explained who I was. I think Charlie hid them because some are a bit risqué – you know, pictures of her naked and erotic poems and stuff.'

'Ah, I see. Have you got them there with you?'

'Yeah.'

'Can you take pictures of any shots with people you don't recognise?'

'Sure. I'll send them over in a tic.'

I'd only just ended the call when Terry appeared wearing only his boxer shorts.

'Someone pinched my bathrobe,' he said, yawning. He stopped and gave me a hard stare. 'And you've got that Miss Marple look in your eye.'

I was holding my phone to my chest, no doubt looking like I'd been caught in the act. I left it face down on the worktop and opened my arms to him. He swamped me in a firm embrace. I buried my face in his neck; he smelt of toasted sugar and sex, and I didn't want to let go.

He sneezed and rubbed his hands together. 'I'm going to have to turn the heating up. And you need to bring your own dressing gown.'

'Does this mean this might happen again?' I asked, twisting coquettishly on one bare foot.

'I bloody well hope so!'

I couldn't hide a big smile. 'Coffee?'

Terry was in the shower when the pictures arrived. There were three shots of a man on his own. The first showed him in a raincoat leaning against a bus stop looking into the distance, another sitting in a restaurant looking up at the waiter. In the third, he was holding a thick volume beside bookshelves in a library. Capturing his defined cheekbones and a moody stare, all were posed like fashion portraits.

But the main thing was I'd seen his face before. Without question.

I thumbed through every one of the case file shots I'd taken and there it was. From the investigation into Lorna's death. Neville Larch. The man she'd mistakenly picked out in the line-up. I felt an iceberg in my stomach.

Could he have been Charlotte's mystery boyfriend? The man who'd been harassing Lorna and had been brought in by police as a suspect.

46

———

'I've found a link. A concrete link between the two cold cases.'

Terry looked nonplussed as he joined me in the kitchen, fully dressed. 'I thought you were making coffee.'

'I was...' I glanced up, trying to locate the kettle, the mugs. 'I am.'

'The two cold cases? How did this happen?'

'Don't ask me how, just yet. I must speak to Fenway, but I need to check something first.'

Terry sighed and pulled up a stool at the breakfast bar. 'I guess this is what it must be like being involved with a detective. Oh, no – wait a minute, you're a psychologist.'

'Ha ha!' I slapped a loud kiss on his cheek and put my arms around his neck. 'You said "involved". Are we involved then?'

'I think so. I hope so. What do you think?'

I pretended to mull it over, rocking my head from side to side. 'I think you might be right.'

He pushed a knuckle into my ribs, something he used to do way back when we were studying for our PhDs and it used to drive me mad.

I slapped his hand away. 'But just because we're together, doesn't mean I've abandoned my responsibilities.'

He put his hands on his hips. 'Heaven forbid!'

'I need to get over to Stanhope Street to check the cold case files, but can we meet later?'

He nodded. 'I'll take you,' he said, glancing up at the clock. 'Traffic shouldn't be bad this time on a Sunday morning.'

'I wasn't angling for a lift.'

'I know you weren't.' He tapped the granite worktop. 'Bloody nuisance you can't access those files from your own laptop.'

'Tell me about it.'

I poured the coffees then took mine with me into the bathroom. I wanted to get moving.

It didn't take long at Camden police station to get the information I needed. Terry waited outside in the car. As soon as I clambered back into the passenger seat, I got straight on the phone to Fenway. Terry put the car in gear and backed out of the parking space.

'Sorry to ring on a Sunday,' I said, putting the call onto the speakerphone, 'but it's important.'

Fenway moaned something about never getting sleep-ins anymore.

'I've found two new pieces of information about one of the cold cases I've been looking at. It's about Charlotte.'

'Hold on... hold on. You're meant to be scouring the files for signs of psychopathology. How exactly did you find out this new information?'

I sucked in a big breath and prepared myself for a reading of the riot act. 'Er... I had lunch with one of the victim's friends, Wendy Leigh.'

'You contacted her? And then *interviewed* her?!'

'Only a chat in a café,' I said quickly, trying to make light of it. 'Sometimes a police officer isn't the best person to ask questions.'

Terry heard every word and drew the car to an abrupt halt before we left the car park. He switched off the engine and silently dropped his head into his hands beside me. This was news to him too.

'Listen,' I went on, ploughing through Fenway's reprimands, 'according to the police file, Chris Pitlock, Charlotte's ex-fiancé, had an alibi for the period of her death. The record shows his van was picked up by CCTV on a traffic-light job in Brixton, miles away from her flat in Primrose Hill that night. But now it seems his work colleague, Bernie Proud, borrowed his van at that time and Chris wasn't with him. Wendy said Bernie let the police know about it, but I can't find any trace of him on the file. He never contacted the police. He was never interviewed.'

Fenway went quiet, taking in what I'd said, before speaking again. 'So, he needs to be interviewed. This needs following up.'

'Yes, I thought so. And I think I've found Charlotte's secret boyfriend too. And, if I'm right, it creates a direct link to Lorna's case, back in 2010.'

'You have been busy,' he said, without enthusiasm. 'But you've also breached protocol, Dr Willerby. In a very serious fashion.'

I squeezed the edge of the passenger seat, not looking at Terry, waiting to face the consequences.

An icy silence chilled the air between us.

I gritted my teeth. 'Are you going to tell Claussen?' I asked, unable to stand the wait. I knew I'd be thrown off the project in as much time as it took a pin to burst a balloon, if she got wind of it.

'I don't know yet.' Another silence. I glanced over at Terry. He was staring through the windscreen, shaking his head.

'Let's get over and speak to this Wendy Leigh first, shall we?' Fenway said.

I blinked at Terry, my face caught between expressions, wondering if I'd heard correctly.

'She's going abroad tomorrow,' I told Fenway.

He spoke again. 'Can you get to Camden police station before lunchtime?'

'I'm already there,' I said gleefully.

47

I made the call to Wendy from Terry's car, as soon as I saw Fenway's sedan approaching through the gate.

'Just so you know,' I told her, 'the inspector and I will be with you shortly. And he's not too happy I spoke to you on my own.'

'Sailing close to the wind, Willerby,' Terry growled from the driving seat, with a knuckle against my cheek rather than a kiss.

I clambered out of his car, then leant down by the open window. 'Sometimes you have to stick your neck out to get results.'

'You've stretched the therapy regulations before – we all know that, but this is different.' He tapped the wheel with his finger. 'You're playing with the legal system here. Ignoring direct orders. Messing with the law.'

I straightened up to wave to Fenway, before turning back to Terry. 'I know. But things are different this time. It's personal. I didn't know this assignment would involve one of my own patients. I want Lorna's killer to pay for what he did to her.'

Terry gave me a stare sufficiently fervid to singe off my eyebrows and sped away in the opposite direction.

Wendy sensed the atmosphere as soon as she opened the front door. Fenway introduced himself on the doorstep, holding out his badge. He made no reference to me.

'Hi,' I said with a diffident wave.

We all stood awkwardly in the hall.

I kept my eyes on Wendy. 'I know you're getting ready to head abroad for a break,' I said in an apologetic tone.

'It's okay – I'm glad you're here,' she said. 'It means you're taking what I said seriously.'

Fenway took a step between us. 'It's me, and my officers you'll be talking to from now on.'

Wendy looked affronted. 'For the record, I'm glad Dr Willerby approached me.' She glared at Fenway unwaveringly as she spoke. 'Being interviewed by the cops scares the hell out of some people, you know – makes them nervy.'

I could have hugged her. I slipped her a sly wink instead.

Wendy led us into the lounge and offered us seats. Her feet were bare and she wore tiny shorts with a strappy top, as if she was already in the Mediterranean.

'Anything to drink?'

Fenway and I spoke together.

'Nothing for me,' I said.

'Coffee,' was his response.

We glanced at each other. It was toe-curlingly uncomfortable.

After Wendy came back with a mug for Fenway, she sat and answered his questions. It soon became clear that we were learning nothing more than I'd already told him. Nonetheless, Fenway had to hear it for himself. Only then could the information be recorded on the relevant files.

By the time we left, it was evident what the next steps should be. Neville Larch had never been identified as a person of interest for Charlotte's death so he would be brought in afresh. Bernie Proud would also be grilled about the whereabouts of Chris's van on the night Charlotte was killed.

'But you won't be party to any of this, you understand?' Fenway said, as we walked back to his car. 'Your job is to look into the evidence left behind, the patterns involved in the murders to suggest the mind frame and traits of the potential killer.'

I nodded. 'Sure.'

'You'll be able to track the outcome of further enquiries by checking updates on the cold case file.'

'Right.' I opened the passenger door, feeling like a small child. 'By the way, did you manage to follow up on Hazel's boyfriend?'

Fenway grunted as he shuffled behind the wheel. 'Didn't have one. Some guy in a band was bugging her – Ivan Nicholls – but he was performing on stage in Birmingham on the afternoon she fell from the balcony.'

That meant I could confidently tick him off my secret list of suspects.

At my request, Fenway dropped me at Camden High Street. As I opened the passenger door, he called out to me.

'Listen, I've had a word with Claussen.'

My legs almost gave way under me. I held onto the roof of the car, then bent down so I could see him. He waited longer than he needed to, no doubt relishing the look of horror on my face. 'And I'm sending over the cold case files.'

'Sorry?' I was expecting to be hauled in for a good talking-to at the very least, but it looked like not only had Fenway kept my transgressions from her, but he'd made a request on my behalf.

'Claussen agreed that as long as you have a strong password on your laptop, you can have unlimited access to the two cold case files. To save going back and forth to Camden all the time.'

'Really?' I patted the roof of the car. 'You did that for me?'

He shrugged. 'Because even though you're a pain in the butt and ignore all the rules, Dr Willerby – now and again you seem to get results.'

I laughed. 'That's brilliant. Thank you.'

I swung the door shut, but he'd accelerated away before it left my hand.

48

———

I turned off the high street and called Terry.

'Fenway let me off with a warning.'

'You're bloody lucky.'

'I know. Are we meeting up for supper tonight?'

'My place or yours?'

'How about mine. I'll be running with Emily first, but I'll see you there about eight?'

'Where are you now?'

'Heading for CCAP.'

'To see Miranda?'

I stopped walking. 'Sort of...'

I nipped the skin at my neck, nervously. With Wendy's information prompting new lines of enquiry I'd forgotten the reason for my visit until now. I wasn't looking forward to it one bit.

Once inside, I kept my head down and went beyond the café straight to the kitchen. I wanted to know if Miranda was around without bumping into her.

A woman I recognised at the sink answered my query. 'She's fixing up some frames in the studio.'

'And Ralph, is he here?' I added.

202

'Yup,' she said, 'same place.'

I wandered round to the next corridor and took a peek through the small panes of glass in the double doors. Miranda was holding a canvas and Ralph had a tape measure in his hand, bending down beside planks of wood. I turned away, my back against the wall. I didn't want to speak to them together.

I'd kept Ralph Stone's contact details in my records from our sessions the year before, but it would have been highly unethical to simply get in touch with him. Instead, I had to engineer some kind of chance meeting. Then what? Confront him? Warn him off? Plead with him? I didn't know for sure. I hoped that by the time I got to see him face to face, I'd know instinctively how to play it.

I loitered at the entrance, listening for their voices. They were discussing sizes and designs for a couple of pictures. They could be hours. I went back to the café for a drink and came back twenty minutes later. I stood with my ear against the door.

'We'll need them – aren't there any left?'

'No, I checked,' said Ralph.

There was a clunk; the sound of wood on wood.

'... high street... need to go and get them,' came Miranda's voice.

'It's okay, I'll go,' was Ralph's response.

I scuttled away from the door and slipped out of sight under the staircase. His footsteps came past me and I heard them fade as he left the building. As he strode along the street, I took off after him, leaving a gap of a few metres. He was wearing a red jumper, easy to keep track of.

I didn't want him to know I was right on his heels, so at the first pedestrian crossing, I joined a group as they meandered over to the opposite side of the road. I stayed parallel to him, before he turned into an art and craft shop. I crossed over and moments later, he came out with a small paper bag sticking out of his pocket. As soon as he took a step, I faked bumping into him.

'Sorry...' I said, squinting into the sun at his face. 'Oh, hi – er... Ralph, isn't it?'

He appeared not to recognise me at first, then he stretched open his mouth without reaching a smile. 'Ah, Dr Willerby.'

I kept up the bright tone. 'How are you?'

'Fine,' he said dismissively. He glanced at his watch. 'What brings you to this neck of the woods?'

'My sister works near here.'

Ralph stood still as my words hung in the air. He looked beyond me, over my shoulder, as if judging whether to make a run for it.

I decided not to prolong the false pleasantries. 'I take it you know Miranda is my sister?'

His eye twitched, a little mannerism I remembered from our sessions, but he said nothing.

I went on. 'I'm glad I've seen you actually. I understand you're dating her.'

A glimpse of the hostility I'd seen during therapy clouded his features. He stiffened. 'Is that a problem?'

'It is actually. And I think you know why I'd have reservations.'

He sucked in his cheeks, rising taller in front of me. 'I've never committed any crime. No doubt you know that for a fact.'

'I think we both know that isn't the point.' I gave him the steeliest stare I could muster.

'So, what are you saying?' He folded his arms.

Not for the first time, I felt a tremor of fear in his presence.

I stood firm and rose to my full height. 'I think you should leave my sister alone. Let her get the exhibition over with, then find a reason to disappear out of her life' – I puffed out my chest – 'for good.'

He smirked. 'Why should I?'

'Because you mistreat women. You know you do. Perhaps not always physically, but certainly mentally and emotionally. My sister isn't the most stable of individuals. You must know that.'

'Miranda is a beautiful, powerful and self-assured woman and she wants to be with me.' He shrugged as if there was nothing he could do about it.

'And no doubt, before long, she won't be the only woman in bed with the pair of you.'

He came straight back at me. 'What makes you think she wouldn't be up for that, eh?' He delivered it with a smarmy grin on his face and I wanted to punch him.

I stuffed my hands in my pockets, concerned that the urge might get the better of me. 'I'm appealing to any decency you still have within you,' I pleaded. 'To any conscience you've got about the way you handle your private life. You came to me for help once, remember? I appeal to that part of you to spare her.'

I was surprised to find myself on the verge of tears, fighting to keep the quivering out of my voice.

'Or you'll do what, Dr Willerby? Break confidentiality and tell Miranda? Tell the police, even though I've broken no laws?'

I couldn't bear to look at his face any longer and cast my eyes down.

'I thought not,' he went on. 'If you breach confidentiality, I'll make sure you get struck off, you hear me? Preserving confidentiality is the most paramount, unbreakable code for any therapist, and you know it. Tell anyone about this and you've had it.'

With that he stormed off.

49

After my disastrous showdown with Ralph, I went back to my flat and did my utmost to shake him out of my system. Everything about him; his face, his posture, his voice, turned my stomach.

Now more than ever I was certain that when he came to me for 'therapy', he had no desire whatsoever to sort out his 'issues'. He just wanted to watch me squirm as he explained in detail what gave him pleasure. A sneaky way of humiliating another woman.

I put a pile of laundry into the machine and checked the fridge, toying with what I might rustle up for the supper I'd offered Terry. Next, I found myself sitting at the kitchen table staring out of the window.

It was a good spot to see the tapestry of back gardens with their overgrown lawns, collapsing sheds and washing flapping like flags in the breeze. It wasn't the kind of area where people tended vegetable patches or cottage gardens with peonies and roses. Residents here were transient, with little inclination to spend time prettifying their homes beyond a few seasonal plant pots. They were merely getting a taste of the big city before they grew tired of the noise, the crowds, the queues, and moved on to the next stage in their life journeys.

If I leaned forward, I could see as far as the main road. The traffic never seemed to stop, even during the night. From time to time, the house trembled with the low rumble of non-stop high-speed trains zipping through Clapham Junction.

It felt earthy living here; I'd become woven into this place. Nevertheless, I felt a glimmer of desire for a larger kitchen that allowed cupboard doors to be opened without taking someone's eye out. And situated far enough from the loo so that you didn't always have to hear it flush. And a little square of decking where I could sit and watch the blood-orange sun dissolve behind the chimney tops. Maybe one day?

I glanced at my workaday hands interlaced on the table and recalled Lorna's, invariably manicured with a different coloured polish each time I saw her. Always bright, just like her personality; metallic pink, glow-in-the-dark yellow, gold with glitter in it.

I reflected on my presence here, waking each morning, when daybreak had stopped arriving for her. She would forever be in the dark, her last moments on this earth branded by the rattling of the railway tracks beneath her, the train bearing down, the screech when the driver saw her too late. The police report said she'd been struck on the head before she was dragged into the path of the train. I hoped with all my heart that she'd already gone to a place without fear or awareness by then. Prayed that she'd known nothing about that final barbaric act that had robbed her of her life.

True to his word, Fenway sent over both cold case files in an email with special encryption instructions. His message confirmed that new information would filter through following interviews over the next few days.

I used the time before I was due to run with Emily to follow Fenway's advice, for once, and return to my research on delusional behaviour. Delusions often stemmed from external symbolism, so I looked into religious ceremonies and historical acts involving hair.

Within an hour, I'd come up with something.

Several accounts described a Nordic myth involving an age-old witches' test. According to the ancient rite, the hair of a suspected witch was cut off and the woman was kept in a pig pen. If her hair didn't grow back within ten days, the woman was regarded as a sorceress. And put to death. Clearly, like many witches' tests, it had no favourable result.

Could the killer be playing out this myth? It was possible, except the time frame was significant. Ten days was repeatedly given in the documentation as the crucial period the subjects were given in order for their hair to grow back. Always ten days. But in the recent cases, the deaths invariably took place exactly seven days after the hair cutting. It didn't fit.

Emily looked distracted when I joined her outside the tube station. She'd already started her stretches, one leg propped up on a bicycle rack. Her fraught expression didn't change when she saw me.

'You okay?' I asked, mirroring her exercises.

She sighed. 'Can we do short and fast tonight? I need an early night for once.' Her tone was miserable. Not her usual sparky self.

I nodded. 'Has that guy been pestering you?'

'No. I haven't seen him. Maybe it was all in my head.' She bent down to retie the laces on her trainers, then tucked her long hair into her hood.

'Just be careful, okay?' I didn't want to worry her or compromise the police investigations with what I knew.

We ran in silence for most of our route this time, our wide strides covering the ground swiftly.

'You've won the challenge, by the way,' I said, as we turned the final corner.

'Which challenge was that?'

'Your one about getting me to love running. It's not even been two weeks and I'm hooked. Still aching here and there, but I absolutely love it.'

She laughed. 'Then my job is done.'

We returned to the station and drew to a halt. 'I should pay you for your time, from now on,' I said. 'It's only fair. That was the deal. Free only during the test runs.'

Her face dropped and she looked almost insulted. 'No way. I'm enjoying it – and our runs are even better, because you're someone I can talk to.'

She saw I was about to protest and held up her hand. 'And, like you said, if some guy's stalking me, it's best to take a break from running after dark on my own.' She bent forward to release her back. 'So we have to keep going together, okay?'

'That would be great, but–'

'No buts. We're both doing the other a favour, so let's call it quits.'

50

Terry arrived exactly when he said he would, but nevertheless I wasn't ready. By the time Emily and I had cooled down, said our farewells and I'd taken a shower, I was hopelessly behind schedule. I hadn't even put on the oven.

'I'm a dreadful host,' I said, drying my hair with a towel as I invited him inside. 'We might have to get a takeaway.'

I didn't admit that I hadn't even got to the point of deciding what I was going to cook.

'No worries,' he said, with a good-natured sigh. 'I was expecting something to be broken in the kitchen anyway. The fridge, the cooker – there's always something.'

I slung my damp towel over the radiator and wrapped my arms around him. 'No, you shouldn't let me off the hook. You made such an effort with that curry for me.'

'Yeah, well. I'm here. That's all that matters.' He held me by the shoulders. 'And let's face it, I love cooking and... you clearly don't, so that's good. We won't be in competition with each other – in the kitchen, at least.'

He tipped up my chin and gently set his moist lips against mine. A glow of warmth enveloped me at the touch of him, the taste of him. I was still pinching myself over the effortless way our relationship had slipped into this incredible new level. Was it real? Was it too good to be true?

'Why did we never take things further before?' I asked him, as we peeled apart.

'Because we were out of sync. I fancied you rotten at university and you never gave me the time of day.'

I squeezed his nose with my fingers. 'That's not true. We were close friends.'

'The clue is in your last word. Never more than friends.'

I took his hand and led him through to the kitchen I hadn't even set the table. I poured us each a glass of wine. He sat down as I went in search of my stack of takeaway menus. We settled on Chinese, but before I could get hold of the phone to put in our order, Terry had picked me up and carried me to the bedroom.

'I think we'll enjoy a Chow Mein even better if we've worked up an appetite, don't you?' he growled.

I didn't argue.

This time I saw an entirely new side to Terry. It took me by surprise, but there was nothing I didn't relish. The weight of him on top of me, the firm way he nudged my limbs exactly where he wanted them, the eagerness in his breathy hungry kisses. I didn't have to think, not for a moment. It was a banquet for the senses – until at last we finally came up for air.

Neither of us spoke or moved for some time. Then Terry wafted his hot face with the corner of the duvet. 'You're really something, you know that?'

'Me?!'

'Yes, you. I'm not going to be able to function properly when I'm around you. I'm just going to want to get hold of you the whole time.'

I gently kissed the top of his nose. 'Sounds good to me.'

'I'm not so sure. I might have to take out special insurance.'

I laughed. 'I'll definitely cook properly next time.'

From the look on his face, I wasn't sure if he took that as a promise or a threat.

That night, after we finally put in our order and ate supper, an idea occurred to me about Charlotte's death.

It would mean Neville Larch had a motive for killing her.

51

In the morning, while Terry was still asleep, I got out of bed and using my new password, took a peek at Charlotte's cold case file. I checked the post-mortem report, but I was wrong. Charlotte hadn't been pregnant when she was killed.

Damn. That scuppered my latest theory. Aside from that, I couldn't see any obvious motive for Neville Larch to be her killer. I'd need to wait for the police to interview him.

I sat back in my dressing gown, staring at the carpet. Chris Pitlock, her fiancé, did have a strong motive for her death however. He'd been jilted, and according to Wendy, he'd been distraught and humiliated. He didn't have a history of violence, but people can radically change when something devastating happens. I knew only too well that fragile personalities could be tipped over the edge. Was that why Chris lied about his alibi? Because *he* was her killer? I'd have to wait for someone to update the file on that too.

I didn't have to wait long. By the time I'd put together a breakfast for two consisting of lumpy porridge, watery orange juice (carton nearly empty) and a boiled egg without the soldiers (out of bread), a new report had been added. Terry laid splayed out on the sofa sipping coffee, his bare feet flapping over the edge as I took a look.

Bernie Proud had been interviewed by the police. It turned out he didn't report borrowing Chris's van the night Charlotte was killed because he had a criminal record. For burglary. He didn't want to get involved. Under caution, he confirmed he'd been driving when the van was caught on CCTV in Brixton on the night in question. It meant Chris Pitlock's alibi was full of holes.

The police had then reinterviewed Chris. He explained the 'mix up'. In order to help pay for the wedding, he was moonlighting. He'd told his boss he was with Bernie that night on a traffic light repair job, but in actual fact, he was acting as a DJ in a nightclub from 9pm. So, he had a *different* alibi.

I checked the time of Charlotte's death: between nine in the evening and three thirty in the morning. Pathologists couldn't narrow it down as much as they would have liked, due to the gas fire left on in her flat, accelerating decomposition. It had been two days before Wendy had found her body.

I swallowed hard as the egg I'd eaten attempted to make a reappearance. Wendy would probably be traumatised for life by the scene and smell that greeted her the moment she unlocked Charlotte's door.

Terry saw me shudder. 'You okay?'

'More details coming in.'

'Getting anywhere?'

I sketched it out for him. 'Chris Pitlock now says he was at a nightclub. He reckons there would be plenty of people who would confirm he was there. But we're talking three years ago.'

'And it doesn't explain where he went afterwards.'

'And look at this.'

I opened up the original scene of crime report. 'It says Chris was carrying a Swiss army knife. He said he always had one in his pocket.'

Terry gave me a questioning stare. 'So?'

'I need to email Fenway first.' I started typing. 'I need him to check something.'

Terry straightened up with a sigh. 'I think I'd better leave you to it and get to work.'

He got his things together, gave me a lingering smooch on the cheek and left. I had a quick shower and got dressed. When I checked my phone, Fenway had already left a message asking me to call him.

'You're right,' he said, 'Swiss army knives come with all sorts of different attachments and Pitlock had one with small scissors on it.'

A band of heat curled around my neck.

He went on. 'It wasn't remarked on at the time, because no one knew about the assault on her hair.'

'And it wasn't the murder weapon,' I said slowly, thinking out loud. 'What time did he say he got home?'

'Around three fifteen in the morning. His gig ended at three o'clock.'

'So he says.'

'We're in the process of checking his new alibis at the night-club and we're trying to trace the cab company he says he used to get from the club in Kennington to his bedsit in Stockwell that night. If he's right, it would have been too tight to get over to Primrose Hill and smother Charlotte by three thirty. He didn't have his van, remember.'

I let out a little moan.

'We've also got something on Hazel Hart,' he added. 'Her friends insisted she didn't know who it was, but... she had mentioned a stalker.'

I held myself in check, wanting nothing more than to yell: *I knew it!*

Then came the words I'd been waiting for. 'It means we're no longer looking at her death as an accident.'

'That's great news,' I said calmly, damping down my jubilation. 'So Hazel's murder just ten days ago *could* have been committed by the same killer who smothered Charlotte in 2016, and left Lorna on the railway line in 2010?'

It was obvious, wasn't it?

I heard a little huff as Fenway breathed out. 'We're keeping an open mind.'

52

'Oh my god, look at you – you're an item!' Miranda shrieked at the sight of Terry, his arm hooked around me, at the door. She let us both in. 'About bloody time! How many years has it taken the pair of you to get together?'

Terry answered as we shuffled into the narrow hallway. 'I'd say it's over fifteen since this blinkin' woman first stole my heart.' He looked at me warmly, then pulled me close to kiss my hair. I smiled, looking sheepish.

'God – she's useless,' Miranda said, waltzing off into the living room.

I stood motionless in the doorway. The place was in total disarray as though she was in the process of moving house. Long crates used to transport paintings were stacked against the walls and there was barely room to move with boxes in the way, half of them full of glasses, bottles of wine, crockery. Only forty minutes to go to pull things into shape before the doors opened for the grand exhibition. We had a lot of work to do.

'When are the press coming?' I called out, picking up two empty cartons. 'Where are these going?'

'Later.' She pointed through the kitchen. 'In the back yard.'

Terry helped Miranda clear a trestle table for drinks, while I got rid of all the empty boxes outside the back door. When I came back, I began dragging out the large flat crates, being careful not to knock over the canvases leaning against the spiral staircase.

'Don't touch any pictures,' she said. 'I know exactly where everything has to go.'

I glanced up at the walls. At least the hooks had already been put in place, although it would take two people to lift the canvases.

'Did something go wrong?' I asked, hauling another crate across the wooden floor. It made a screeching noise as it went like fingernails on a blackboard. 'How come you're not ready?'

She stared at me. 'What do you mean? We've got bags of time.' She swanned off into the kitchen and I watched her pour herself a glass of wine, then knock back half of it.

That was Miranda all over; laissez-faire, head in the clouds, assuming that everything will go swimmingly. This was too important for us to make a hash of it.

'Is anyone else coming to help?' I was opening a box of beer glasses, alongside Terry who was tipping crisps and nuts into dishes.

The doorbell jangled as I spoke. Miranda came back with two women I recognised from the project. Behind them was another figure dressed in a crisp grey suit. Ralph. We caught each other's eye immediately and shared a mutual deadpan stare. He snapped his eyes away and took great delight in throwing his arms around Miranda, picking her up off the floor. All for my benefit, it seemed.

'How's my little starlet?' he said, his face plastered in smiles. I felt like I'd been punched in the stomach.

I turned away, busying myself with side plates.

The next person to arrive was Emily. I felt a rush of delight when I saw her. She brought an air of upbeat efficiency and seemed to have a kind word for everyone. She'd brought flowers and napkins and various other items everyone else seemed to have forgotten.

'Anyone got a screwdriver?' came Miranda's voice, giggling as Ralph started tickling her.

'There's one here,' Emily called out.

The three of them set about opening the remaining wooden crates that had come over from CCAP. I recognised several paintings that had been on display, alongside other artwork, in the gallery. Terry went over to help lift the paintings onto the hooks. I kept my distance, searching for a corkscrew in the kitchen. I couldn't find one. Miranda hadn't thought this through properly at all. I heard Terry and Ralph chuckling.

'Ralph seems charming,' Terry said, as he came up behind me by the cutlery drawer, wrapping his arms around my shoulders.

'Appearances can be deceptive,' I said, instantly regretting it. It was at times like this when I was relieved no other person could know what was going on inside my head. I turned to him, my eyes hovering below his chin. I had the prickly feeling that he'd not only spotted my awkwardness, but was going to comment on it.

'You look guilty about something...'

Sometimes, I wished Terry wasn't so perceptive.

'Do I?' I looked straight into his eyes, knowing I couldn't say a thing.

He frowned slightly, wiped his dusty hands on a tea towel and wandered off.

Emily joined me once he'd moved away. 'Who's that gorgeous guy?' she asked conspiratorially.

I felt a rush of heat colour my cheeks. 'Oh, that's Terry.'

She waggled her finger between me and his figure at the far side of the room. 'Are you and he?'

I fluttered my eyelashes at her. 'I'll tell you another time,' I whispered.

With five minutes to go before the door opened, Miranda disappeared to change and the rest of us worked like bees in a hive, each with our own jobs, tracing our individual paths between the kitchen and main room. Thankfully, at the eleventh hour, someone produced a corkscrew from their pocket.

By then, a new panic had set in. 'Where are the catalogues, Miranda?' I shouted up the iron staircase.

It was Ralph who answered from behind me. 'All in hand,' he said pompously. He reached down to a carrier bag and pulled out a wad of brochures. I drew back, my hands up in surrender as if he were holding a revolver. I turned my back on him and strode into the kitchen even though I had no reason to go in there. I loitered, pretending to look for something, but really using it as a refuge. I couldn't bear to be in the same room as him. Breathing the same air. Under pressure for Miranda's sake, to be polite.

'I think we're ready,' came Terry's voice. I spun round and fell into him, burying my head into his chest.

'You okay? What's going on?'

I mumbled something vague about that night being so special to Miranda and hoped he wouldn't probe further. We'd barely broken apart when the doorbell rang and the first visitors arrived.

53

Miranda flew down the stairs like a wood sprite, in her trademark bare feet, wearing a floaty chiffon dress.

'I think we can declare the Miranda Willerby art exhibition open,' said Terry, as we hung back at the kitchen door. I let my shoulders drop and puffed out a loud whoosh of air.

From then on, the doorbell rang every few moments and people kept flooding in, so much so that Miranda decided to leave the front door wide open. I recognised many faces from CCAP, but there were also tutors, media critics wearing name badges, gallery scouts and members of the public. Camera flashes went off and there was a lively buzz as viewers took in my sister's work and shared their reactions.

I tried to eavesdrop as I trawled the room with wine, making sure everyone had top-ups to their drinks. The overriding atmosphere was positive; with erudite comments such as 'bold and austere', 'ominously complex', and 'biomorphic mix of horror and humour' wafting around. Viewers were nodding, smiling. Sales were being made.

My heart sang as I watched Miranda accept praise, putting her hand to her chest, hugging strangers, giving people a little piece of herself. My sister. It was such a delight to see her happy, doing so well. Then I caught Ralph watching her too and my perfect moment was poisoned.

I turned to the wall, pretending to engross myself in one of Miranda's new paintings. Then did another round with champagne. When I returned to the drinks table, we were low on red wine. With visitors still piling in, I picked out Miranda's vanilla-blonde hair in the crowd and wove my way towards her.

'You'll have to get someone to go out and buy some,' she instructed. 'Get Ralph, he came in the car.'

'Can't *you* ask h–?' She was whisked away by the arm of a suited man, before I could finish.

I found Terry. 'We need more wine.'

'And more orange juice,' he said, 'I've just opened the last carton.'

'You couldn't possibly get to an off-licence, could you?' I turned around, trying to remember where I'd left my bag. 'Get it on my debit card,' I said, heading towards the kitchen, remembering I'd left it hidden away at the back of the pan cupboard.

'I'll get them,' came a husky voice behind us. It was Ralph. He patted Terry's arm. 'Shall we both go?' he said, not looking at me.

'Sure.' Terry winked at me. 'Won't be long.'

I had a sour taste in my mouth as I watched the pair disappear. I didn't like the idea of Ralph being anywhere near Terry. Just as I didn't want him within spitting distance of any of the people I cared about. I could feel venom coursing through my veins and if Miranda hadn't come into the kitchen at that moment, I probably wouldn't have said anything. I'd have managed to keep myself better in check. But the words were out of my mouth before I could stop them.

'I hate interfering, but there's something you should know,' I said, pulling her towards me, away from the vibrant hum beyond the door.

She looked bewildered.

'Ralph's not right for you,' I said clumsily.

She shrank away from me. 'What do you mean?'

'He's got problems and–'

'What are you talking about? What's he done?'

'Nothing…'

Her startled expression sank into indignation. With her hands glued to her hips, she was waiting for me to explain myself. I couldn't. I wanted to with all my heart, but I couldn't.

'Ralph and I are together and that's that. What's wrong with you?!' She didn't wait for a response. 'I knew you'd be all funny like this. That's why I didn't tell you about him.'

'It's not disapproval – it's protection,' I said, faltering. 'He's… unsuitable. He's going to hurt you, I know he is.'

I wanted to tell her everything – about his abusive patterns with women, about his glib approach to therapy – but I had to keep quiet. I couldn't even say he'd been my patient.

She screwed up her face. 'I can't believe this. It's my magical moment in the limelight and all you want to do is ruin it, with rubbish about my new boyfriend being "unsuitable". I mean – "unsuitable" – what the hell does that mean?!'

Our torturous confrontation was interrupted by sudden applause breaking through like the sound of thunder, then cries of *Where is she?*

A face popped around the kitchen door.

'Here she is!'

Then more faces and arms beckoned her away from me. 'Miranda, quick!'

I followed them, as the tinkling sound of a spoon against glass brought the room to a hush.

'We have a bit of an announcement,' called out the woman I

knew to be Miranda's latest tutor, Betty Dixon. 'It's all very last minute, but one of Miranda's pictures has been selected for the Rex Carlton Award.'

A rambunctious cheer came as Betty threw her arm up and pointed to the new painting I'd just been trying to fathom out. It wasn't up my street, but it had clearly gone down well with the people who knew their stuff.

Miranda stepped alongside her, open-mouthed, dazed. Betty put her arm around her.

'For those of you who aren't familiar with the award, it means a week on show in the Tate Modern, lots of publicity and a cheque, of course!'

More roars and clinking of glasses followed.

Miranda looked on the verge of tears. She held her hands together in front of her mouth like she was praying, her thin bare legs twisting together. Vulnerable and overwhelmed. Just like I remembered her at six years old.

Betty hushed the crowd. 'And there will be a posh ceremony next week in Mayfair.' She dropped her head in mock regret, 'but that will be invitation only, I'm afraid.'

Three cheers went up, followed by rowdy singing, chanting and stamping. Miranda was ecstatic, standing in the centre of the room, accepting hugs, kisses and pats on the back. I couldn't get to her for the swarm of well-wishers.

'I can't believe it!' I heard her call out. 'There'll be a ceremony and everything!'

I wanted to share in her joy, tell her how proud I was, but I hung back, knowing my face would not be welcome so soon after my heavy-handed accusations.

54

The wind was hostile when I left my cosy flat for our next run. As I speed-walked towards the station, the wind swatted at my hair and reflective jacket like I was an insect that needed obliterating. The world had turned aggressive.

'Are we still going?' I asked plaintively, when I found Emily warming up. The rain had soaked through my trainers already and my toes were squelchy and turning numb inside wet socks.

'Of course. You'll get used to it.'

I grumbled, but I knew she was right. Commitment to anything meant carrying on in the face of adversity. For some reason, Lorna's face, sincere and hopeful, popped up like a bubble in my mind. The renewed investigation didn't seem to be uncovering much about her death and I felt like I was letting her down. Neville Larch was the sticking point, but perhaps there were clues in the tapes of our sessions I had yet to listen to. I needed to make them my priority.

We ran in silence for the first stretch to save shouting into the frenzied hiss of spitting traffic. As soon as we could, we took a turn off the main road away from the tyre spray.

Emily broke through the steady chug of our breaths. 'Since

we met, I've told you a few bits about my life, but you've told me nothing about yours.' It wasn't said with malice, more that she was stating a fact.

'There's not much to tell,' I said lamely.

She glanced sideways to look at me. 'Er, excuse me – a new bloke for a start.'

'Oh, yes, Terry – he's wonderful.'

'You said you don't have patients at the moment, so what are you working on?'

'Ah, that's a bit tricky.' I wiped a drip of rain off the end of my nose with my glove. 'It's confidential. Sorry. I'm not allowed to share what I'm doing with anyone.'

'That's tough.'

I shrugged. 'I'm used to keeping secrets as a therapist. I have to do it all the time.' I laughed, attempting to make light of it, but inwardly feeling repulsed at the thought of Ralph and his dirty little secret.

'So, tell me about this Terry guy,' Emily said, curling her lip.

Chatting wasn't easy for me at this pace, so I gave her the edited version. 'Well... I first met him in my early twenties when I was doing a doctorate in psychology. He works in the police. He's strong, funny, gentle, generous – everything. Our history means he knows me really well. We're being low-key about it...' I came up for air. 'But it feels pretty special, actually.'

Her face blossomed into a grin. 'You're totally into this guy! He seemed approachable and easy-going at Miranda's do. Kind of no rough edges.'

'Ha! That's Terry, exactly – you're very perceptive.'

'You didn't fancy him before?'

'No. I thought of him as a good mate, that's all. A kind of brother figure. Mr Reliable; he always seemed to be there when I was having a rough time. I never thought of him in *that* way.' I snatched an extra lungful of air hoping she'd take over.

'I know what you mean. I had a dream about a bloke once. It completely changed my view of him overnight. He was the courier manager at work. He went from being Mr Boring to Mr Gorgeous by the next morning. For no real reason whatsoever!'

'Strange isn't it? How you change your view about people... when they haven't really done anything different.'

'So, how come Miranda said only yesterday afternoon that you were single?'

'Ah, she didn't know until the exhibition. I haven't told anyone properly except you.'

'Why not?' Emily's directness was refreshing, but it also kept me slightly on edge.

'It's kind of only just happened. In any case, many of my friends have left London; we email a lot, but not with something like this. It's early days, anyway. I'll tell friends from work when I get back.' I took an extra breath. 'As for Miranda – she and I have had a bit of a falling out.'

'Oh, sorry to hear that.'

'Nothing major and it happens all the time!' I turned to Emily and threw my eyes heavenwards.

The rain didn't abate, but Emily was right; I got used to the squelch inside my trainers, the raindrops gathering on the lip of my hood dripping onto my face. It should have been deeply unpleasant, but it wasn't. It felt like the time I went on a school camping trip when I was ten and we woke up to find our sleeping bags sitting in pools of water. Fun, an adventure, in tune with the elements.

'You're quite an insular person, aren't you?' Emily said. 'I looked you up online, but there aren't many references to you. A few mentions of you working at St Luke's and links to various papers you've written. Nothing else.'

'You're right. I'm not on social media – it's not good practice for a therapist.'

'Why not – isn't it good for patients to see you as a real person?'

'It doesn't work like that. In my style of therapy I'm meant to be a blank screen. When people tell me things, I get out of the way and merely clarify what they're trying to say. It means patients are getting to know themselves better, not me.'

'Ah. That makes sense.'

'I don't have a wide network of friends in any case. Compared to most people, it's almost embarrassing actually!'

'Billy no-mates?'

We both laughed.

A touch of defensiveness made me speak again. 'I like to cut through the masks we all wear to find out how people are *really* feeling underneath. Not everyone is up for that.'

'Is that why you became a therapist?'

'Partly.' I decided to tell her the truth. 'Miranda was the main reason. I stupidly thought that if I learnt all about psychology, in some vicarious way I could help her, but it totally backfired.'

'How come?'

'She thinks I'm always trying to "fix her". She thinks I'm constantly watching for signs of "psychopathology".' I grimaced. 'She's right, really. All I've done is alienated her.'

'At least you care.'

We ran the final stretch into the bright lights of the station entrance and out of the deluge. As I stretched over to one side at the start of our cooldown, I spotted a figure. Someone seated on a high stool at the window inside one of the cafés. He was staring straight at me.

I shot upright, the rush of blood making me light-headed. The black and white stripe. It sent a sharp prickle up my throat. I'd seen it before. His hair was thick and black, but with a distinct white stripe running through the side; what people call a *Mallen streak.* The man saw me peering in his direction and abruptly got up.

'Emily, quick, look...' She straightened up too late. I pointed at the window, but the space was empty. 'I think it was him...'

'Who? Where?' She strained to follow my line of sight.

It clicked. 'The guy from the tube.'

I hurried over to the café entrance and scoured the inside, but couldn't see him. I came out, tutting. 'Shit – he's gone...'

Emily stood with her hands on her hips, a frown quivering between her eyebrows. Before I reached her, a flash of green in my peripheral vision made me jump and the man darted past us out into the rain.

'There! That's *him*!'

He yanked up his hood against the elements and we both charged after him.

'Hey! Stop!' I called out.

With warm limbs and a robust pace still in our legs, we caught up with him at the first corner. He took off to the left, but Emily put on a spurt and sprinted past him. She stopped sharply to block his path as I came up behind.

Emily saw his face before I did. Her expression changed from suspicion into one I wasn't expecting.

'Oh, my god, it's *you*...'

She knew him.

'Have you been following me?' she growled.

'No, I... I only wanted to talk to you. You won't return my messages, my calls.'

'That's because it's over, Stephen.' She glared at him. 'It was ten months ago! And you're still pestering me.'

'You've been blanking me; you moved house, you changed your number, what choice did I have?'

'Wait,' I said, stepping in. 'It was *you*, wasn't it?'

His eyes darted around furtively, as if considering whether to make another dash for it. Emily grabbed his sleeve. She wasn't letting him go anywhere. 'You were the one who pushed me on the platform at Camden station,' I snapped. 'I thought the black and white stripe that stuck in my mind was a scarf or a hat, but it was your *hair*.'

He burst into animation like a wind-up toy that had been let loose on the ground. Emily hung onto him as he tried to shake her free.

'I didn't *push* you. I was trying to get to Emily. I didn't want anyone to get hurt. I just wanted to get her to listen to me.'

Emily let go of his sleeve, shaking her head. 'Bloody hell. You nearly killed Sam.' She squared up to him, her chin jutting forward. 'You were following me the other day as well, weren't you? You were behind me at the bar, right? You tried to grab my hair.'

He shook his head, wide-eyed. 'What? When?'

She turned to me, pulling me away. 'I should have realised. It must have been him – the guy who's been following me, hanging around outside my flat. I didn't recognise him.' She called to him, hanging onto me as she continued to walk backwards. 'Leave me alone okay? Or I'll report you to the police for stalking me.'

He started to come after us. 'I'm not stalking you! I want to talk. Can't we try to sort out what happened between us?'

She stopped. 'We already did that, Stephen. We talked for bloody hours, months ago. I'm just not into you. I'm sorry. There's nothing to discuss. Leave me alone.'

She threw her eyes up and linked arms with me. Together we made our way to the station without looking back.

55

I sent Fenway a message as soon as I got home, then jumped in the shower. After our encounter with Stephen, I'd insisted Emily get a taxi. Stephen hadn't followed us back to Clapham Junction as far as I could tell, but I didn't like the idea of her being easy prey on her way home. He obviously knew where Emily lived, which wasn't good, even though she said he'd never got as far as ringing her doorbell.

While we'd waited to flag down a taxi, she told me his full name was Stephen McVey. 'There was nothing to it,' she stressed. 'We went out for a few weeks and I realised I didn't fancy him. Simple as that. I met him at the gym. He was into rock climbing and is a brilliant table tennis player. Physically, I thought he was hot, but it turned out he was pretty feeble-minded when it came to his personality. You know the type, agreeing with you all the time, waiting for you to decide where to go on dates, pussyfooting around like I was made of porcelain. I got sick of him and ended it. It took him months to get the message and I thought he'd finally stopped harassing me. Except I was wrong...'

I'd barely registered what she was telling me. All I could

hear in my head were the words she'd uttered earlier: *You tried to grab my hair.*

I stuffed a ten-pound note in her pocket before I ran off, so she'd have no chance to hand it back. At least she'd get the opportunity in the taxi to call the police and report him. I thought she'd done that already, but she said she didn't think she had enough to go on.

Fenway got back to me the following morning. He'd actually followed up my request this time. Perhaps my account of events the previous evening had sounded sufficiently unnerving. It turned out Stephen McVey – the meek and dithering ping-pong player had a police record for GBH. He'd headbutted a man four years ago after a minor car crash, which resulted in a broken nose and fractured cheekbone.

'Sounds like someone with anger issues.' I was chomping on a piece of toast and tried not to sound like my mouth was full. 'So his DNA will be on record?'

'Yup. We're checking through everything now to see if there's a link with your cases.'

I felt myself sit up taller at the sound of Fenway's concluding words. He made it seem like I was finally part of the team, not some annoying add-on he was having to put up with.

'As you're on the line,' he said, 'I might as well update you on Chris Pitlock's alibi.'

I took a quick gulp of orange juice to send the last scrap of toast down.

'The nightclub in Kennington confirmed he was their DJ the night of Charlotte's murder, between nine and three, like Pitlock claimed. Clocked off at three in the morning on the dot, they said, then he had to pack up his gear, get paid and so on. The cab company wasn't so helpful, unsurprisingly. We're talking 2016, don't forget – and they couldn't confirm his journey to Stockwell at around three fifteen in the morning. They don't keep records that long. But if Chris finished his gig then, he's not looking like a viable suspect.'

'Because the estimated time of Charlotte's death was three thirty at the very latest?'

'Exactly. You see my point?'

I thanked him for ringing, but ended the call feeling deflated. I hated loose ends. I liked things to be clean and neatly sewn up.

I spent the rest of the morning having another go at identifying legends, rituals, fetishes and historical records involving cutting hair. There were several cases of serial killers clipping hair *after* they had murdered a victim. Sometimes strands were kept as mementos, other times attacks involved hacking off all the victim's hair as a form of insult. One recent case involved a Spanish man who left clumps of hair by the hands of his victims, but he stabbed the women he chose.

The murders I was investigating involved 'clean' deaths. Gravity ultimately killed Hazel, a train killed Lorna, and there was no blood at the scene in Charlotte's death. Besides, the Spanish killer had been behind bars since 2012.

I drew a blank when it came to anything involving the exact pattern I'd discovered. Hair-hacking followed by a seven-day waiting period, then a 'clean' murder. This pattern was specific to these murders. I could only assume the procedure had personal significance for the killer.

After another cup of black coffee, I moved on to the next of Lorna's tapes. The second and third were similar to the first; saturated with the same level of distress and guilt, as she relived the incident when the van mounted the pavement.

But the fourth tape, dated September 2010, marked a turning

point. Lorna mentioned that she'd spoken to college staff and they'd agreed to organise a fashion show. 'To raise money for those who were injured in the collision. I can't believe they're going to do it.'

It was the first time I'd heard her sound the least bit enthusiastic about anything.

'The place they use has this beautiful wide staircase that fans out into a marble hall at the bottom,' she'd told me. 'They want to have models parading down the stairs in outfits the students have designed. I'm working on my range of equestrian gear, but I need to get involved in something.' There was a little gap on the tape as she hesitated. 'To get away from myself, if you know what I mean. I've been wondering about getting a puppy, but Mum said I should really think about the day-to-day reality of having a little dog around the place. But the fashion show will give me something positive to get my teeth into straight away. I can help plan the outfits and do some modelling myself. Otherwise, I'll be sitting around feeling miserable.'

I remember she'd worn a cropped polo-neck in canary yellow that day. I'd always thought that particular colour clashed with long blonde hair, but that wasn't the case with Lorna. She looked like a golden statue. The kinks in her hair were even more pronounced on that occasion; like a row of zeds down her back. I remember it made her seem more alive.

By our next session, students and tutors had rallied to the cause and the show had been scheduled. Lorna was to play a minor part on the day, helping the models change backstage. Nevertheless, over the next few tapes, I heard her grow mentally stronger. I remembered she'd begun to smile, to laugh, during our sessions. She showed a wit and spontaneous humour I didn't know she had.

The event was due to take place in early November. After our last session and a few weeks before she died. There was no mention of it on her police file. Could it have held a clue as to what happened to her?

I turned off the tape machine. I couldn't face listening to the final session with Lorna's chirpy voice full of hope and anticipation as she looked forward to her special night. I didn't want to hear us share that final goodbye as I wished her well.

On nineteenth November she was found on the railway line. I still couldn't believe I'd known nothing about her death; it must have been on the news, but evidently, I missed it. But it was like that in my line of work. Patients came for a short while, often forming a powerful bond between the two of us, then they disappeared into their own world. More often than not, I didn't see or hear of them again.

I dropped the machine back into my bag, together with the remaining cassette. I'd have to return to it when I was feeling less choked.

56

LORNA

Nine years earlier

I feel sick when I think about it. Obviously, the whole evening had to be abandoned. How could something so freakish have happened? It was supposed to be an evening of remembrance. Suddenly, everything was worse than it was before.

Once the ambulance had gone, most people were in shock and we had to call it off. It was one of those awful one-in-a-million calamities. And none of the other models had issues with the stairs; there was nothing loose and the carpet wasn't ruckled.

Up until that point, everything had been going swimmingly. Not only had tickets sold out before the night, there were people queuing at the door. Mum and Dad came. I was nearly in tears because they looked so proud. All the extra dressmakers and models gave their time for free, as it was for such a good cause. The flute and harp duo were perfect, playing soothing music. Loads of people took photos and someone from *The Evening Standard* was there. The tutors did an amazing job; an elegant refined affair to honour the victims of the van collision.

In spite of all the goodwill, it was turmoil behind the scenes, getting everyone dressed in time. Thankfully, I knew exactly who was meant to be wearing what, even though wigs, hats and shoes got completely mixed up. Everyone was in a muddle about the order they were due to come down the stairs, but we did our best.

I was one of the first to parade, so I could go behind the scenes and help with everything. I loved gliding down that luxurious staircase with its silky-smooth gold bannister. The red carpet was soft and spongy, and it was such a thrill to hear everyone break into applause when I came into sight. Mum was right at the front, clapping like a maniac. The harp flourished into a crescendo, the chandeliers sparkled, the cameras flashed.

Once that fateful night was over, the run of bad things didn't stop. Soon after, I started being followed by someone. Then there was the night at the pop concert. I was in bits when Julia pointed out that someone had snipped my hair off at the back. I was so angry and humiliated, like I'd wet myself, or something. Once I realised what had happened, I had to leave. I was in such a state, I needed to be on my own, away from everyone.

I managed to get an emergency appointment at Giovanni's that Saturday and he said the best way to rectify it would be to take off all my hair above the collar. I was devastated. With each snip of his scissors, I sobbed my heart out. They gave me tea, then one of the girls ran out and returned with a brandy on ice! How lovely. Everyone was kind, but inside I felt I'd been physically abused. My gorgeous long hair – it's just... *me*. It's who I am. Not this new version, with hair that doesn't even reach my neck.

Everyone I know had the same reaction after my traumatic 'restyle' at the salon. I could see people looking at me, baffled and disapproving. As if they were saying to themselves: *What on earth possessed her to ruin her hair like that?* Then they snapped plastic smiles on their faces and were overly bright with their compliments. But I know every one of them was fake. Every single one. They hate how I look. I hate it. I hate whoever it was who did this to me.

I'd been doing so well since the collision at the ATM, but it was all too much for me. Mum suggested I go to see the nice therapist again. She said Dr Willerby would help me get everything into perspective. But there was a longer wait than last time. I was offered someone else instead, but I turned it down. I didn't want to start again with someone new. I like Dr Willerby, so I've asked to join her waiting list.

In the meantime, I've decided the puppy idea is the right thing for me. I think having something else to love and care for will help me feel better and Mum said she'd look after it when I'm at college. I told everyone on my course I'm on the lookout for a pure-bred beagle and someone even shared it on Facebook. A few days ago, I got a text from someone called Alistair. He said he's the brother of one of the foundation-year students and he knows a breeder selling puppies off at discount price, because the litter is bigger than they expected.

You'll need to get in quick, as she's already sold three, he'd put in his message.

Kennels are near Barnes Bridge train station. Get there tomorrow at 6pm. Mum will come with me after work, so it won't just be me. I'll be wearing a denim jacket and my mum's got ginger hair.

I got straight back to him and it's all arranged. I'm glad he's bringing his mother; I would have been wary meeting a bloke I've never met before on my own. Especially after what happened with my hair. When I think of that khaki combat jacket, that figure tailing me, I get the shakes and can't breathe properly. Thank God he seems to have given up. No one's been hanging around since my hair was hacked off. Doing that must have given whoever it was the stupid thrill they wanted and they've got no reason to follow me anymore.

57

LORNA

Nine years earlier

It's nearly dark when I get off the train. The sky is inky black with stars and curls of clouds. I can see the moon. I'm thinking I should have brought Mum with me, after all. But this stage is just about choosing one of the puppies, not to actually bring one home. That'll be next week, once all the vaccinations have been done and they've had the final go-ahead from the vet. She can come with me then.

I spot a figure in a denim jacket at the far end of the platform, but there's no one with ginger hair standing alongside. As the figure gets closer, it's not the stranger I was expecting.

'Oh, it's you,' I say. 'I was expecting someone called Alistair.'

'He asked me to come instead. His mum's got a migraine and couldn't get out of bed.'

'You know him? You know about the dogs? How weird. I'm relieved it's you actually. I was beginning to think it was a bit stupid to agree to meet a stranger.'

We come out of the station, across the bridge and join a narrow path alongside what looks like wasteland, where buildings have recently been demolished. It's deserted here and poorly lit.

'What is this place?'

'There's going to be a new development. That's why it looks such a mess.'

There's a chain-link wire fence that's been squashed down here and there, allowing people through to the railway cutting. I shiver. It's not just the cold; I'm uneasy, wandering so far from civilisation.

'Is this right?' I asked. 'It looks like we're in the middle of nowhere.'

'We're not going to someone's house. The breeders need space to keep the dogs. They've got horses, too, so there are stables and a paddock. It's not far. You'll love it.'

'Blimey, I'm glad I didn't have to find it on my own.'

'Nearly there. It's quicker if we cut through here.'

We step over a torn-down section of the wire and walk alongside the railway line. I can see the red light from a signal floating in the distance.

'The owner said they'd already sold three of the pups. Don't want you to miss out.'

'Of course. Thanks. It's good of you to take me. How do you know about them?'

'My uncle knows someone who works there.'

I turn to look at the lines beside us: they're shiny and silver, illuminated only by the moon. 'Are you sure we're allowed on here? Aren't trains going to come right past us.'

'It's fine. It's not far. Can't you hear the dogs barking? We're nearly there.'

We turn off and head into the bushes, but it's like walking into an underground cave and I hesitate. I can't hear any dogs. All I can hear are alarm bells clanging loudly inside my head, telling me to get out of there. This isn't right. I need to return to the station, to where there are other people. There will be other puppies, another day.

'Listen, I'm sorry. I don't feel too well. I'm going back.'

'But we're nearly there.'

I turn around and start clambering over the low branches and broken bricks as fast as I can. My heart is bolting. It was stupid to have come this far.

I don't make it as far as the station. I don't even make it out of the undergrowth. Before I can stagger into the meagre glow of dusk, something heavy and hard whacks me on the back of the head. I hear the crack as it hits my skull and my body buckles under me, like a puppet with broken strings.

I feel crisp leaves under my cheek as I flop down with a crunch and take in the musty mossy smell of the earth. My grip on existence falters. I need to get up and keep going, but I can't make anything move. My legs, my arms are set in stone.

I'm dragged towards the track. I try to dig my heels into the earth, to anchor myself, but that simple action is beyond me. I try to make myself heavy. It's all I can do. I can't even get my eyes to open.

With a jolt, my lip slaps against the cold metal of the railway line and I hear the rumble, feel it vibrate under my ribs.

A train is on its way.

I don't need to open my eyes to know the red light up ahead has turned green. Full steam ahead.

It's as though a supreme being in the sky has decided there are too many like me in the world. I scrunch up my eyes; it's all I can manage. Someone must go. I think it's going to be me.

58

SAM

The Present

The run-up to Miranda's award ceremony wasn't easy to navigate. CCAP were given complimentary tickets and it was Emily who went out of her way to make sure I was given one, not my sister. Not surprisingly, ever since I'd tried to warn her to steer clear of Ralph, Miranda had been totally off with me. She was ignoring my calls and messages. It wouldn't normally have bothered me; it wasn't exactly unusual, but my concern for her had roots in very murky water. I wasn't going to be backtracking.

Fortunately, I got regular reports about Miranda's well-being through Emily, who saw more of her than I did and seemed to have become a regular at the project between shifts of gym work.

She had no idea my casual questions about my sister had any ulterior motive. By her account, Miranda was sparky and brimming with exuberance, looking forward to her big day on the red carpet. She was on an even keel. That was all that mattered. I didn't know for how long that was going to last.

During the days before the event, Emily and I went out running every evening except for the weekend. That time was ring-fenced for Terry. He and I spent from Friday evening to Monday morning at his place, barely getting out of bed.

When we did peel ourselves away from our love nest, we went for coffee or brunch in local spots, holding hands like we were having a holiday romance. We walked arm in arm across Regent's Park and took the train further out, over to the water gardens and Tudor deer park near Hampton Court. I spotted a kingfisher, glistening fluorescent blue through the branches, but Terry claimed I was daydreaming.

After dark, he cooked sumptuous suppers while I sipped wine and read. Every so often between stirring sizzling dishes in the kitchen, he'd come up behind me and kiss the back of my neck. It was the most relaxed I'd felt in years.

I should have returned by then to St Luke's, but I had a call from my clinic to say the original two-week 'sabbatical' had been extended. Someone – I couldn't imagine it being either Claussen or Fenway – had decided I was doing a worthwhile job and the Met didn't want to lose me just yet.

It was tempting to think I was on vacation. With everything so new and delectable with Terry (and not only the food), it would have been easy to continue walking on air, but regular updates on the murder cases pulled me back to stone-cold reality.

A couple of hours before Miranda's ceremony was due to start, I was back at my flat, meant to be choosing an outfit, but instead I decided to take another look at Lorna's crime report.

Sitting cross-legged in my bathrobe, I rested the laptop on my knees. I already knew Lorna had been found on a mainline train track near Barnes Bridge station. It was some distance from her flat in Parson's Green. The report explained how she'd gone to meet someone to look at a litter of puppies. I'd remembered from the tapes that she'd mentioned she might get a dog.

Texts found on Lorna's phone showed she'd been intending to meet a young man called Alistair Madeley at Barnes Bridge station. His mother was meant to be there too. They had both been interviewed in 2010, but claimed they knew nothing about the arrangement.

It was Alistair's phone that had been used to send the texts, but he insisted he hadn't sent them. He told police he'd lost his mobile that same day. Aged twenty at the time, he'd been working at Pepe's Pizza in Brixton. He thought a customer must have pinched it. His mother said she'd been constantly nagging him about tucking it in his back pocket. 'It was too easy for someone to nick it in a crowd,' she'd explained to police.

In 2010, the police didn't appear to have anyone else in the frame for Lorna's death. But Neville Larch, the man she'd mistakenly accused in the line-up, had been dismissed too easily for my liking. While it looked like Chris Pitlock was out of the frame for Charlotte's murder, Larch was a definite link between both cases.

I got up to stretch my legs and wandered over to my wardrobe. There hadn't been a spare invite to Miranda's do for Terry and he had to work that evening anyway, so I was turning up on my own. As I flicked through the hangers, I found myself looking at clothes differently, now he and I were together. I could sense myself considering outfits with an eye for whether Terry would like them or not. It was ridiculous!

I pulled out a navy-blue suit with a pencil skirt and heard the words 'too prim' in his voice in my head. I moved on to a slinky cocktail dress in claret velvet and held it up against me in front of the mirror. I couldn't hide a smile as I imagined his reaction. A stare, a clearing of the throat, then a low groan as though he was tasting the creamiest chocolate in the world.

I laughed out loud at myself. So much seemed to have changed in such a short space of time. Suddenly this man was in my life full-time. It felt right, it felt completely normal, as if he'd always been there.

On the other hand, it was hard to grasp I was no longer single; I was used to doing everything on my own. Was it dangerous to feel so at home in this new situation? I didn't want to rely on this 'being in a couple' thing; besides, I didn't really know where our relationship was going.

I put the dress back and pulled out a simple silk blouse and smart trousers. *My* choice. Without Terry's voice in my head. No matter what happened between us, there was no way I'd ever be relinquishing my independence.

I pulled on the long jacket over my blouse, added a pearl necklace and swept my hair into a knotted updo. My stomach did a loop the loop when I considered how shocking it would be to discover a huge chunk of it had been hacked off at the collar. Instinctively, my hand went to the back of my neck to check, as I fitted the diamanté clips. What a nightmare it must have been for those innocent women.

59

I still had a few minutes before I needed to leave, so I went back to Lorna's online file. There was an update: the police had interviewed Larch and a transcript of his recent interview was attached. I hurriedly read on.

There was certainly a cloud hanging over him. It turned out he'd been Charlotte's former English teacher at school and was 'happily' married. Two strong reasons to want to keep his relationship with Charlotte clandestine. Two strong motives to get rid of her if she'd started to demand more or made threats to expose him.

He claimed the secret affair had been going on for two months, during which time he'd never set foot inside Charlotte's bedsit. Sure enough, there was no DNA match at the scene to contradict this. Nothing. He also had a strong alibi for the narrow time slot when her hair had been clipped; giving a lecture at the University of East London. A note was attached that confirmed his alibi had been checked and it held up; a roomful of students, together with tutors, could vouch for him.

Then there was Larch's account of the day Charlotte was killed. I flicked through to the full transcript to get a feel for

Larch's own words. It started with Fenway asking him his whereabouts:

NL: I was getting ready to go on holiday. To Guernsey with my family.

DI Fenway: Where were you exactly that day?

NL: I spent nine to five at work, as usual, then I was at home, with my wife and son, from around six thirty. We were packing. Sorting out last-minute things. We caught our flight mid-afternoon the next day.

DI Fenway: On 24 October?

NL: Yes.

DI Fenway: What about late that evening on the 23rd, from say, eight o'clock onwards?

NL: I was at home, like I said. I didn't go out at all that evening. My wife will vouch for me.

DI Fenway: Okay, so what if you'd gone to bed as normal and then left the house during the early hours? How would your wife have known if you'd slipped out for a while?

NL: [NL laughs] She'd have heard me get out of bed. The dog would have barked. He'd certainly have made a fuss when I came back. My wife's a light sleeper. She'd have known.

DI Fenway: Okay. Moving on: when did you return from your holiday?

NL: It would have been around the 8 November — I can check.

DI Fenway: We'll be checking ourselves. When did you hear about the death of Charlotte Walsh?

NL: Not until after I came back.

DI Fenway: How did you find out?

NL: I knew something was wrong when she didn't turn up to meet me. She'd never missed our rendezvous before. I went to the dental surgery where she worked and the first thing I saw was all the flowers. Then I looked her up online…

DI Fenway: Why didn't you come forward when you heard she'd been killed?

NL: Because it wasn't anything to do with me.

DI Fenway: We knew she had a secret boyfriend; it would have saved us a lot of time.

NL: I was… I am married — I didn't want to kick up dust. It wasn't serious, but it would have ruined everything for my family.

DI Fenway: How did you and Ms Walsh normally contact each other? We found no trace of your number on her phone.

NL: I made it clear to her we had to be careful, so we didn't use phones or social media at all. We had a regular meeting place. At the library on Green Road. Monday nights at 7pm. I told my wife I ran a school drama group.

Charlotte and I had an agreement to wait
fifteen minutes and leave if the other
person didn't show.

A note at the end stated that according to the airline, the
dates Larch had given were correct. His ticket had been scanned
ninety minutes before the flight and he was out of the country
until early November. A follow-up interview with Larch's wife
corroborated his alibi, but it still meant he was in London the
night Charlotte was killed.

It all looked perfectly watertight. Unless Mrs Larch was
lying...

60

The hall was full by the time I got to the Campion Hotel in Mayfair. I'd hung around reading the police files for too long and by then there was not time to go for the train. I ditched Plan A, then waited over ten minutes for a taxi at the corner of the high street.

I sneaked in at the back, but not before Miranda spotted me as I ducked down searching for a seat. Another black mark in my copybook, no doubt. At least I'd turned up.

There was a short interval after the initial speeches and I moseyed over to the display table at the side, not really reading anything, just biding my time watching people, taking in the surroundings. I recognised Betty Dixon from Miranda's exhibition, hovering around with her arm glued to Miranda's back, introducing her to people. I stayed out of the way.

It certainly was a posh event; plenty of dignitaries in the art world had turned up clad in long gowns or black tailcoats. Together with the opulent backdrop, the scene seemed to belong in another century.

I glanced up at the ostentatious chandelier in the centre of the gold and white domed ceiling. It sparkled like a waterfall. I wondered what it would look like from the upper balcony that ran around all four sides of the space. The intricate geometrical design in marble under my feet reminded me of patterns in a kaleidoscope I used to have as a child. It seemed a pity to stand on it. I wanted to clear all the people away, so I could take a proper look.

Someone tapped my shoulder and I spun round.

'Glad you made it.' Emily handed me a glass of bubbly.

'Only just,' I said with a grimace.

Her eyes trailed down my outfit. 'Blimey, you look like royalty,' she whispered. She glanced down at her drainpipe jeans under a long jacket with large splashes of orange and red. 'Cripes, I feel dreadfully underdressed in this.'

The jacket reminded me of one of Miranda's paintings.

'It makes you look arty though,' I said, with a chuckle, 'like you're meant to be here.'

Emily laughed. I couldn't imagine her being fazed by many things.

She looked up in awe, as I had done. 'I bet this ballroom spends most of its life hosting weddings,' she said with a hint of melancholy. She took a tiny sip of champagne. 'Have you spoken to Miranda?'

'Not yet. I think she's got more important people to see right now.'

'She's a bit wired, by the looks of things. Ralph is helping to calm her down.'

I followed Emily's line of sight and spotted him, looking smarmy, bent on one hip sweeping his hair back with his fingers. He had the air of a true gentlemen; charming, self-effacing, respectful. But I knew it was all fake. I turned away.

'Miranda said there's something a bit special lined up for the presentations,' Emily added, 'but she didn't say what.'

I took in the full space from right to left, wondering what

might be about to happen. A lone trumpeter parading on the balcony playing a fanfare? A golden carriage appearing through the double doors?

Someone rang a little bell at the front before I could reply.

'Ladies and gentleman, for the presentation of the awards, please take the door on your right into the entrance hall.'

'Ah, here we go.' Emily strode out. I followed her through. When I'd arrived originally, guests had been shown through to the ballroom using a side entrance, so it was the first time we'd caught sight of this impressive scene.

The hall was dominated by a grand staircase on a marble chessboard floor, surrounded by tall pillars. Two sets of stairs came down from the floor above, joined at the landing, then fanned out into the centre before us. It was breathtaking.

'Oh, God...' Emily put her hand over her mouth.

'I know... how amazing...'

I was aware she'd dropped her head beside me, searching for something in her handbag. 'I've got to find the loo,' she said, a pained look on her face.

'Are you okay?'

She briefly held her stomach. 'Sorry, not feeling too good. I'll find you later.' With that, she carved a path through the crowd and disappeared.

There was no trumpet voluntary, but what came next was equally as impressive. The awards came in different categories and when each one was announced, the winner appeared on the balcony and made their way down the imperious staircase to the sound of cheers and applause.

Miranda's turn came towards the end. She floated down the stairs like she was born to it; not even glancing at the red carpet, in spite of her ridiculously high wedges.

Just like during her exhibition, she was swamped with people afterwards wanting to congratulate her and ply her with questions. *Would she be selling work in any London galleries? What would she be doing with the prize money?*

I stayed back, watching her joyful face – her cheeks pink, her smile never ending – thrilled for her. I scanned the faces for Emily, but couldn't find her anywhere, so I left the celebrations and went in search of the nearest ladies' toilets. Perhaps she was still in there.

I waited by the basins until figures had emerged from every cubicle, but she didn't appear. I sent her a text, but didn't get a reply. I left it at that. If she was feeling ill, she wouldn't want me pestering her.

On the way back to the entrance hall, I spotted Ralph walking slowly ahead of me, chatting quietly with someone beside him. Two people were in front of me, so I couldn't see who it was. As the couple broke apart, I saw it was Emily with him. I slipped behind a tall pillar to stay out of sight.

Ralph had taken off his jacket, so was wearing only a dress shirt and trousers. The two of them turned to face each other and in an instant, I felt he was standing too close to her. It was as though she felt it too, because she stood back a fraction, holding her handbag in front of her chest like a barrier between them.

She shook her head and he cocked his on one side with a slimy smile. Everything about him was predatory; the way he leant too close, the way his eyes roamed blatantly into her cleavage, the way his gaze lingered on her hair as though he might reach out and stroke it.

I fought the urge to break cover and demand he get away from her. I was saved by his phone. He stopped ogling her and reached into his back pocket. As he looked at the screen, he nodded at Emily and held up his other hand to her in farewell.

As Emily walked on, Ralph turned round in my direction, pressing the keypad on his phone. A chill rippled up my breastbone and I gulped as his footsteps drew closer. I closed my eyes, desperately trying to conjure up something plausible to say when at any second, he'd see me.

Then his steps stopped. He must have taken a detour into the carpeted cloakroom.

Seconds later, Miranda burst out of a door up ahead, looking flustered. 'Ralph?' she called out. 'Where are you? What happened?'

I curbed my sisterly urge to rush towards her.

Within seconds, Ralph shot out of the cloakroom, looking like a burglar caught with his hands in the till. I stayed where I was, making sure I could see them both.

There was no sign of his phone. I scanned his backside for the telltale shape, but it wasn't there.

Miranda grabbed his arm. 'You were meant to be there when Professor Acton spoke to me. I wanted you to meet him.'

'Sorry, honey,' Ralph said, wrapping his arm around her. 'Someone spilt wine down my front and I had to wash it out.' He unhooked his arm and tugged at his shirt as if examining the result. 'Looks presentable, I think. I've just spent the last five minutes under the hand dryer in the toilet.' He kissed her cheek. 'I didn't want to stand beside you looking like a dog's dinner,' he said with a chuckle.

He glanced behind him towards the entrance to the cloakroom, as if he was reluctant to leave. Miranda interlaced her fingers with his and led the way back to the entrance hall.

I was left with silence. There was no one around. The resonant marble floor would have alerted me if there had been.

I took the chance and slipped into the cloakroom. One minute he had his phone, the next he didn't. He must have left it in there somewhere. I began separating coats and jackets that hung from a long rack, then when I found nothing, I moved on to a couple of chairs by the wall.

I couldn't believe I was snooping around like this, but it was too good an opportunity to pass up. Ralph's body language with Emily and his blatant lies to explain his absence had instantly set alarm bells ringing inside my head. All because Miranda wouldn't listen to my protestations about Ralph. I couldn't blame her. All I could offer were vague hints of my unease. I needed proof. She had to see something concrete with her own eyes.

I moved past a collection of umbrellas to more coats. Then I found it. On another chair under a row of men's jackets. It was still switched on. I picked it up and pressed to light up the screen.

He'd been replying to a text when he'd been disturbed by Miranda's call. The words: *Let's arrange...* were as far as he'd got, so I swiped up to see what he was responding to. The previous message simply said *okay,* so I looked for the text Ralph had sent before that.

As I stared at it, my stomach scrunched into a tight ball:

How long is your hair and can you send a photo?

No wonder he'd left his mobile out of sight when he heard my sister calling him. I took a shot of the message with my own phone and was about to read more of the exchange, when I heard laughter. I threw down the phone and shuffled over to the long coats, in a genuine search of my own this time.

The couple I'd heard came in, followed by others as people began to leave. Soon the cloakroom would be packed. There was no more I could do.

Within seconds, I was out of there.

61

Once I was outside, I strode away from the emerging guests until I was alone. I rang Terry. When he didn't answer, I remembered he was at work, so I made my way home and rang him again from there. He sounded formal when he answered.

'Ralph could be involved with the hair-cutting murders,' I blurted out. 'We've got to get Fenway to arrest him now.'

'Hold your horses, Sam. What's going on?'

I hurried through a rundown of the interplay I'd just witnessed and the texts I'd found.

'And you're saying he could be responsible for three murders on the basis of a couple of vague texts?'

'He *could* be – and he's dating my sister.'

'Is she worried about him?'

The panic in my throat made me flounder. 'No. Not yet, but–'

'You think he's cheating on her?'

'Planning to, at the very least,' I said, being careful not to reveal anything I shouldn't about Ralph. 'It certainly looks like something unsavoury is going on.'

'If he's promiscuous, that's not great news, understandably, but you don't know the context of those few words you saw. And even if he's two-timing Miranda, it doesn't mean he's a serial killer.'

'Can't you get Fenway to look into him?'

'You'd need something more specific than this to initiate any kind of investigation. Just mentioning someone's long hair... I don't mean to sound patronising, but people talk about hair all the time.'

'But–'

Terry cut across me. 'Come to think of it, Ralph told me he was in France the week Hazel died. At a wine festival. He mentioned it when we left Miranda's exhibition to get more bottles. Showed me photos as we waited to be served in the off-licence.'

I stalled. 'So... maybe he was lying about the dates.' An uncomfortable silence sucked out all the air between us. 'You should have seen the way he looked at Emily. I've got a really bad feeling about him.'

Yet again I was confronted with my oath of confidentiality to Ralph. I couldn't get past it. I was only entitled to reveal information to anyone if a patient had broken the law or had revealed to me the intention to do so.

'I think you're overreacting, Sam. Your sister's with a new guy and your instinct's saying he's not right for her, but–'

'Can't you run a check on him? He's called Ralph Stone. He lives in Battersea. Can't you just see if he's got a criminal record?'

'No! I really can't. It's unethical and I'd be putting my job at risk. You of all people should know that.'

I let out a groan. I certainly did.

There was no way I could tell Terry about Ralph's grubby sexual history. Not yet. Terry was right. Ralph's behaviour didn't make him a killer. I didn't have enough to go on.

Catch twenty-two again.

I rang Emily a couple of times the following morning, but couldn't reach her. Her phone was switched off. I called Miranda instead.

'Hi, I just wanted to say how wonderful it was last night. I'm sorry I didn't get to speak to you.'

'That's okay.' She was crunching something in her mouth; cornflakes probably.

'It was a splendid do, I'm so proud of you!'

'Yeah, it was pretty special. Made a few new contacts. I'm going to talk to a gallery next week. Betty set it up. She's been brilliant.'

I'd caught Miranda at a buoyant time. She also seemed to have forgotten she was cross with me.

'Good turnout,' I said, edging my way towards the subject I really wanted to ask about. 'I saw Ralph and Emily.'

'Yeah – lots of artists from CCAP were there. Did you speak to anyone?'

'Only Emily. Have you heard from her since?'

'No. She got very upset about something at the ceremony. I didn't get a chance to ask her what had happened.'

'Oh, I thought she was unwell. She said she had stomach pains and went to the loo.'

Miranda made a little humming sound. 'No... I don't think it was that. Anyway, she left early. I hope she's okay.'

While Miranda chatted on about who was there and what people said, my mind was elsewhere. Could Emily's early departure have had anything to do with Ralph?

'Let me know if she gets in touch, will you?' I asked Miranda as we drew the call to a close.

I did some yoga postures in my sitting room and, just out of interest, tried on my tightest pair of jeans. For the first time in months I managed to get them over my hips. The top button still wouldn't fasten without a gargantuan intake of breath, but I was nearly there. I tugged them off with a flourish of jubilation. Running with Emily had made a huge difference already.

Fired up with my achievement, I pulled on my outdoor gear. It was time to take to the streets on my own for once. See how it felt. After all, Emily wouldn't be coming along with me forever.

Before I went, I checked my diary. Nothing planned for the weekend. Terry and I had talked about possibly going to a French film, but we hadn't finalised anything. I hated the way we'd left things the previous day so I rang his number.

'Are you at work?' I asked him.

'Not yet. I'm in at lunchtime. Are you okay?'

'I don't like the way we left things last time. I feel like we've fallen out.'

He chuckled. 'I'm not sure too much damage has been done.' I could hear Sibelius playing in the background, then the tinkle of cutlery. No doubt Terry was cooking something. 'I hope you can see why I can't run a police check on Miranda's new boyfriend.'

'Hmm... I suppose.' I felt a glint of frustration. 'It's just that I'm banging my head against a brick wall when I try to discourage her from seeing him.'

Terry coughed a staccato laugh. 'What's he done that's so dreadful? Apart from this text you mentioned... which, let's face it, isn't exactly damning. And the way he was looking at Emily.'

'I can't really say.'

'What do you mean? Is there some kind of issue here?'

'Yes and no. It's tricky.'

'Oh, wait a minute.' Terry's voice took on a hoity-toity tone I'd rarely heard before. 'Do you and Ralph have history?'

It was my turn to laugh. 'No way! Well... not in the way you think.'

'You *do* have history!' There was joviality in his voice, but not enough to hide the starchy undertone.

I didn't answer.

He went on. 'Did you know him before he and Miranda got together?'

I hesitated.

'It's a simple question.'

'I... he...'

'You *did* know him. It doesn't matter. I mean your previous relationships aren't anything to do with me, but I can't see why you're hiding it.'

'I'm not.'

'You are. You just admitted you have history with this guy, but you're also telling me you don't.'

'We were never in that kind of relationship.'

'What then?'

'I can't say.'

His voice shot up in register. 'You can't say. Sam, I'm... how can I put it? I'm disappointed. I thought you of all people would value honesty above everything. I thought it would be a given between us. I'd hoped we wouldn't keep secrets or bend the truth.' I could feel him slipping away from me. 'I don't know what to say.'

'Think about it,' I said, my voice clear and strong. 'How might I know Ralph in a different way?'

There was a prickly silence. Awkwardness. I was about to make things clearer when he spoke again with conviction. 'Listen, I've got to work again at the weekend, so that film we talked about... we'll need to give it a miss. Sorry.'

With that the phone went dead.

62

I ran to the common at full pelt, brimming with rage. The misunderstanding with Terry was totally unfounded. He'd got the wrong end of the stick entirely and now we'd fallen out. It was stupid. Pointless. And I'd let it happen.

I skirted a group of tall trees and ploughed across the wet grass. I hadn't done any stretches and just as I reached the playground, my ankle tweaked. With the next step I was forced to pull up.

Now I was furious with myself for not doing what I was supposed to do. 'You must warm up before you run,' Emily always said. 'Every time.'

I hobbled to the nearest bench and sank down. The rain on the soggy wood bled through to my skin in seconds. Shit!

I felt for my phone in my anorak pocket and called Fenway. Perhaps he might get things moving with Ralph. I was still jittery about something happening to Miranda; every moment she was with him she could be at risk. I kept revisiting the creepy way he'd glared at Emily's hair too.

'Is that all you've got? This one text,' Fenway exclaimed, an almost-exact repeat of Terry's response.

'There's more, but it could compromise my job.'

'Oh – that confidentiality business, you mean.'

'Exactly. Ralph was a patient.' There, I'd finally said it.

'If you were in a court case, any therapist would be required by law to hand over all relevant patient files.'

'I know, but we're nowhere near that, are we?'

'You might as well come clean now. Save all the pussyfooting around. You see my point?' That little phrase of his was starting to annoy me.

'Okay, but if you find something incriminating about this guy, he mustn't know the tip-off came from me. It could cost me my job. Can you agree to that? Can you promise me?'

For once I heard a glimmer of empathy. 'I realise you're treading a fine line on this secondment. Half-psychologist, half-investigator. I'll do my best.'

I only hoped his best was good enough.

'So, what's he done?' Fenway asked.

I explained how Ralph had come to me for therapy regarding his sexual practices. 'He likes three in a bed, but he doesn't make this clear at all at the start,' I said, 'and he's also a sadist.'

The DI seemed to find it amusing. 'What you've told me is not exactly a big deal. Some women *like* that kind of thing. It's up to individuals to come forward if he's assaulted them.'

'But it's not straightforward rape or assault. It starts as consensual sex, then turns abusive.'

'Maybe it's some kind of S&M thing. The stats say one in ten people experiment with it. That includes women too.'

'I'm not being naïve here,' I snapped. 'S&M is totally acceptable and plays a valid part in some relationships – when the couple trust each other. That's the key thing. Trust. That's not how it goes with Ralph's little operation. That's why he's always on the prowl for his next victim.'

Fenway sounded intrigued. 'What does he do exactly?'

'He gets friendly with woman one, has sex for a while, gets bored, then brings woman two into the mix. He sets up the threesome which involves sadistic acts, beatings, bondage – but only to woman one, then he drops her. Woman two usually disappears too – they're often scared and no longer interested. Ha – I wonder why? If she doesn't scarper, he finds another woman.'

'Don't any of them report him?'

'Ralph told me no one had. Not one. That was his prime defence. But maybe he *has* been accused. That's where you come in. I need to see if there could be links between Ralph Stone and Lorna, Charlotte or Hazel.'

'Hmm... Lorna and now Ralph – two ex-patients coming to light in a matter of days. Bit odd, isn't it?'

'Not when you consider that I see around twenty-five patients every week and some only come for a couple of sessions. It's not surprising they crop up from time to time.'

'I keep forgetting how long you've been in this business,' he said, his tone laden with sarcasm.

'Are you going to do something about this or not?'

'Okay, okay. It's worth looking into and I'll try to keep your name out of it.'

After my shower, I sat on the bed with Lorna's final tape next to me. I should have listened to it sooner, whether I felt up to it or not. It could be too useful to put off any longer.

I slipped the cassette into the machine, then hovered over the button without pressing it. Maybe I should do it later and prime myself first with a brandy.

No. It could hold vital information that could lead to her killer. I needed to do it for Lorna. I pressed the play button and closed my eyes.

As I let Lorna's words fill the space around me, it didn't take long for my tears to bubble up to the surface. She was swept up in the glamour of the fashion show the college had organised, chattering on about the music, the posters, the dresses. She was in high spirits, looking forward to it. In many ways it was harder to bear than if she'd been upset.

'You helped me see how many positive things there are in my life,' she said. 'Thank you.'

Hearing those words was heart-wrenchingly poignant, knowing how little time she had left.

Then Lorna went quiet. I strained to hear, not wanting to miss anything.

'I've got a bit of a secret,' she said in a whisper. I could visualise her playing with the locket that was always around her neck. 'I've met this guy. He's been helping me a lot with the show.'

'Ah, you like him?'

'Yeah. He's twenty. And cute. We're sort of going out, but he's very shy and not much has happened yet.' She stopped. 'Silly to bring it up really. I haven't told anyone else, but I thought if I mentioned it here, you could kind of look after the secret for me, now our sessions have finished.'

'How do you mean?'

'Telling you about him makes him real. It takes him and me beyond just something in my head. Does that sound stupid?'

'Not at all. I feel very privileged. I'll look after your secret for you with pleasure.'

I heard the chair creak. She must have got up to leave. 'I'd better tell you his name,' she said, laughter in her voice.

'If you want to.'

'It's Chris.'

63

———

I stopped the tape with a shudder.

Chris...

It couldn't be, could it?

Hurriedly, I did the maths. Pitlock's date of birth indicated he'd recently turned thirty. It fitted.

Police had discounted him for Charlotte's demise on the basis of the estimated time of death, but it was only an estimate. The time frame was between nine in the evening and three thirty in the morning. It seemed pretty open-ended. What if the pathologists were mistaken by just half an hour? Chris could have found a way to get to Primrose Hill in that time. And what if he had also known Lorna?

I toyed with this new potential piece of the puzzle, but knew it wouldn't be enough for Fenway. How many twenty-year-olds called Chris were there in London, at any given time? Thousands. I could hear Fenway's annoying voice in my head: *You see my point...*

～

I slept on it, thinking my nocturnal subconscious might help me make a decision about what to do next, but I still had no idea once morning broke. By then, Fenway had left a message:

Person of interest has no criminal record

I called him.

'This is Ralph Stone we're talking about, right?'

'Uh-huh.'

'Are you sure? No complaints made against him? Ever?'

'Diddly-squat. He's never been in for questioning over anything. Not even got a speeding fine.'

I swore under my breath.

'It's good news for your sister, isn't it?'

'Not entirely... he's still got a very dubious track record.'

'There's some other bad news, I'm afraid,' Fenway said. 'We can't find any links to your three cases for Stephen McVey, your friend's pestering ex. He was in jail serving his GBH sentence when Charlotte Walsh was killed. He was playing a rugby match on the day Hazel fell off the balcony. We're still waiting to confirm an alibi for 2010, but already that's his involvement with two of the three deaths wiped out.'

I ended the call with a heavy heart. As far as I could see that left only Neville Larch and Chris Pitlock as potential suspects.

I was crushing an avocado and spreading it on sourdough toast when I finally heard from Emily.

'Thank goodness you're okay,' I said, sucking melted butter from my fingers. 'I was getting worried about you.'

'I'm sorry. You shouldn't have worried. I'm fine.' She didn't sound fine. 'I let my phone run out of juice, that's all. I didn't feel like being sociable with anyone.'

'You seemed unwell at the ceremony, then Miranda said you were upset about something...' I let my words hang there simply as facts. I didn't want to probe or make Emily feel I was pushing her into explaining herself.

'Yeah. I know. I'll tell you later. You up for a run or are you seeing your bloke later on?'

'I'm up for a run, if you are.'

'Good. Shall we try somewhere different tonight? I fancy running along the Thames.'

We arranged to meet at Waterloo station at eight.

64

Emily was jogging on the spot under the station clock when I came through the ticket barrier. She looked tired, her face in shadow inside her thick hoodie. Even so, I could see her cheeks looked raw, her eyes puffy like the flesh of an oyster.

She didn't make eye contact, so I didn't ask any questions. She'd tell me in her own good time if she wanted to.

We began with a loose jog when we left the station, passing the bars and restaurants towards the walkway beside the river. Heavy rain and a stiff northerly breeze had kept tourists away. Up ahead, the blue lights of the London Eye oozed across the surface of the water, the white face of Big Ben replicating the moon. Beyond Westminster Bridge, the spires of the Houses of Parliament poked the patchy charcoal sky, reminding me of fantasy castles in animated films. Beside us, the river murmured and lapped. I eased into a lengthier stride alongside Emily, letting my body find its own cadence.

'I could never have too much of this view,' she said, staring out across the water.

'I know what you mean. I love this area.' As I glanced down, I noticed trails of mist reaching us, wrapping around our ankles, turning the walkway into swirling whirlpools.

'How's your sleep been?' I asked.

Ahead, the white orbs along the walls of the embankment hung as liquid light, floating against the black sky.

'Oh, crap. The irony is you don't have to *do* anything to get to sleep. That's the whole point. You just have to switch off. I can't even get that right.'

I hadn't seen this side of her before. Coloured by despondency and failure. She'd always appeared forthright and eminently capable, even when she was out of sorts. It took me by surprise.

'I struggle to sleep sometimes. Switching off means letting go. For those of us who like to be in control, it goes against the grain.'

She tossed up her eyes. 'Tell me about it.'

When I looked up, a quicksilver halo had surrounded the moon. I was tempted to stop, to take in the scene in its glorious entirety, but it was too cold; we had to keep moving.

'My dad was a poor sleeper,' I told her. 'Used to spend half the night doing chores. Like polishing his shoes.'

She managed a chuckle. 'My brother, Kipper, annoys the hell out of me – he can fall asleep at the click of a finger. He slept through a gas explosion in our street once.'

We ran without words for a stretch, with only the slap of our trainers against the pavement, the shunting of our breath. The rain was getting heavier, batting into our faces, lashing into our eyes and forcing them shut. It soaked my woolly hat and dripped inside my collar.

Without warning, she grabbed my arm. 'Careful,' she gasped, pointing to my feet. I looked down to find a pizza with one bite out of it discarded on the pavement.

'Could have gone flying...' she said, steering me around it.

'What a shame. It even had pineapple on it.'

She made a puking sound. 'I hate them. Used to work in an Italian joint. Since then I can't bear those little balls of mozzarella. And the smell of oregano makes me throw up.'

'Miranda had a thing about sherbet fountains when she was about ten. Only she was the opposite. She was obsessed with them.'

'Those yellow paper tubes... with liquorice sticking out?'

'They're the ones. Miranda kept a stockpile without anyone knowing. She'd have at least three before bedtime. Every night.' My words were clipped as I snatched my breaths. 'We'd find half-eaten ones in her sock drawer... under her pillow. . hidden in her hiking boots. That summer, we came across boxes of them in the garden shed. But the mice had got to them before she could. Such a mess. Put me off them for life.'

Emily giggled and I felt a tingle of pleasure at making her laugh. 'I'll have to buy her one. See what she says!'

We ran through a park, away from the raw exposure of the main road, distanced from the heckling of traffic It was suddenly hushed, as though we'd crossed into another world.

'It was nice you were worried about me,' she said, without any preamble. 'I had a bit of a meltdown after Miranda's ceremony.'

'Are you okay now?'

'Getting there. I had a nasty shock.'

She said no more and I thought that was all she was going to give me. She reached into her pocket and pulled out a tissue to blow her nose, then spoke again.

'My friend died falling down stairs years ago. It was a big grand staircase like the one at Miranda's award night.'

I recalled Emily's reaction when we'd walked into the entrance hall. I'd thought, like me, she was in awe of the majesty, but instead she was calling out in horror.

She went on. 'The shoes she had on were too big and she slipped. Tumbled down around ten steps. But that in itself wasn't what killed her. On the way down she cracked her head open on the exposed stone beside the carpet.'

I reached out and squeezed her arm. 'Oh, my god, I'm so sorry. What an awful reminder.' I couldn't tell if the water coursing down her face was rain or rain diluted with tears.

'Miranda's ceremony brought it all back. Sorry I scared you.'

'Is that why you had to rush to the loo?'

'I thought I was going to throw up. I didn't have time to explain.'

Still the rain came down, thrashing the pavement, stabbing our faces with thousands of icy needles. The adversity seemed to bring us together, fighting the ravages of winter side by side.

'I left straight away.' She let out a moan. 'Or I tried to. I got caught by Ralph before I could get away. He was asking me if I knew when Miranda's birthday was. I said I hadn't a clue. He was a bit weird actually. He stands way too close. Stares too much. He's a bit creepy.'

'I know what you mean.' I decided to test something out even though it meant telling a white lie. 'He tried to touch my hair once.'

'Oh, God – yes, me too! What is it about men and long hair? I suppose Miranda's hair is really short – maybe he misses running his hands through thick curls or something. Maybe he has some kind of fetish about it.'

Her words were like barbed wire across my face. 'I'd be very careful around him,' I warned her. 'I don't like him one bit.'

65

In spite of literally being soaked to the skin, I felt categorically euphoric when I got home. That's endorphins for you. In fact, those feel-good chemicals had sent us into fits of hysterics by the end. We'd found a stretch of deep puddles near the Royal Festival Hall and stamped in them with both feet together, like little kids. We danced and messed about as if we were drunk.

'When are we running next?' she'd asked, kicking a cascade of water as far as she could.

'Not sure. The new man of my dreams and I have had a tiny falling out.'

'Already?! That's not good. You need to sort that out, girl. We'll run on Monday, shall we? Give you the weekend to fix your love life.'

I grimaced, stepping away from the last pool. 'Got anything nice planned?'

'I'm working Saturday morning. Then the girl downstairs is helping me paint my sitting room. On Sunday I'm supposed to be having lunch with a guy from the gym.'

'Whooo,' I called out childishly.

She threw up her eyes, but nevertheless looked bashful. 'At the place around the corner from Clapham Junction as it happens. We've been running past it. French place.'

'Camille's Bistro? I know it.'

'Any good?'

'Worth a visit. Definitely.'

That night I had harrowing dreams. It took me by surprise after feeling so buoyant. Maybe I was too hyper when I got into bed, but my brain wouldn't settle down. Like a terrier, it jumped from one thought to another, tugging and gnawing, in a bid to get my attention.

A familiar gurgle charged through the ancient pipes running alongside my bedroom and I heard the front door close. Someone coming in or going out?

I closed my eyes, then realised I must have opened them, because I was staring at the powdery shapes of the curtains, the cupboards. I watched the way triangles of light appeared on the ceiling and slid over the wardrobe every time a car passed by. Sleep felt a long way off.

In the early hours, I got up and made cocoa and after that I must have slept, because by morning the remaining wisps of dreams were already haunting me.

They were about Chris Pitlock. I could picture him from several photographs I'd seen on the police files. His cheeks were hollow, his mouth rounded into a pout. His eyes appeared sunken as if he was shrinking back from the world with something to hide.

In my dreamworld he was dragging Lorna out of prickly bushes onto the railway line, then he was in a room, squashing a pillow over Charlotte's face.

Neither soft classical music on the radio nor the nutty molasses aroma of brewing coffee could shake those images from my mind. As I held a hot flannel to my face in the bathroom, I knew that even if Fenway held his tongue long enough to hear me out, he wouldn't take my suspicions about Chris any further. Lorna's voice on the tape had sent my pulse racing when she mentioned the right name and the right age. But I had no actual evidence – only the frantic urge to do something more to find it.

I pulled on the first dry clothes I could find and opened my laptop. Once again, I scrolled through the police reports of the three murders, one by one. The answer, the truth, was right there under my nose somewhere. If only I could see it.

I had a choice. I could sit there fretting as I stared at the screen or I could get out and do something. What held me back was simple. I wasn't meant to interview anyone involved with the cases. I'd already had my wrists slapped for doing just that. Without the opportunity to speak to people and find out more, however, the whole exercise seemed pointless. My hands were tied.

The jangling of my phone burst through my thoughts like a bell hanging right over my head. It was DCS Claussen. My heartbeat pattered as I said hello.

'DI Fenway has kept me informed of your progress, she said, her tone starchy. No *How are you?* Or *Good to talk to you.* 'I'm sure it's not a reflection on your capabilities, Dr Willerby, but I'm not sure we're making a great deal of headway.'

'What? I disagree,' I jumped in defiantly. 'We've linked three murder cases now and new suspects have been coming to light. I'm not sure what more–'

She cut across me, ignoring my response. 'I think it was a little optimistic on our part to revisit cold cases from this angle. I'm sorry you've wasted your time.'

Wasted my time?!

She said it in that bogus 'apologetic' tone people use when they know they're rubbing salt into a wound. I wanted to fling the phone at the wall.

'We gave you an extra week, Dr Willerby, but I think it might be best to call it a day.'

That was her polite way of saying I was utterly useless. I stood still but the floor beneath me felt like it was shifting. She hadn't finished. 'St Luke's are expecting you back on Monday.'

Monday? My eyes were wild with outrage. But there wasn't much I could say. Within seconds the call was over. I chucked the phone onto the sofa in disgust. I'd been 'sacked'.

With that thought came a burst of adrenaline. I had no more to lose.

I jumped up in search of a pen. Then wrote down an address from the police file and stuffed it in my pocket. Without bothering with breakfast, I grabbed my coat, hurried down the communal stairs and caught the first bus over to Stockwell.

66

The bus left me on the edge of a high-rise estate. Each tower block was distinctive, however, with its own unique daubing of graffiti. As I strode down steps into a central square, lads doing wheelies on bikes criss-crossed the open space, making a point of narrowly missing me. Women carrying plastic carrier bags, many also pushing buggies, skirted the edges with their heads down.

Further on, groups of teenagers were hanging around watching me. Others sat on walls banging their heels into the bricks. Most were smoking, empty cans of beer strewn on the ground. Loud reggae music came from somewhere. Even at ten in the morning, it felt intimidating.

On the journey over, I'd made a plan about how I was going to play this. I hated the idea of deception, but if it ultimately led to the police arresting a serial killer, it was going to be worth it. I swatted Fenway's disdainful face out of my mind. Then I thought of Terry and gulped hard. If he found out what I was up to he'd be simmering with disapproval too. But I needed to do this.

A woman edging towards fifty answered the door. She wore a

pink miniskirt and tight low-cut top. Her legs were bare. Chestnut roots bled through her blonde hair.

'Mrs Pitlock?'

'Might be. Who's asking?' She held the edge of the door firmly, giving the impression of someone well-practised at slamming it shut.

'I'm Dr Willerby from St Luke's Hospital, near London Bridge.' I held up the photo ID card I wore around my neck. 'I'm involved in research looking into–'

'Bugger off!' she snarled.

'There's a fee,' I called out, just as the gust of air from the slammed door hit me in the face.

The door opened again slowly, seemingly of its own volition. Her face slid into view. 'A fee?'

'We usually offer between one to two hundred pounds,' I said in a matter-of-fact tone. 'Depending on how useful the information is to us and how willing people are to–'

'What information?'

A couple of front doors on the same floor had opened. A little black girl wandered out of one of them, sucking a lolly, and at the other, a woman in a dressing gown was leaning against the door frame, chewing gum, her eyes glued to me.

'May I come in?' I said, pulling my gaze back to Mrs Pitlock.

She grunted something and stood back, then led me through to a sitting room, heated like a sauna by a roaring gas fire. Mrs Pitlock gave a cursory wave to the nearest sofa and flopped into a rocking chair, which squeaked as it tipped back with her weight. I perched on the edge of the cushion, forced into that position by collapsing stacks of knitting magazines behind me.

'So what do I have to do and when do I get the money?'

She was at least two stone overweight with chubby white flesh bulging out above her waistband. Judging by the lattice design imprinted on her cheek resembling a nearby cushion, I'd say she'd been fast asleep until I'd rung the bell.

'We understand there's been some renewed interest in your son, Chris, regarding the tragic death of his fiancée.'

Mrs Pitlock threw me a fierce look. 'How does St Luke's know about that?'

'I'm sorry, I can't reveal my sources,' I said, bluffing my way through as I went along. 'What we're interested in is how bringing it all up again has affected you and your son. Mental health is big in the news these days, as you might be aware. We're looking into whether people think the police are sensitive enough when handling this kind of thing.'

Mrs Pitlock took a laboured breath. 'Sure, it's shaken us all up again. That poor girl's death was nothing to do with Chris,' she said, picking up a couple of knitting needles embedded in a pile of lime-coloured wool that had been stuffed down the side of her seat. 'I'm making a pair of gloves for him.' She waved a leaflet at me, showing the pattern.

'Complicated...' I said, blinking hard. They resembled something you might make for a ten-year-old for a Halloween party.

She shrugged, as if she made such items all the time.

'Are you happy to go ahead with the interview?'

'And you'll pay me at the end?'

I hesitated. 'It doesn't quite work like that. I have to take my information away and... once it's processed we sort out the paperwork for the payment.'

I hated myself for my blatant lies, but knew I'd pay her out of my own pocket, no matter what she was able to tell me.

'Yeah, all right then,' she said.

67

I pulled out a spiral-bound notebook and pen. Mrs Pitlock smoothed back her hair and made herself comfortable, as though she'd been transported to a television studio.

I plunged in. 'Great – to start with, can you tell me which schools Chris went to? Was he born around here?'

'Why do you have to know all that?'

'We need to get a bit of background about your son first, Mrs Pitlock. You know, get a sense of who he is.'

She gave me the details from infant upwards and I jotted them down. I was looking for any links with Lorna.

I scanned the room, noticing a box of tools and a white hard hat in the corner. 'Does Chris still live with you?'

'Yeah. When the wedding fell through, he never moved out. Been here ever since.'

'What are his hobbies?'

She looked confused. 'Well, he works.'

'What about his free time, what kind of things does he like to do?'

'Oh, you know, football, going down the pub, playing darts.

Has a flutter on the horses. He goes fishing when he can, collects them toy soldiers. Is that the kind of thing you mean?'

I nodded. 'Has he ever been interested in fashion, at all?'

She spat out a hoot of laughter. 'Have you seen him?! He wears nothing but jeans and combat gear, like those army waistcoats and military jackets. His wardrobe is green and grey, that's about it.'

'Was he living at home in 2010?'

'Yeah.' Her eyes strayed up from her needles with suspicion. 'What's so special about then?'

'I'm just wondering about his girlfriends before Charlotte.'

'If he was seeing anyone then, he never mentioned it. He's a private lad. Always has been. Never says much. One of the quiet ones, you know?'

'Right.'

'He was doing training on mending washing machines in 2010, I think, then he moved that summer on to clearing drains. Didn't last long though. Left that and went on to electricals. He was taken on by the council a couple of years later. He does street maintenance; sorting out street lights, traffic lights, holding up those stop-and-go lollipops when there's roadworks and stuff.'

'Did he ever mention anyone called Lorna at that time?'

The clickety-click of Mrs Pitlock's knitting needles stopped in mid-stitch. 'Lorna? Nine years ago? Dunno. Maybe.'

'Lorna Sullivan? Very pretty girl with long blonde hair – she'd have been around the same age as Chris in 2010.'

Mrs Pitlock looked like she was reaching back into the past in an attempt to grab hold of something.

She blew out a breath. 'Dunno. Sorry. You'd need to ask him. You gonna ask him for a chat, so he can get paid too?'

'Um... possibly. We're most interested in the views of family and people close to "persons of interest" at the moment.'

I cringed inwardly. Without doubt, my line of questioning sounded ludicrous. I certainly didn't want to talk to her son. I knew I'd be stepping over the line by a mile. It might even seriously jeopardise the case.

She shrugged. No doubt all she could see were pound signs before her eyes and the nitty-gritty of the what and why didn't interest her in the least.

I asked a few further general questions of the kind she was probably expecting, but it didn't lead to anything. All in all, it was a useless visit. I decided to call it a day.

I gave her my thanks and stood up. 'This is all very much confidential at this stage, so we do ask everyone to keep these visits to themselves.' I tapped the side of my nose. 'It's all separate from the police too, so it might be better if you don't mention this if they ever get in touch about anything.'

'What – don't tell anyone?'

'That's right. Some people have had to forfeit their fee because they've told other people and then bits and pieces have ended up in the press.'

'Oh, right. So I won't get my money unless I keep my gob shut.'

'Best not take the risk. I'm glad you understand.'

It was hard to imagine a time when I'd hated myself more than in that moment. I felt physically sick preying on the poverty and naivety of this woman who had committed no crime of any kind.

'Better have your number then,' she said. I wrote it on a scrap of paper for her.

In my bid to get out of there as quickly as possible, I stumbled and knocked over another stack of magazines teetering on the edge of a coffee table.

'Sorry,' I said, picking them up. They weren't her ubiquitous knitting magazines. The top one was a brochure with a villa on the front and a mountain in the background.

Mrs Pitlock was right behind me so I handed it to her. She tutted. 'Ah, that ain't going to happen no more,' she said dolefully.

'You were thinking of a holiday?'

'Nah, my husband came into some money and we were thinking of moving out there. To Spain. One of them places in the sun. Like the ones you see on TV.'

'Sounds lovely.'

'Chris was gonna come too. He was gonna put in his share for it. Arthur and me don't have much family here and I don't have any proper friends – not really. We was gonna make a fresh start...'

'Oh, I see. But you've changed your mind?'

'Sort of. I found an advert and called the number and this woman came round. Played us a DVD and gave us brochures like this.' She rapped her nails against it. 'It got Chris and me chatting about it. He never usually says much, but he liked the idea.' She sniffed and the bloom of cheeriness faded from her face. 'We were all set to put down a deposit, but things got a bit uncomfortable.'

'Can I ask why?'

'We realised who she was. Her family had done wrong by us in the past. It was all very unfortunate and brought up a lot of hurt, I can tell you, but it wasn't her fault. She was a babe in arms at the time. Anyway, I said I wanted to let bygones be bygones. I said I'd be happy to go ahead.' The edges of her mouth drooped. 'But, she stopped coming soon after.' She dropped the magazine back onto the table. 'So we put it on the back burner.'

I felt the niggle of something scratching at the back of my brain. 'Did the woman come from an estate agents?'

'Yeah, one of those posh ones in Dulwich Village.'

I felt a jolt in my chest. 'Can you remember the woman's name? The one who talked to you about it?'

Mrs Pitlock stared at her bare feet. 'Of course. Friendly girl. Chris asked her lots of questions and she knew her stuff.' She shuffled past an empty bird cage. 'I've got her details here, somewhere.'

She reached into a straw beach bag and plucked out a business card.

My hand shook as I took it:

Hazel Hart
   Sales Agent, Home and Abroad
   Dentworths in Dulwich

68

I raced down the concrete stairs and kept going until I was clear of the estate. It was too noisy to use my phone on the main road, so I hurried to the bus stop. As I clutched the mobile in my slippery hands, I was chanting to myself: *She'd been there! Hazel had been there!*

I had to tell Fenway. I had to make sure they got their hands on Chris Pitlock as soon as possible. Not only had he got a strong motive as the jilted fiancé for Charlotte's murder, it was clear that he'd met Hazel and they'd chatted together in his own home.

The traffic was heavy and with the bus nowhere in sight, a bunch of commuters had rapidly built up around me. With my thumb hovering over Fenway's name on my contacts list, I had second thoughts. There were too many people about for the kind of call I had to make.

I pulled out of the queue and wandered over to a low wall opposite a church. I sat down. I had a massive problem on my hands. By visiting Mrs Pitlock I'd defied Claussen's authority hook, line and sinker. My plan had been to tell Fenway that any new information had come purely from Lorna's confidential tapes. But Lorna died in 2010. How could I tell Fenway there was a link between Hazel, the most recent murder victim, and Chris Pitlock without getting myself into a shitload of trouble?

I really shouldn't have done the 'interview'. Even if it had been with every good intention.

I slipped the phone back into my coat pocket. I couldn't tell Fenway. Not yet.

There was only one thing I could do.

Now I knew there was a definite link between Hazel and Chris, I had to go back. I had to speak to Mrs Pitlock again. I'd only scratched the surface.

With my insides churning, I rang Mrs Pitlock, using the number I'd got from the police file.

'What? Straight away?'

'I've just spoken to my manager,' I lied. 'She's delighted about our conversation and is eager to hear more. It might mean another fifty pounds.'

'Oh, all right then,' she muttered.

On the way back up, I had a call from Terry.

'I'm a complete idiot,' came his words.

'Why, what's happened?'

'I've just twigged what you were getting at with Ralph Stone. I kept going over it in my head, then the penny finally dropped. What a dimwit. Ralph's been a patient of yours, hasn't he?'

I chuckled. 'Yes!' I wanted to skip into the air with joy now that the kink in communication between us had been ironed out.

Terry went on. 'And, of course you can't say anything about him. I'm so sorry I put you in that position.'

'It was mostly my fault. I didn't know how to explain.'

'I feel terrible.' His voice dropped into a deep slow drawl. 'I missed you last night. We could have been together and I got myself into a silly huff and–'

'I know. I'm sorry too. Let's do tonight, shall we? Shall I come to you again?'

'You're not going to tempt me with one of your culinary delights then?'

'Er... not if we're going to keep seeing each other.'

He laughed and I wished I could reach out and hug him.

'Come over for eight,' he said.

Mrs Pitlock was halfway through eating a muffin when she let me back in.

'Do you want some?' she asked, waving the wrapper at me, dropping crumbs.

'No thanks.'

I took off my coat in the hall, prepared this time for the blast of Saharan heat that awaited me.

'So what do we have to talk about now?' She returned to the squeaky rocking chair.

Out came my notebook again. 'The idea of relocating to Spain...' I said, figuring out on the spot how I could feasibly bring Hazel back into the discussion. 'Was that originally your idea or Chris's?'

'Both, really. I rang to arrange the first visit.'

'You said Chris asked Hazel lots of questions. Did you think leaving the UK was a good idea for him?'

'To help him move on, you mean?'

I nodded.

'He never mentioned it specifically, but it crossed my mind, certainly. He was terribly shaken up after Charlie left him. Then when she was found dead... and all that. It was a lot for him to cope with.'

'Of course.'

'This idea about Spain certainly perked him up.' She gave me a sly grin. 'And the girl who came... I mean, she was gorgeous, no two ways about it. His eyes lit up when she showed up at the door, I can tell you. All that lovely long hair.' Mrs Pitlock plucked a crumb from her cleavage, popped it in her mouth and licked her lips. 'I joked she must trip over it getting off the bus. Not to her face, obviously.'

I joined her in laughter, my heart pattering fast.

'Do you have any photos of Chris and Charlotte you could let me see?'

'Not many, everything's online these days, isn't it? There'd be plenty on Chris's phone, if you wanted to wait for him.'

'No, no – I don't need to bother him.'

'Arthur's probably got a few too, but he's gone down the bookies as per usual. Got a day off.'

Mrs Pitlock tackled the living room assault course and disappeared. Finally, she made it back with a dusty photo album under her arm. She sat beside me on the sofa and opened it between us, flicking pages towards the back. I recognised Charlotte; there were various pictures, but none of them very good. Blurred close-ups of the pair of them, pictures taken on a pier somewhere, others in a nightclub.

'Charlotte had lovely long hair,' I mused innocently.

Mrs Pitlock pressed her greasy finger fondly into Charlotte's face. 'Yeah, we talked about how she was going to put it up into something fancy with flowers on her wedding day.'

'Did Chris talk about her hair much?'

She puffed out her bottom lip. 'Not specially.'

'Did Chris like going out with women with long hair?' The

words were out before I realised how inflammatory they sounded, but she didn't seem to notice.

'Never known him date anyone else except Charlie. Like I said – he was a shy kid growing up.' She stopped to think. 'Someone said she cut it all off in the end. Charlie did. Such a shame. Wasn't long after that she got… she was… you know.' Mrs Pitlock's gaze fell sombrely to her bare feet, then she straightened up. 'Would you like to see some pictures of Chris as a kid?'

It was the last thing I wanted, but it seemed impolite to decline. She was in her element. With a son who didn't talk to her much, a husband at the betting shop on his day off, and with no real friends to leave behind if she moved abroad, she struck me as a lonely soul.

She drew the album onto her lap and flicked through the pages so fast I couldn't see any of them properly. All I noticed was that several pages had white spaces, as though various snaps had been removed. As she reached the page she was looking for, a loose picture flew out. I picked it up from the carpet.

'Oh, that's Roy, Chris's dad. He's not with us anymore.'

I made a warm consoling sound. 'I'm sorry to hear that.'

'Don't be. Long time ago. I've got Arthur now…' She tailed off.

In spite of her words, she gazed longingly at the photograph. 'You know, this is the best picture I have of him.' She flipped it over and I caught the date in pencil on the back. 'He'd finally had his hair cut properly. He used to snip it himself in front of the bathroom mirror. Men do that, don't they? Make a pig's ear of it. Not that day though. He was sitting smug as pie in the kitchen with a smart trim when I came home.'

She found a space on the correct page and slid the picture under the transparent plastic film.

She closed the album, seemingly forgetting why she'd

opened it. 'Chris will be back any minute,' she said brightly. 'Looks like you'll get to meet him after all.'

I took a horrified glance at the door and shot up, grabbing my coat. That was my cue to get out of there. And fast.

'I'm very sorry,' I said, making a point of checking my watch. 'I really must be going.'

69

———

I was in a daze as I made my way back home. I could see pictures from the album flashing before my eyes; Mrs Pitlock's words coming and going in my ears, as I attempted to process what she'd told me.

Were there any crucial clues embedded in our encounter that put Chris in the frame as the serial killer? He'd liked Hazel and his father used to cut his own hair – that's all I could hold onto. Was I trying to make him fit so I had something concrete to show Claussen?

I stomped up the stairs to my flat, banging my fists on the banister. It was like trying to get two live ends of a wire circuit to touch each other when they were simply too short.

Miranda rang just as I reached my door.

'You okay?' I asked, letting myself in. It was always my default response whenever she called me.

'I'm fine,' she snapped. 'Don't always sound so worried. I can look after myself, you know.'

'Sorry.' I dropped my keys on the ledge in the hall and peeled off my coat with one hand.

'It's Emily I'm ringing about. Have you seen her?'

'We went for a run last night.'

'I'm a bit worried about her. Did she tell you why she went home early the night of the ceremony?'

'Yes, she did.' I strolled into the kitchen, dying for a cup of tea.

Miranda went on. 'Something about her best friend? How she died falling down a flight of marble stairs?'

'Yes, that's what she told me.'

'She was in tears about it at CCAP. She said it was because her friend's shoes were too high. She kept going on about it. The shoes, the shoes. Sounded awful. I think she's seriously traumatised even though it was years ago. She hasn't been back in since.'

'Really?' I leant against the draining board, staring longingly at the empty kettle. 'She said she had plans for the weekend; she didn't sound like she was in a terrible state.'

'She was supposed to teach a self-defence class yesterday and she didn't show up. If you're running again, I just thought you could see if there's anything we can do. Let her know she can talk to us. She's been such a help at the project. I hope she's going to come back.'

'We've arranged to run on Monday, so I'll let her know,' I reassured her.

'That would be good,' Miranda said. It was the most grateful she'd sounded for months.

Spending that night with Terry was just what I needed. I fell into his arms at the door to his flat and we stayed entwined almost until it was time for me to leave, fifteen hours later.

My questions surrounding Chris Pitlock and the cold cases temporarily fluttered out of my head and settled somewhere out of sight the entire time. For the first few hours, we drank, ate, flirted, teased and laughed, always touching. Then Terry led me to his bedroom. I didn't think of Lorna, Charlotte, or Hazel once.

'Can I tell you a secret?' he said the next morning. Where the floating voile curtains didn't quite meet, broad strokes of gold broke through and fell on his shoulder and bare back. I reached over and pressed my lips into the warmed skin.

'Go on,' I muttered, looking up at his debonair features.

'I've never made love that many times in one night.'

I let out a racy laugh. 'No – nor have I.'

He gripped my hand. 'We'd better fall out more often.'

I hooked my naked leg over his, relishing the velvety touch of his body hair. Because we'd already known each other for years, we had all the dizzy excitement of a new relationship without any of the usual awkwardness. 'Was it really a falling out?' I asked. 'More a misunderstanding, I reckon.'

'Okay, but we need to get our wires crossed on a regular basis from now on.' He drew a forefinger down from my armpit to my waist and it made me shiver. 'Oh, a tickling spot,' he said, sounding delighted. 'I didn't know you had one, Dr Willerby. Fancy that!'

I pulled away and bounded onto all fours astride him on the mattress. 'Right – in that case, I'm going to find yours.'

'Ah, well, I'm not ticklish anywhere, as it happens,' he announced. 'And I don't do weak spots.'

I jabbed my fingers at the edge of his ribs and watched as he squirmed and wriggled, pretending I hadn't hit the right place. I tried both sides at once and he coiled up like a spring with a loud howl.

'I lied!' he cried. 'Have mercy!'

I carried on tickling until he nearly fell off the mattress. 'Okay, okay,' he pleaded, his arm up in surrender. 'Let's say you won that particular contest.'

He rolled beside me again, sweeping my hair back, taking my head in his hands. He drew my head towards him and kissed my lips hungrily. We weren't finished yet.

As he stepped out of the shower, Terry told me he'd promised to have lunch with an old university friend who was going through a divorce.

'Come if you like. Oliver won't mind,' he said, towelling himself down in front of me, unabashed at his own nakedness. 'I can't guarantee it'll be much fun though.'

'I don't think your friend would be best pleased confronted with a stranger at a time like this,' I replied, untangling my blouse from his jeans where they'd been flung, last night. 'I'll give it a miss, thanks.'

He took his damp towel back to the en suite.

When he came back, I was combing my hair in front of a mirror.

'How's it going with the haircutting cases? Can I ask?'

I pulled a bleak expression. 'I've got a few leads, but nothing conclusive. Not enough to satisfy Fenway, at any rate.'

'These women who get their hair cut at the back...' Terry pulled on his jeans. 'I was thinking about it – wouldn't you know if someone was cutting off your hair?'

The same question Fenway asked. 'Not if other people are brushing up against you legitimately in a crush – like in a queue. That's how it happened with Lorna, Charlotte and Hazel, by all accounts. Busy, noisy public places – or dark, like in a cinema. If the music's loud you wouldn't hear the scissors. I've often had people catch my hair by accident as they grab the back of the seat to get off a bus. That could disguise a furtive snip.'

'Wouldn't you feel the cold steel against the back of your neck?'

'Not if it's just the top layers of hair. Nevertheless, I agree, it's quite a skill to do it undetected. You'd need nerve and a steady hand.'

70

Terry and I shared a late morning coffee, then I left after a lengthy goodbye hug. It seemed we were both still a little clingy after our near bust-up.

As well as being bright, it was mild outside, so instead of jumping on a bus, I walked from Earl's Court. I was in no rush to get home.

As I reached my local high street, I remembered Emily saying she was having lunch at Camille's Bistro. I glanced around for her, knowing it was unlikely I'd spot her.

My thoughts drifted back to Miranda's ceremony. Something was niggling at the back of my mind. As a psychologist, it's my job to pay attention to words – to the exact words people use to explain and describe events and experiences. Emily had been upset on Wednesday, because the occasion reminded her of the death of her friend. Miranda had said the friend had fallen down a stone staircase because her shoes were too high. But Emily herself had said the shoes were 'too big'. There was a difference.

Emily also said 'the shoes she was wearing'. What did that imply, exactly? Did Emily mean the shoes didn't actually belong to her friend? It was an unusual way to put it otherwise.

I looked up to see a crowd flooding onto the main road, heading towards me. With it came the loud banging of drums and banners; a march against local council cuts by the look of it. Hundreds of demonstrators filed past, striving to stay off the road. Mostly good-humoured, they were chanting or blowing whistles, punching their fists into the air. Uniformed police were dotted here and there, some dressed in riot gear with dogs.

I pressed on against the tide, forced to a snail's pace. At one point there was a scuffle and the horde bunched up, squashing me momentarily into a tall hedge. A group holding yellow balloons tumbled like dominoes almost on top of me. Then a crushed beer can flew right before my face from nowhere. Someone pushed my head down, so I didn't get hurt. I turned to thank whoever it was, but no one was looking my way.

'Move along!' the nearby police officer shouted and just as quickly, the crush dispersed.

I was about to turn off the main road when I thought I caught a glimpse of Emily, after all, on the other side of the road. Like me, she was forcing her way against the surge of protestors. I recognised the way she walked; head held high, confident. I was about to call out when I saw my mistake. Her hair was the right colour, but it was in a completely different style; an inverted bob that reached down only as far as her collar. Wrong person.

Someone bumped into her and she turned her face to one side. Thick tar seemed to fill my lungs as I snatched a breath. It *was* Emily. Only her hair had been cut off.

I yelled at the top of my voice, but she couldn't hear me over the clamour of the crowd. I burst into a run, but had to stop to negotiate the busy road. By the time I got to the far side, she'd disappeared into the throng.

I jogged to Camille's Bistro, but the place was empty. A sign on the door said it was closed due to a break-in. Emily must have moved on somewhere else.

I hurried along the main street, checking inside the cafés and restaurants, but there was no sign of her. I called her phone, but it was switched off.

There was nothing else I could do. I headed for home in a state of shock, feeling as though I was on a ship in stormy seas lurching towards the rocks.

Emily's lovely hair. It hadn't reached down to her waist like Hazel's, but it was much longer than mine. She'd had it all cut off into a new style. Surely, it couldn't be for the reason I was dreading.

With trembling hands, I tried her phone again. This time I left a message, but kept it light. I didn't want to frighten her in case I'd got it wrong.

I strode from one side of the sitting room to the other, back and forth, my fingers toying with my lip. Had someone snipped off her hair at the back? Was that the reason for this complete restyle? Emily didn't know the significance of an assault on her hair. But I did. I knew exactly what it meant.

71

I was twitchy, marching from room to room, huffing and puffing; hot one minute, shivering the next. All I could see flickering before my eyes was Emily with her long hair cut off. She still hadn't called me back.

I put laundry in the machine, then forgot to switch it on. Then plugged in the iron, ready to press a shirt for my return to St Luke's the next day. Going through the motions.

Barely aware of what I was doing, I found myself scrolling for updates on the police files. I knew the clock was ticking and any moment I'd get a call from Claussen or Fenway ordering me to delete them. Now I was declared 'off the case', my access would be revoked and I'd be shoved out into the cold with no involvement whatsoever.

I flicked through my notes from my visit to Mrs Pitlock again. Hazel's long hair. Chris taking a shine to her. There was the photo of Chris's father. *Hair cut. Not with us anymore.*

Mrs Pitlock had been talking about her first husband. The date I'd spotted on the back of his photograph was 16 June 1997. The date of his one and only smart trim. *Finally had his hair cut properly,* she'd said.

But when did he die?

I went back to my laptop and trawled the records for a date. It wasn't on the police file.

I had to try something else.

I opened the search engine and punched in key words: Roy Pitlock, Stockwell, obituary. I stalled when nothing popped up. Then another idea came to me using an ancestor search website. I signed up for a trial membership and entered his name. One record was retrieved and it was the right location.

I let out the breath I'd been holding inside my lungs. The date of Roy Pitlock's death was recorded as 23 June 1997 – exactly one week after his first proper haircut.

I gripped my hands together against my chest. *Yes!*

I stopped myself from doing anything rash, and slowly and deliberately wrote down all the pertinent details about Chris Pitlock. I needed to make sure I'd got everything straight in my mind; I couldn't afford to get this wrong.

The next ten minutes seemed like the longest and most nerve-wracking I'd had to endure since getting a tooth pulled when I was nine.

But it all made sense. It was there in black and white.

When his father died, Chris was ten years old. The kind of age when children grasp the finality of death. When they're likely to dwell on it and feel more complex emotions about it. Like anger. My theory was that Chris had created his own myth linked to his father's death. He believed in his ten-year-old mind that his first proper haircut had somehow *caused* his father to die.

According to my recent training, this was exactly the kind of belief that could bring about a delusion in later life. It was entirely feasible for Chris to have turned the circumstances of his father's death into a secret magical power in his own mind: a 'grandiose delusion'. The belief being that if the haircut led to his father's death, then perhaps Chris, himself, could ensure that selected individuals died, seven days after he lopped off sections of their hair.

Chris could have hidden his 'secret power' from everyone. Many individuals with delusions, even grandiose delusions, socialise and function quite normally. They generally don't behave in an obviously odd or bizarre manner. They don't necessarily hear a 'voice', unlike people with other psychotic disorders.

It was easy to see how Chris could hold a grudge against Charlotte for abandoning him, but what about Hazel? What had she done to upset Chris?

Seconds after thinking I'd pieced everything together, it fell apart in my hands. What about Lorna? I didn't even know if he was the Chris she knew. And it was nine years ago. How could I find a link between the two without confronting him directly? Without a link to all three, my theory wouldn't hang together.

I banged my fist on the table. As it stood, there wouldn't be enough to goad Fenway into action – I was sure of it.

72

I was brought back to the here and now by a scorching smell coming from the living room. As I ran to the iron I'd switched on half an hour ago, my mobile pinged with a message.

It was Emily.

I've found out something really important about Stephen McVey – the guy I used to go out with. Something weird's happened and I think he's dangerous. He wants to meet. Can you come with me? The gardens on the Fulham side of Putney Bridge. ASAP.

I rang her straight back, but once again I reached only her voicemail. I left a message to say I'd get there as soon as I could and instructed her not to approach Stephen on her own.

My instinct was to let someone else know where I was going, especially when I wasn't sure what I was getting myself into. I called Terry, but remembered he'd be knee-deep in discussions about divorce with his friend. I left a message giving him the exact location.

As an afterthought, I told him what I'd learnt about Chris Pitlock, briefly explaining how the circumstances of his father's death exactly matched the MO of the murder cases. I also mentioned that Chris knew Hazel Hart.

'Could you pass this on to Fenway as soon as you can? I know it's not concrete evidence, but Chris could be the haircut killer,' I stressed, ending the message in dramatic fashion.

It occurred to me as soon as I pressed send that Terry and I had been so preoccupied at the weekend that I hadn't got around to telling him I was off the cases. He'd find out soon enough when he got through to the DI.

I grabbed my coat and bag, only just remembering to switch off the iron before I ran to catch the next train to Putney.

As I climbed the steps up from the platform, I spotted a co-worker from St Luke's. Gwen Barker. A busybody and trouble-maker if ever there was one. She and I were from different planets and I wasn't in the mood to stop and be charming to her. As I neared the top of the steps, I dropped my head and pretended to search for something in my bag. Then I felt a touch on my arm.

'It *is* you,' said Gwen, in a tone that sounded more reproachful than pleasantly surprised. I'd been rumbled.

'Oh hi, Gwen. How are things?' I reluctantly stepped to one side, getting out of other passengers' way.

'Oh, same old,' she said drearily. 'Actually, I'm thinking of leaving St Luke's.' She pulled on a pair of expensive-looking gloves. 'Been headhunted. A clinic in Toronto is doing ground-breaking research into postnatal depression. Have you heard about the latest PCP tests into neuropeptide inhibitors?'

I opened my mouth to explain that this particular research must have passed me by, but she jumped in before I could utter a word. 'Of course you haven't. Well, it's fascinating – and lucky for Sunnymede Health Services, I'm a bit of an expert in PND.'

Gwen always did like dropping in her acronyms. She tossed them around like most people fed scraps to the pigeons. She watched my face, waiting for me to look dumbfounded by her news.

'Congratulations,' I said with a plastic smile. 'I'm so sorry, but I need to be somewhere.' I hooked my bag over my shoulder and took a step past her towards the ticket barriers. A tinkle of laughter made me hesitate and turn round.

'Is it the new trend?' she said, with a smirk.

'Sorry?'

'Is this the new fad?'

I frowned, irritated at being held up.

'You didn't know?' she said, turning me round by my arm. 'There's a clump of your hair missing at the back.'

73

I broke away from Gwen and shot through the ticket barrier, clutching the back of my hair. There was a clump missing only on the top layer – that's why I hadn't noticed. Now I ran my fingers through, it was obvious. *Who'd done this to me? Was it Stephen? Or Chris? How long has it been like this? How many days have I got?!*

My memory went into fast forward. I was with Terry until that morning. Surely he would have noticed. I recalled sitting in front of the mirror, combing my hair. No, it was fine then. I was certain of it.

Think! I'd been walking home from Earl's Court. The demo. People pushing into me, getting jostled and shoved. The tall hedge. The balloons behind me. Someone pushing my head down to avoid the flying beer can.

It must have happened then.

I hurried past a library and the usual array of high street shops and cafés, until I reached Putney Bridge. The gardens Emily mentioned were on the far side. I was hurtling down the steps when my phone rang again.

'Where are you?' Emily was running, out of breath.

'I've just crossed the bridge. What's going on?'

'I can't explain. Stephen's taken off. Cross back over the river.' Her voice came in little bursts. 'Go past the pub and turn right into Saltern Road. Go to house number twenty-seven, it's about halfway down.'

'Emily, we should call the police.'

'I have. They'll be here any moment. I can't say any–'

With that the call broke off. I rang back, but there was no reply.

Before I set off running again, I redialled Terry's number, then cut the connection. Better to wait until I actually got to the final destination, as things might change again. In any case, Emily said the police were on their way, so we'd be safe. I could tell them then about my hair.

I was passing The Bugle when a call from a number I didn't recognise came in.

'Hello?'

'It's Doreen Pitlock, love. I need to check something about the fee for the interviews.'

Damn! I should never have given her my mobile number. I smothered a heavy sigh. 'Go on.'

'When I get paid it needs to be in cash. I can't be doing with any of these online bank transfers or cheques, okay?'

'Yes, of course.' Anything to get rid of her.

'And I've been thinking,' she went on. 'That lass you mentioned. Lorna thingummy. I was chatting to my neighbour and we remembered all about it.'

She had my full attention now. 'Remembered all about what?'

'That's when the girl died, didn't she? The model. Isabel Grace. Smashed her head in – falling down the stairs.'

Falling down the stairs. Snippets of conversations I'd had recently with Emily and Miranda pummelled my brain like a swarm of bees. Could it be the same girl?

Mrs Pitlock went on. 'This girl, Isabel, was wearing high-heeled shoes that were too big for her. It was technically an accident, but a few people secretly blamed the person who gave her the shoes. That was her. Lorna Sullivan. She was backstage and made Isabel wear the wrong shoes.'

The fashion show in 2010.

'So you *knew* Lorna?'

'Not really, but my neighbour remembered her name from the papers. This Lorna girl had caused trouble before, accusing an innocent bloke in a road accident.' She hesitated. 'It was Isabel Grace we knew. The one who fell on the stairs, poor love.'

I asked the big question that was bursting to trip off my tongue. 'Did Chris know Isabel?'

'Er... he might have done. Local girl. But he never tells me anything, so I can't be sure.'

My thoughts were bubbling away. What if Chris *did* know Isabel? What if he was fond of her? If people had blamed Lorna for Isabel's death, maybe he had too. It would give him a motive for killing Lorna.

'Did you know Lorna was killed soon after?'

'Ooh, was she? No, I didn't know that.'

My stomach curdled as I absently lowered the phone from my ear. I was replaying other voices in my head. Voices talking about a girl who'd fallen down stone stairs. Miranda telling me the girl's shoes were too *high*. Emily telling me the shoes were too *big*. A broken neck. Isabel Grace. It had to be the same girl.

I turned into Saltern Road and glanced up at the house numbers, my mind diving all over the place. As well as having a motive for Charlotte's death and a connection to Hazel Hart, Chris Pitlock could have known Lorna too, through Isabel. He could indeed be the boyfriend Lorna had told me about all those years ago. Surely Terry had put a call through to Fenway by now. There was no point in me trying Fenway again, he probably wouldn't even answer my call, given I was officially off the case.

I thought again about the likelihood of Chris being able to get from Stockwell to Primrose Hill to smother his fiancée within the time frame established by the post-mortem. It was unlikely, but not impossible. There was also the army knife Chris admitted to carrying which had an integrated pair of tiny scissors. Is that what he'd used to snip off my hair? Tricky to do without me being aware of it – but again, not impossible.

I quickened my step. There was no point in speculating right this minute. The facts were what Fenway needed and hopefully he'd have them by now.

I turned my attention to Emily. What was so urgent about Stephen McVey?

74

I reached the house with number twenty-seven on the gate. There was a sticker on the front door:

Take the outside steps to the roof garden. Emily

Mrs Pitlock was still on the line, chuntering on about what she was going to do with the fee from the 'interview'.

'... and some tanning sessions, seeing as I'm not moving abroad. And one of those designer tote bags would be. .'

I tried to end the call, but she didn't hear me. She hadn't finished. I didn't want to cut her off, so I let her carry on chatting to my palm, not paying any attention.

As I opened the tiny gate at the top of the fire escape, I felt a jolt of amazement. The roof garden was exquisite. The only problem was the lack of shelter, which left it exposed to all the elements. In the summer it would be a haven for sipping cocktails and some serious tanning, but right now it was bitterly cold and everything was on the move. Terracotta pots with hellebores, pansies and cyclamen were being cast around in the wind; many already on their sides, several broken. Behind them, stems of bamboo in raised beds clawed and swayed, swishing around like an angry sea. Running around the edge were low glass panels allowing views in all directions. My mouth fell open. You could even see the Thames from here.

Emily stepped out from behind a wicker panel. 'I love this place,' she said, spinning around, her arms wide, as if she'd just magically conjured it up. 'A friend's mother runs it on Airbnb. A two-bed pied-à-terre with roof terrace. Not bad, eh?' Emily dangled a bunch of keys in front of me. 'She's in Paris, so I've got exclusive use for a few days.'

I was confused.

'Where's Stephen?' I said, looking around me. 'Is he here? Did he cut your hair? What's going on?'

Emily stared at my face with a blank expression, as though taking me in for the first time. I shivered in return. Loops of unlit fairy lights swung violently with a life of their own and smaller plant pots looked like they were about to take off in the wild gusts. It was also spitting with rain, not the weather for standing about. Emily was in her running gear; trainers, lycra and a zip-up top. She flipped up her hood, but otherwise seemed impervious to the elements.

I took a step closer to her, bracing myself against the lashing wind that seemed intent to blow me over. 'You said Stephen McVey was up to something. What's happening?'

She flopped onto a white metal chair in front of a round table, as though we were expecting tea.

The tinny buzz of a distant voice made me falter. I still had Mrs Pitlock rabbiting on through the phone in my hand. I pressed it to my ear. 'Sorry, I really do need to go now.'

'Did you hear what I said?' came her voice.

'About?' I shouted, pressing my gloved finger in my other ear to block out the roar of the wind. I mouthed 'sorry' at Emily, who was slouching with her hands in her pockets.

I leant against the glass panel around the edge of the garden, waiting for Mrs Pitlock to finally dry up. 'Isabel Grace,' she said. 'The girl who fell down the stairs. You asked me if Chris knew her.'

I stood up tall. Acutely tuned in to what she had to say next.

'That's right, yes. You said "we" when you mentioned her name. You said you knew Lorna's name only from the papers, but it was Isabel Grace you knew. You and someone else.'

Emily rose from her seat and was slowly coming towards me.

'Yes, that's what I just said. She was gutted,' said Mrs Pitlock. 'Isabel was her best friend.'

'Who was gutted? Who was Isabel's best friend?'

75

Emily slipped out of my line of sight behind a trellis covered in fake ivy. I turned to keep my eyes on her, wondering what she was doing.

'Who was Isabel's best friend, Mrs Pitlock?' I bellowed into the phone.

'Em...'

'Sorry? Who?'

'My daughter. Em–'

Before I could hear more, the phone was snatched from my hand. Emily switched it off and hid it behind her back. 'You got tracking on this?' she asked, her eyes narrowing.

'No...'

'Better to be safe than sorry,' she said as she flung it as far as she could into the graphite sky. It soared over wet rooftops in the direction of the river and disappeared.

'Emily... what the hell–?'

The expression in her eyes shifted from unreadable to downright hostile as she turned to look at me. At that moment, a firework went off, shooting high above the chimney stacks, peppering into a thousand slivers of crackling white light.

Another followed. My mind fizzed and popped in tune with them. *Em. Emily.* Her best friend died at the fashion show.

A crumpling realisation steamrollered over me. Her mother was Mrs Pitlock. She was Chris Pitlock's sister.

'Your n-name?' I stuttered, staring back at her. 'Emily Chambers...'

'Oh, that. My coach suggested changing it when I was eighteen. There was another elite cyclist called Pitlock and people kept mixing us up.'

Emily Pitlock. She must have known Charlotte, her brother's fiancée, as well as Lorna, through Isabel's death. And Hazel came to her mother's house with her 'homes in the sun' brochures. The three murder victims. She knew them all.

'Your mother never mentioned you,' I said, my voice breathy.

'We don't get on. Never did. My brother was the one who stayed at home. Her little mummy's boy. I spread my wings and she more or less disowned me. She only gets in touch if she wants something.'

I recalled the missing pictures in the photo album. Perhaps this explained the gaps.

'I think we should sit down, don't you?' Emily said, flinging off her hood. Her tone was matter-of-fact, without obvious enmity. The rain had stopped, but swollen black clouds hovered above us. I was in a daze as I sidled over to the table at her side. Emily wouldn't hurt me, would she? Not after the bond we'd built between us? Nevertheless, I pulled out the chair that was closest to the staircase.

'But, your hair...?' I said, as I sat on the edge of the metal seat, the cold rain bleeding through my jeans.

She sat down, her new short style settling around her neck. 'I did it myself. To throw you off the scent. I've always been good with a pair of scissors. Mum never knew I was the one who gave Dad his first smart trim shortly before he died.' Emily casually stretched out her legs as though nothing had changed between us.

'*You* cut his hair...'

'I used to cut my own hair when I was little, but once I turned eight, Dad let me have a go at his. We waited for Mum to go out. We never told her. I made a really good job of it.'

Instinctively, my hand went to the back of my head. 'And mine?'

She nodded without emotion. 'That was me, obviously. When I saw you in the crowd near the French restaurant.'

A sharp pain lashed down my spine as the truth finally settled on me.

Emily had given me a death sentence – I was her next target.

76

'How did you know?' I asked Emily, genuinely mystified. 'How did you know I was working on cold cases?' We were still sitting around the patio table, like two chums waiting for the party to start.

Emily smiled. 'Way back in 2010, I had to speak to the police when my friend, Isabel, was killed falling down the stairs. I hit it off with one of the officers and we stayed in touch, going out for a drink every now and then. Not long after Hazel fell off the balcony, we met up in a pub. I wanted to make sure the police were treating it as an accident.'

'They were – to start with.'

She shrugged. 'My officer friend let it slip that someone was being brought in to look at old murder cases. He was angry. Said it might get in the way of his promotion.'

'How did you know it was me?'

'After a few drinks, he told me it was a psychologist from St Luke's. So I looked up the staff list online. Then I rang the mental health unit and with a few strategic questions, found out which psychologist was on secondment. Once I had your name, it was easy. You were conspicuously absent on social media, but I found a photo of you through your sister.'

Emily must have seen my face drop. She chuckled. 'Miranda isn't quite as guarded as you are! She'd tagged you a few times, even though you hadn't posted anything for years.'

This was news to me. I tutted under my breath.

'Then I got to hear that Tamsin had been visited by someone questioning whether Hazel's fall was an accident. Facebook is a wonderful thing. I knew I needed to keep a closer eye on you, so with the help of Miranda's timeline, I tracked your sister down to CCAP.' Emily clapped her hands together. 'Then I was in!'

A frown dug deep into my forehead. 'How did you know which cold cases I was looking at?'

'It didn't matter to start with. I just wanted to know if any links were being made between Hazel's death and any other cases.'

'But you never asked me once about what I was up to.' I was genuinely intrigued by her back-door approach.

'I watched, waited. I knew from your reactions that you were miles off target. I made use of Stephen, poor love, even though he didn't know a thing about it.'

'You made use of him?'

'He'd been popping up now and again, trying to get me to talk to him, so I exaggerated things a bit. Turned him into my mystery "stalker". I knew he was there behind us, in the underground. He was trying to tap me on the shoulder, but I made out it was someone "pushing" you. I shooed him away with everyone else. I was certain sooner or later you'd question whether it was *me* he'd shoved instead. When you asked me to take a photo of him, I knew you had him pinned as a potential suspect.' She sniffed. 'When I pretended someone had been trying to grab my hair in the bar that time, your face said it all.'

'That wasn't Stephen?'

'That wasn't anybody!' She sent her eyes up to the sky. 'I made it up to follow the story you were building in your mind. So you'd suspect him. I knew then I was safe.'

'Until today.'

She slapped her hand down on the table. 'My brother told me you'd gone to speak to my mum. How dare you trick her with promises of a payout for "research"! I thought you were better than that.' Emily said it not only with her words, but the whole of her face.

The brief spectacle of fireworks had petered out and it felt suddenly colder, darker up there on the rooftop. Metallic clouds had cut out much of the twilight glow and Emily's face had taken on an odd sheen like a silverfish, as a result.

'I didn't do it lightly and she'll get her money,' I said, glancing over at the gate, wondering how many steps it would take for me to reach it. 'It was the only way I could get more information. I had so many pieces of the puzzle and Chris Pitlock's mother – your mother – knew more than she thought she did.'

'My brother was devastated when Charlotte called off the wedding. Stupid, flighty little bitch. Kipper's life was ruined. He was never a robust kid. I've always had to look out for him.'

'Kipper?'

'He couldn't say Christopher when he was a boy.' She flapped her hand at me as if it was obvious. 'He could only manage Kipper and it stuck with me.'

'It didn't start with Charlotte, though, did it?' It was my turn to throw some flour into the fire. I drew up straight. 'I *knew* Lorna. Bet you didn't know that.' Emily looked as though she'd walked into a lamp post and I savoured the moment. For a second or two, I felt a glimmer of the upper hand.

Her surprise rapidly dissolved into a knowing nod. 'Ah, of

course. She was traumatised by that collision outside the bank, wasn't she? Must have had therapy with you at the hospital.'

I slid my eyes away from her, thinking back to our last run together. How candid Emily had seemed; genuinely vulnerable. 'Why did you tell me your friend had died falling down the stairs? You must have known that could link you to Lorna. Wasn't that a bit of a risk?'

Emily folded her arms. 'I didn't know you were going to speak to my mother. She was the one who told you the full details, not me.' Emily looked down. 'And I liked you, in spite of my reasons for getting close to you. You're easy to talk to – and for a short time...' She stalled, unable to finish.

She sighed. 'You asked my mother the right questions. I underestimated you.'

'But, Isabel's death was an accident. Lorna wasn't to blame.'

'Oh, yes she was! She was clueless. Lorna made Isabel wear a pair of stilettos that were way too big for her. She would never have slipped and had her skull cracked open otherwise. Silly cow. Isabel was my best friend. She didn't stand a chance. Just so she'd look right for the dress. Unbelievable.'

Emily's desire for revenge bruised me. I'd never seen this side to her before. In that moment, I had a true glimpse of who I was up against.

77

Emily got up suddenly and walked behind my chair. 'I like taking risks.'

I blinked fast. A hotchpotch of street lights were creating the illusion of a night sky beneath us. The entire situation felt upside down, surreal.

She squatted on the decking beside me and must have plugged in a cable, because the fairy lights came on. Their white sparkle gave the place a glowing festive feel. Emily smiled as though we were friends. It made me think how easily disturbed individuals could blend into society.

I'd grasped the truth of it by then. Emily had some kind of switch inside her that flipped whenever she was deeply traumatised, originally set in place the time she found her father dead. It triggered a murderous response whenever a similar extreme trauma recurred. Always involving those she cared deeply about. That's when her grandiose delusion kicked in – the drive to punish those she felt deserved to die. It was love curdled into revenge – right under my nose and I hadn't spotted a thing.

'I think we should try jumping to that shed down there.' She pointed to a shape a long way down in the neighbouring garden.

'The one with the corrugated roof. What do you think? Could you make it?'

I didn't dare look. 'What?! No way – it would be madness. We'd break our necks.'

She grabbed my collar, savagely tugging me to my feet, nearly choking me. 'You should go first. Your hair's been cut now. You've been chosen. There's no escaping what happens next.'

'Tell me about Hazel,' I said, playing for time while I urgently tried to figure out an escape. No one knew where I was. I'd left a message for Terry, but it was for the wrong place.

'I was in awe of her,' Emily said, still holding onto me. 'Taking selfies from the tops of buildings. So freeing – once you're that high, no one can stop you. The world is yours.'

She leant casually against the glass panel, swapping her grip at my neck for the belt around my coat. 'She was a challenge, for sure. I didn't know who she was at first. Then it clicked. Her family moved to America when I was young, but not before they'd put my dad out of business. Set up a new bakery two doors down from ours. All flashy and modern, with a deli and café, undercutting Dad's prices with three-for-two offers. Stole all his customers.' She spat out the words. 'It was callous and cynical.'

'But it wasn't Hazel's fault.' My voice came out a hoarse whisper.

'She was born the year before Dad died, so she was part of it. He'd gone totally downhill by then. Kind of gave up on life. The Hart family was celebrating soaring sales and their new addition to the family and Dad had to stand by as his earnings fell to nothing.' A wistful expression softened her stare. 'I met Hazel a couple of times when she came over. Her parents were still abroad, but she'd come back. I was nice as pie to her at first, telling her I loved her Instagram posts. That bit was true. Then I told her to stop coming. Told her exactly what her family had done to us, but she wouldn't listen. I even slapped her across the face to let her know how angry I was. I wanted to give her a chance, but she wasn't paying attention.'

'You were at Hazel's party the day she died?'

Emily nodded. 'It wasn't difficult to find out about it. One of Hazel's "friends" on Facebook mentioned it. Said she was bound to do one of her daredevil selfies on the balcony. Social media has a lot to answer for when it comes to handing out useful details.' Emily sucked in her cheeks. 'She was made of steel, that woman. I couldn't risk hand-to-hand combat with her in the way I'd dealt with the other two. I stalked her for a bit, finding the right time to make my mark on her hair and declare her a victim. Although, she hadn't a clue what it meant, of course.'

'Hazel's friends said they thought a man was following her.'

Emily laughed. 'I'm sure they all thought that! I'm fit, aren't I? I'm fast, take long strides like a man. I borrowed Kipper's combat gear so I looked like a bloke. Always with my hood up so no one saw my face.' She gave me a smug grin. 'I thought it was a rather clever irony that it was Hazel's beloved sun – exactly what she was trying to sell to my mother – that killed her, in the end. I wore large mirrored cufflinks that day. My secret weapon, right there in plain sight. I tilted them so the sun shone straight into her eyes, just as she hoisted herself onto the rail.'

It sounded methodical, entirely detached, as if Emily was explaining how she'd mended a hairdryer. 'I was lucky it was a bright day, otherwise I would have had to think of something else.' She blinked as though bringing herself back to the present. 'Come on,' she said, pulling me with my belt, like a dog on a lead. 'Take a leap of faith. Give it a go. If the shed's too far for you, how about the garage this side of it?'

My mouth fell open. She *had* to be joking. The idea of jumping anywhere from up here was ludicrous. A death wish.

Emily was strong. She bent my arm up behind my back and pressed me against the glass. 'We'll have to clamber over this first and stand right on the edge,' she said in all seriousness. Her hair brushed my face and I could smell something rancid on her breath.

I peered over the glass panel to the tiny ledge beyond it. It was less than half the width of a brick. All I could think, in my blind panic, was how useless I'd been on the gymnastics beam at school. And the long jump. My legs turned to rubber and she had to take my weight.

'I thought you'd be tougher than this, Sam. I'm a bit disappointed, to say the least.'

I was no match for her strength. If we got into a struggle, she could tip me over in a matter of seconds.

Think!

I cleared my throat to stamp out the whimper I could feel about to emerge from my mouth. 'I'm not sure you've thought this through,' I said, appealing to her controlling ego. 'Your method is very precise – you've established that. You cut the hair of your targets, then kill them seven days later. That's what happened to your father, wasn't it? He died seven days after you first cut his hair. It's always seven days.' I dug my heels into the slippery decking against her weight. 'You can't bring that forward. You can't kill me now. Today. It would ruin your system. You cut my hair this lunchtime – you have to wait six more days.'

A vestige of confusion fluttered across her face. It was enough. During her split-second hesitation, I broke away. I charged towards the little gate in the corner, bolting down the stairs so fast I tripped over my own feet. I stumbled, scraping my cheek against the wall. Ignoring the searing pain that followed, I fled along the street, snatching gasps of air, spiky with ice.

I knew Emily would come straight after me. One runner against another.

78

As I raced onto the pavement I heard a yell of pain behind me. Emily must have slipped on the wet decking like I had, only fallen harder. For a fleeting moment I thought about stopping to help her, but the moment passed. I couldn't afford to wait. Instead, I ran as fast as I could to the far end of the street.

I wasn't used to sprinting; Emily and I had raced our last twenty metres every now and again just for fun, but we'd not done anything sustained like this.

The sound of a police siren brought with it a flurry of relief and I began to slow down at the corner. *Terry's found me! I'm safe: thank God!*

I bent over, my hands on my knees, snatching wheezing breaths, that awful gone-too-fast nausea washing over me. All I had to do was stand up and throw out my arms so they'd see me.

But the flashing blue lights went straight past. It was an ambulance. Heading somewhere else. They hadn't come for me. I snatched a glance behind me, but Emily hadn't yet come out of the gate.

Dizziness hit me like a surge of seasickness, but I had to get moving again. I needed a phone. I desperately needed a payphone. I scanned the street both ways. Nothing. I dashed for the next junction and scrutinised the area. There was a booth on the next corner. I hurtled towards it, praying it wasn't out of order.

Pick up, pick up, I hissed into the receiver.

Vital moments scooted past as I waited for Fenway to reply. *Not the answerphone – please not the answerphone.*

'This better be important,' the DI grunted. 'I've just had your mate Terry Austin blasting in my ear.'

'Listen, okay?' I didn't wait for his consent. 'Chris Pitlock–'

He cut across me. 'Yeah, yeah – the one who's created a deluded myth in his own mind about his father. Austin's told me all this. But Pitlock would have needed a helicopter to get to his fiancée's place and kill her within the timescale confirmed by the post-mortem.'

I screwed up my face. It was like a painful moment in a quiz show where the person you thought would win doesn't have a clue. 'I'm not talking about him!' I yelled. 'He has a sister...' I garbled my way through what had happened.

'Where are you?'

I gave instructions as concisely as I could, turning round every few seconds to check on Emily's whereabouts.

'Isn't Austin with you? He said he was heading over to Putney Bridge.'

Shit! She was there, in the distance, coming straight towards me.

I dropped the phone and bolted.

79

I flew across the road and took the first turning towards the high street. The lights were turning red and the traffic was closing up, bumper to bumper. Squeezing my hands into fists, I ran flat out between the cars, praying no one would run me over. Shouts barked behind me once I got to the other side. Probably an irate driver. It seemed like more than one voice, but I didn't dare slow down. I careered along the first road I came to with no idea where I was going. My legs simply kept me on the move, just like Emily herself had taught me.

Before the next turning, I risked another glance back. Emily was fifty metres away, stuck at the other side of the road now the lights had changed. There was another figure near her, wearing almost identical running gear, but I was too far away to see who it was.

My lungs were on fire, my tongue glued to the roof of my mouth. I thought of ducking into someone's drive and hammering on their door, but the chances of anyone answering and letting me in before Emily caught up with me were negligible. I thought of dodging behind a wall so I could climb inside a wheelie bin, but it was too risky. I'd probably pull the bin over and draw attention to myself.

So I carried on, zigzagging, until I finally arrived at a green space on the edge of the Thames. There was a footpath alongside the grass, but the street lights came to an end. It was like dropping into a tunnel.

When I first met Emily, she struck me as fearless, gutsy and defiant. Moreover, I saw a hint of Miranda's vibrancy in her. I responded instantly to that, and wanted to be part of it before I took in anything else about her. But I should have stopped to question the way she'd suddenly popped up out of nowhere. I should have looked deeper at the impact of her tragic past. At the layers of her pain. Then perhaps I would have put two and two together.

My thighs were burning, turning to lead with every step. All I wanted was to collapse in a heap, but I couldn't stop. As I kept to the unlit footpath between the grass and the water, I felt a sting of sadness that Emily wasn't the person I thought she was. I genuinely liked her. I thought tender sprigs of friendship were blossoming between us, but it was all fake. How better to climb under my defences than by revealing her hidden childhood hurt? She knew my job. It was a well-judged ploy to play the willing patient – opening up, enticing me with the subject matter she knew I cared about, following her swift reconnaissance enquiries at CCAP. All so she could find out what I knew and keep one step ahead of me.

The path led inland a fraction, skirted on both sides by bushes; a dense mix of holly and evergreens. A tremor of fear scooted down my spine as I grasped the realisation that this was close to where Emily lived. It was her territory and she'd know it inside out.

It was too late to change course.

80

I had no time to react when a black shape sprang out of the bushes. Off balance, I let out a shriek as I buckled to the ground. Emily landed on top of me and pushed my face into the tarmac. My nose was bent against the knobbly surface and she ground her fist into my spine. I was winded and had no strength to fight back.

'You can't get away from me,' she hissed into my ear. 'You're wasting your time.' She grabbed my hair and twisted it into a tight coil. Stabs of pain splintered across my scalp.

Where was Terry? The police?

I craned my neck to look behind me, but her grip was too firm. She hoisted me up and dragged me through a narrow gap between the shrubs. I knew I'd be no match for her if I lashed out – she was a self-defence expert after all. My only chance was to break free and run until... until what? Emily was a trained athlete. She'd catch me. She always would. The brutal truth that I couldn't escape her hit me like a blinding light. This was the beginning of the end.

The river was only a few feet away. I glanced over to see swirling shades of mossy green and black running into each other, hiding a secret world beneath the surface. The tide was coming in fast.

Fearful of being interrupted, I reasoned she'd want to get the job done quickly. She'd want to get me over the railing and into the water and let the river do the work for her. That had been the pattern with her other victims; she'd let the pillow, the train and gravity do the damage. A common passive-aggressive approach typical of female killers. Often, they don't like getting their hands dirty. They don't like mess. Surely it would be the deep and turbulent tide for me.

We were bathed in shadows with only the distant grumble of traffic for company. The park area was deserted. Where were all the tourists and commuters when you needed them?

Emily wrenched my arm up my back, the other still tugging my hair. Everything about her exuded insurmountable strength. I tried to shrink down. Maybe if I made myself small I'd be able to duck under her arm and make a run for it. Run as far as the road and stop the traffic. Give Terry and Fenway's team time to catch up.

I had a better idea. I went floppy for a few moments, letting Emily believe she'd got the better of me, then I took my chance. My gloves having long since been discarded, I lunged up and jabbed my thumb in her eye – no one has strong eyes, do they?

She yelped and while she was half-blinded, I swept her feet from under her. Her backside hit the mangled undergrowth with a crunch. I aimed a kick at her legs, but she was too quick for me and caught my foot mid-air, twisting it. I lost my balance. I reached out for something to hold onto, but clutched only a feeble branch that snapped off with my weight.

It happened so fast; her knee against my chest, a zip against my cheek, the sound of crumpled fabric against my ear. It was a mad kerfuffle and I couldn't make out the order of things. One minute we were in the bushes in the park, the next she was hauling me across grass, tarmac, then steps leading upwards.

At the top, a thunderous roar filled my ears and violent thudding shook the wooden boards beneath me. She'd dragged me to a railway bridge.

81

———

A shooting pain in my head convinced me my skull had been split open. It brought with it a reverberating racket between my ears as though I was inside a threshing machine. Tentatively, I patted my hair and found a raw spot sticky with blood. Emily must have hit me.

I was blinded by dazzling lights and couldn't figure out exactly where I was. The clattering faded away, replaced by the lull of light waves coming and going. There was a slightly salty rotting odour. It was almost calming.

Hands grabbed me under my armpits and I was propped up against a wooden builders' board. I was fighting the dizziness, the temptation to close my eyes and give in to the darkness. Then came sounds of splintering wood, cracking and splitting, like someone breaking down a door. More heaving and pulling. Then I was bundled over a railing, landing in a heap on the other side. I was expecting to hear the splash of water, but there was a crunch of gravel instead. Emily was crouching beside me.

I couldn't think straight.

Waves of lucidity rolled over me, followed by flashing lights and closing curtains of blackness. One, then two coloured lights floated before my eyes; green and red. Long shiny poles were reaching up into the sky. I couldn't tell what was real and what was my mind playing tricks. I wasn't even sure if my eyes were open or not.

No, the shiny poles weren't leading upwards. They were stretching alongside me. On the ground.

Rails.

With a jolt of dread, I knew exactly where we were. Beside an overland section of the tube line. On a bridge across the Thames. Emily had broken through tall construction panels so we'd be out of sight of passers-by. She wanted me to follow in Lorna's footsteps. She wanted the wheels of a tube train to end my life.

I blinked, tried to sit up, striving to bring the fuzzy shapes around me into focus. But my neck gave way, my head smacking back down into the sharp stones.

A thunderous rattle brought a grey and red blur shooting past me. Emily gazed into the distance, listening, then she looked down at me. 'It'll be quick,' she said, once the roar had faded. Her familiar voice sounded strangely soothing. 'If the train doesn't get you, the live rails will. Two of the tracks have a deadly electric current.'

I stared to the side. *Which two?*

She knelt down, bringing her face close to mine, under her hoodie. Almost as if she was cradling me. It was the first time I'd had the chance to look closely into her eyes and I rapidly searched for the signs I'd missed. Who she really was. What she'd done.

I had to admit she'd played her role extremely well. She'd pulled the wool over my eyes good and proper; gently tipping events and circumstances towards the light so I'd grasp them in the way she wanted: the shove on the tube she'd generated herself to make it look like one of us was in danger. The stalker she dreamt up at the bar; the accusations thrown at Stephen claiming he was trying to grab her hair. And making out Miranda's new boyfriend was a threat. All the while she carefully bided her time, observing from the sidelines, never asking questions, never prying, covering her tracks so meticulously. A tour de force.

I thought I heard footsteps, cries, running. *Was it wishful thinking?* The pain in my head got worse. Like a spear lodged inside my skull. Then another sound broke through. The rumble of another train. Emily was pulling my arms, shuffling me across the gravel. *This is it.* I dug my heels into the stones, wriggled and writhed against her. The thunder getting closer.

On the fringes of my awareness there were more footsteps, yells, a scuffle. Then a tranquil pause, after which everything seemed to float in slow motion. With one final surge of energy I kicked out at Emily, blindly punching with everything I had. I hit something; her leg, her chest, I couldn't say what, but the sound of a slump followed.

When I finally managed to lift my head, a shape lay still across the wooden sleeper. Somehow, I'd knocked her down. Part of my woozy brain was telling me it didn't make sense. She'd gone down too easily.

The rumbling filled my ears as I got to my knees. I had to tug her off the rails. I didn't know which ones were live. *If the train doesn't get you, the live rails will.*

Then I saw my mistake. Not dark hair beneath the hood, but blonde. A bloodcurdling wail exploded from my mouth. The figure wasn't Emily.

It was Miranda.

I'd struck her instead. Where had she come from? The footsteps, the shouts – she must have been behind me.

Frantically, I pulled at her arms, but her weight was too much for me. My legs had turned to custard. I kept slipping away from reality, unable to keep my eyes open. Flashing lights. *Focus!*

I pulled with all my might, but any remaining strength had gone. I couldn't shift her. It was too late.

The train bore down on top of her.

I watched helplessly as the carriages flashed past. I saw her hand beside the track. The torn pocket of her hoodie. A trainer on its side. Then came a deafening squeal of brakes as the driver reacted. Too late. Sparks.

I flopped against the barrier, my head in my hands. There wasn't enough time. I didn't have enough energy. I'd killed my own sister.

82

———

I was lying flat, tubes draped across my chest, on the move. There was a strong smell of antiseptic, the wail of a siren. Someone was leaning over me taking my pulse.

'You're on the way to hospital, Samantha,' came a voice.

I was trying to figure out how this stranger knew my name when a different voice followed the first. It was Terry's; deep and soothing, telling me everything was going to be okay. I allowed his words to seep in like dripping warm honey and could almost imagine it was all a terrible nightmare. None of it was real.

A bump jolted me.

'Sorry – pothole in the road.' The words of a stranger.

That's when the truth hit me for real.

'Oh, God,' I wailed, 'I killed her.'

'No, she's safe.' Terry's words made a clacky sound, sticking together, as though his mouth was too dry.

He wrapped my hand in his.

'No – you don't understand.' I tried to rise up, but had no strength. 'It's Miranda. She was wearing a hoodie. I thought it was Emily. I lashed out at her, knocked her unconscious and she fell in front of the train.' My scratchy voice came between desperate gasps. Stabs of truth. 'I made a terrible mistake; she'd come to save me. I killed her – my own sister.'

Terry let go of my hand. Rightly so. After what I'd done, it would all be over between us. I had to be punished. I'd done a dreadful thing.

I dropped away.

In my mind I went somewhere else. Another time by the Thames. Warmer, before the last days of summer had died. The sun had dodged dense clouds and fragments of light twinkled like crystals on the water. I could sense the surge of the tide; imperceptible, resolute and mesmerising all at the same time. I wanted to stay there. Never come back.

A hand, smaller than Terry's and fitting snuggly into mine, replaced his.

'It's okay,' the voice said with a firm squeeze.

It was a cruel quirk of fate. The nurse, the paramedic, I didn't know who it was – had a voice just like her. My sister. But I knew it was the glimmer of fantasy. I knew what I'd done. Miranda wasn't here. She never would be.

'Sammie, don't cry.'

I must be dead.

It was Miranda's voice, it really was, but the only way I could possibly hear her was if I was with her. Dead too. On the other side.

'I'm so sorry,' I told her disembodied voice.

'I'm so glad you're okay...'

I tried to twist round, to look behind me, but it made my head spin.

The first paramedic leaned over me again, telling me to stay still.

There was a shuffle behind me and suddenly Miranda was there. Right in front of me. I must have been in some strange purgatory place where life and death crossed over. In the middle, with a foot in both worlds. It was the only way it made sense.

'I was so frightened she'd hurt you,' she said, her voice choked with emotion. 'Terry rang me. I ran like hell to catch up with you.'

I watched her mouth move. Confused. Miranda wasn't dressed like an angel. She wore jogging pants smudged with patches of oil and her face was scratched. There were spatters of mud and blood in her hair. I blinked hard, a rush of heat inside my chest.

Unless...

At some stage between being bundled into the ambulance and getting to the hospital, I caught up with reality.

Miranda was alive. She was flesh and blood right there beside me.

What I couldn't understand was how that could be possible. I'd tried to pull her out of the path of the train, but I'd failed. She was too heavy. She was stuck. I wasn't strong enough. I'd watched the train plough right over her.

83

London Chronicle
4 February
Suspect in Daredevil Arrest

Police investigating the recent murder of Hazel Hart, aged 23, and two historic murder cases, made an arrest yesterday.

The suspect, a 32-year-old woman from London, was detained while trespassing on the tube line between East Putney and Putney Bridge.

Police made the arrest after she is believed to have rescued another woman, Miranda Willerby, who had fallen unconscious onto the tracks. Ms Willerby narrowly escaped death as she was pulled out of the path of the train in an extraordinary act of bravery.

A witness videoed part of the incident on his phone. He later commented: 'One woman was out cold, almost touching the live rails. Another woman tried to grab hold of her, but she couldn't shift her. The suspect took over and dragged the unconscious woman to safety, just as the train got to them. I don't know how she did it,' said the witness, 'she stepped in when it counted and put her own life at risk.'

Since the news broke, the footage has gone viral on social media. Viewers are calling it the most daring rescue they have ever seen.

338

84

I didn't need to stay overnight in hospital. I was checked over, then discharged with only cuts, bruises and exhaustion. Terry had taken me to his place. I didn't want to be on my own that night. Miranda insisted on coming too. She'd curled up on the sofa.

Once I'd slept for a solid ten hours, my brain was sufficiently up and running to take in the full picture. Emily had saved my sister's life. Miranda would have been killed for certain if she hadn't acted so decisively. She risked her own life to pull my sister free.

Miranda stood and watched me get out of bed as Terry popped his head round the door with a mug of coffee. 'I don't think I'll be going running any time soon,' I said to the pair of them.

'Thank God we were both wearing rubber soles,' Miranda said later, as we sat together at the breakfast bar. 'It was only by chance I had my trainers on. I'd just been playing football with my friend's little boy.'

She got up to find an apron. She'd announced she was making poached egg on toast for us all. Terry and I had exchanged a look of resignation. We preferred our eggs boiled, but we had no say in the matter.

I'd already had calls from DCS Claussen and Fenway, all whistles and bells, congratulating me on tracking Emily down, as if they'd had every faith I'd come good. I kept the conversations short.

Miranda plonked a chunk of butter the size of a bar of soap inside one of the poaching cups, then scooped most of it back out again. 'I don't understand. I don't get it. Emily seemed so... lovely.' Miranda chewed the end of a wooden spoon between breaths.

'I know... but people are so complex. What you see on the outside isn't usually what's going on inside.'

'But she was a *serial killer*. And she was about to kill you too. How could she do that and seem so normal?'

Miranda's words sent a chill down the back of my neck and I could feel my heart pattering. *Emily, the serial killer.* She wanted rid of me to stop me getting any closer to the truth. It was a profound irony that she was the one – ultimately – who saved me too. By teaching me to run.

I explained what I could to Miranda, but I was still mystified. The woman Emily really was seemed a million miles from the laid-back running chum I'd got to know. It didn't seem possible she was the same person.

'During my training at Guy's, we'd discussed some extreme examples of delusional behaviour,' I told Miranda. 'The historical case of the baker, for instance, who thought he was made of butter and was terrified of melting near heat.'

She swung round. 'Seriously?'

'There was also the woman who thought she was dead, suffering from a condition known as the "walking corpse delusion".'

Miranda's mouth dropped as she cracked open the eggs.

'Such patients often get themselves killed; they starve to death or wander onto busy motorways. Many are harmless to others, but as I discovered, they can also kill.'

Terry set out cutlery for us and poured orange juice. He watched Miranda at the hob in the same way you'd keep an eye on a clumsy child; on high alert, ready to put out flames or catch anything that went flying.

'So, Emily had a grandiose delusion connected to her father?' Miranda went on.

'It looks like it. A grandiose delusion gives someone an inflated sense of their own importance. They see themselves as special, chosen – sometimes by God. They get locked into their own way of thinking and don't notice when aspects don't make sense.' I took a sip of juice. 'In Emily's case, I think she'd been traumatised by her father's death when she was eight. She found his body and had no idea what to do.'

Miranda took a seat beside me, leaving the eggs to cook. 'It's really sad,' she muttered. She looked like a glum toddler, cupping her chin in her hand.

I went on. 'Emily must have worked out that he'd died seven days after she'd given him a haircut.'

'She thought she'd killed him? She thought it was her fault?'

'Not quite. At that age, she didn't see it like that. It was the trauma associated with someone she deeply loved that had the biggest impact.'

'I still find that hard to grasp – that an eight-year-old could cut hair so professionally.'

'Good enough to convince her mother, at any rate. Emily had cut her own hair all her young life,' I told Miranda. 'She'd had a lot of practice and wanted to make a fine job of it when her father finally allowed her to cut his. It held a significance it should never have had. The death, the seven days and the haircut had all stayed together in Emily's mind as a kind of fantasy. Then later as an adult, it was as though cause and effect existed between them. It's called reasoning bias.'

'But why did she have to kill people?'

'Her fantasy evolved into a full-blown delusion, but her attacks weren't random. That's why she saved you. In her mind, her targets were only ever people for whom she felt over-whelming anger. Associated with people she deeply loved. That's how her grief came out. Each murder was triggered when Emily was deeply hurt or traumatised again, bringing back her original distress. She saw Lorna as responsible for killing her best friend, Isabel, because she gave her the wrong shoes. Then when Charlotte called off the wedding with her brother, Emily had to punish her. Chris was older than her, but she felt it was her job to protect him.'

'Hazel was trying to sell the Pitlock family a home in the sun,' Terry cut in. 'But that wasn't the reason Emily was so furi-ous. She realised Hazel was part of the family who had put her father out of business. That's what triggered her murderous response.'

'It all stemmed from love,' I said, with a sigh. 'Her delusions turned circumstances based on love – for her father, her brother, her best friend – into revenge.'

Miranda set the eggs on the plates. 'Oh, shit, I've forgotten the toast!' she wailed.

'Don't worry, I'm not that hungry,' I protested.

'Nor me,' Terry echoed.

Miranda sat down, lifted her knife and fork, then stalled mid-air. 'This probably isn't the best time to mention this' – she snatched a breath – 'but I've split up with Ralph.'

'Oh...' My eyes slid inadvertently towards Terry's. One of his eyebrows lifted a fraction.

'What happened?' I asked.

'Certain things started to put me off. Small stuff at first. A few times I found him on his phone and he looked like I'd caught him masturbating or something. Then one time he snatched his phone away so fast, it was like he thought I was about to swing an axe down on it. He blatantly lied about where he'd been a couple of times too.'

I felt my face take on a mock-surprised expression.

'Then I saw him once, when he didn't know I was there, and he was eyeing up this woman. He tried to touch her. It was really gross. I don't know. There's just something slimy about him.'

I cleared my throat. 'I hope you're not too upset.'

'Blimey, no. He was awful when I told him. He grabbed my arm and shook me – he was really aggressive. On the verge of hitting me. He swore at me and stormed off. I'm glad I saw sense in time.'

She seemed to have forgotten about my objections to him.

I glanced down at my lap and silently cheered.

85

Miranda took off late morning, leaving Terry and I curled up in a tangled knot on the sofa. He should have been at work, but he refused to leave my side.

'The day is yours,' he said. 'What do you feel like doing?'

'Sleeping,' I said, stretching through a yawn.

'Mmm, I think I can help with that,' he said, mischief twinkling in his eyes. 'Then what?'

'Go back to my flat and get ready for work, I suppose.' I nuzzled my face into his neck.

'So soon?'

'I'm shaken, but I'm fine. My patients will be expecting me.'

He tutted. 'Ever the consummate professional.'

'I need to see Emily at some point too. It feels important to thank her for risking her own life to pull Miranda to safety.'

He drew back. 'Seriously? Even though she tried to kill you?'

'I owe her that much.'

He gently traced the line of my jaw with his finger. 'You've got inordinate amounts of compassion – that's your problem. And nosiness. And headstrong audacity,' he added, with a wink.

'I'm sure it won't be long before you find some new impossible enigma to sink your teeth into.'

I raised my eyebrows. 'You reckon?'

He ran his hands through my hair, then hesitated. 'There's one thing you've got to promise me though,' he said, his tone harder, 'before you do anything else.'

I fixed my eyes on his. 'What's that?'

His laugh was tender. 'Get yourself a haircut.'

THE END

ACKNOWLEDGEMENTS

This novel has been helped on its way by many people. Huge thanks to my early readers: Mike, Ruth, Helen and a special thanks to my sister, Ruth, for her brilliant attention to detail. Heartfelt gratitude to Betsy at Bloodhound Books for structural guidance and editor, Morgen, for doing a fantastic job teasing out a myriad of errors and clunky sentences. Thanks to Fred, Tara and Heather at Bloodhound Books for sending this book out into the world, together with my recent novels, and for embracing the series.

A big thank you to my lovely ARC readers on Facebook and those of you who have read all my books and seem to keep coming back for more. I am indebted to you for your loyalty, kind words and humbling reviews.

My biggest thank you goes to my wonderful network of friends, in particular: Jo, Kerry and Anna, whose support and encouragement is invaluable.

And finally, to my husband Matthew, who is always my first reader and has been my rock in all that I do. I hope you know how amazing and special you are. Being by your side is the greatest honour I could ever have.

ABOUT THE AUTHOR

AJ Waines is a number one international bestselling author, with sales of over half-a-million books. She topped the entire UK and Australian Amazon Charts in two consecutive years, with *Girl on a Train.* Her fourth psychological thriller, *No Longer Safe,* sold over 30,000 copies in the first month, in thirteen countries.

AJ Waines has been featured in *The Wall Street Journal* and *The Times* and has been ranked a Top 10 UK author on Amazon KDP (Kindle Direct Publishing). Following fifteen years as a psychotherapist, she has publishing deals in UK, France, Germany, Norway, Hungary, Czech Republic and Canada.

She lives in Hampshire, UK, with her husband. Find her books online at: http://viewauthor.at/AJWaines. You can also visit her website at: www.ajwaines.co.uk. For news of forthcoming releases, join her Newsletter at: http://eepurl.com/bamG-uL.

9 781913 419424